Photo © Ginny Filer Photography

Mia Sosa is a *USA Today* bestselling author of romantic comedies and contemporary romances that celebrate our multicultural world. Her books have been translated into nine languages and have been praised by numerous outlets, including *The Washington Post*, *Bustle*, NPR, *Entertainment Weekly*, *POPSUGAR*, *BuzzFeed*, and *Oprah Daily*. A New York City native, she now lives in Maryland with her college sweetheart, their two book-obsessed daughters, a gentle Cavalier King Charles spaniel, and one adorable rescue cat that rules them all.

Connect with Mia Sosa Online

miasosa.com
MiaSosaRomance
MiaSosaAuthor
MiaSosa.Author

BY MIA SOSA

When Javi Dumped Mari
The Wedding Crasher
The Worst Best Man
The Starter Ex

LOVE ON CUE

Acting on Impulse
Pretending He's Mine
Crashing into Her

SUITS UNDONE

Unbuttoning the CEO
One Night with the CEO
Getting Dirty with the CEO

Praise for Mia Sosa

'Sosa has a gift with words that's infectious and wry, one that keeps the pages turning in delight'
Entertainment Weekly

'[Mia Sosa's] hot and swoony romances are always ones that we know we're going to obsess over as soon as we pick them up'
Cosmopolitan

'Mia Sosa is among the elite authors writing truly laugh-out-loud-funny romantic comedies'
Book Riot

'Mia Sosa's writing is so entertaining and engaging'
POPSUGAR

'Mia Sosa has enchanted me with her rom-coms. They provide the perfect amount of laughs and swoons you need in a book, and they always deliver!'
Buzzfeed

'All of Mia's rom-coms are *chef's kiss*'
The Nerd Daily

'Mia Sosa has written some truly incredible romances'
Culturess

'A delightfully playful and prank-filled romance from the Queen of Rom-Coms'
Alexis Daria

Praise for *When Javi Dumped Mari*

'*When Javi Dumped Mari* is Mia Sosa at her absolute best! Friends to lovers, with a little second-chance romance sprinkled in, the sexual tension and laugh-out-loud humor will have you turning the pages and sighing in satisfaction at the end'
Farrah Rochon

'The most fun that I've had reading a book in a long time. Mia Sosa expertly strikes the balance of crafting a story that makes you laugh out loud and also pulls at your heartstrings'
Kristina Forest

'Mia Sosa is the reigning queen of the modern rom-com, mixing hilarity with heat and so much emotional wisdom when it comes to families, work, and love. Each time she releases a book, it's an event for me and a cause for great celebration, because she's the master of feel-good romance'
Olivia Dade

'Mia Sosa is the undisputed queen of the unputdownable romance. The yearning is divine, the tension is delicious, and the chemistry is explosive—*When Javi Dumped Mari* is friends-to-lovers perfection. Sosa has delivered her signature combination of wit, heat, and heart, and I can't stop talking about this completely devourable book'
Denise Williams

'*When Javi Dumped Mari* is everything I want from a friends-to-lovers romance! Full of swoons and tension and steam and so many laugh-out-loud moments, no one does humor and heart and heat like Mia Sosa! If you love *My Best Friend's Wedding* but have always wanted it to have an HEA, this is the book for you!'
Naina Kumar

'A funny, thought-provoking, and delightful friends-to-lovers romantic comedy full of heart and sizzling chemistry. Mia Sosa never misses!'
Farah Heron

'With *When Javi Dumped Mari*, Sosa pens a sublime romance that leaps off the page with humor, heart, and heat. Her ability to craft the perfect rom-com is the best I've ever seen'
Tracey Livesay

'A sexy, banter-filled, humorous ride that rom-com lovers are sure to adore. This book kept me on the edge of my seat until the very last page'
Gabriella Gamez

'Another absolute banger from the queen of laugh-out-loud rom-coms. There is simply no one else writing rom-coms that deliver so many laughs with equally delicious tension, chemistry, and sizzle. Mia Sosa does not miss, and this banter-filled homage to *When Harry Met Sally* might be her best yet'
Adriana Herrera

'Mia Sosa gives us all the rom, com, and yearning you could ask for in this endlessly entertaining, chemistry-filled journey between two best friends. Layered with surprises and a tension-packed dual timeline, *When Javi Dumped Mari* is friends-to-lovers gold!'
Lauren Kung Jessen

'I want to live inside a Mia Sosa romantic comedy! Full of so many hilarious moments that are sandwiched between careful emotional development. Bold, funny, and dynamic, Mia Sosa has written another banger!'
Danica Nava

'*When Javi Dumped Mari* has it all. It's funny and sexy, and delivers an incredibly satisfying happily ever after. The perfect homage to the one that got away'
Neely Tubati Alexander

'With *When Javi Dumped Mari*, Mia Sosa adds yet another sexy, fun, and satisfying romance to her oeuvre. I savored it from beginning to end'
Rachel Runya Katz

'Full of chemistry, humor, yearning, heat, and raw emotion, Mia Sosa has written an addictive friends-to-lovers romance. The will-they-won't-they drama had me hanging by a thread! Every page was infused with delicious tension; there are scenes in this book that are going to live rent-free in my head, and I'm not mad about it'
Aurora Palit

'Full of heart and hijinks, *When Javi Dumped Mari* is Mia Sosa at her most delightful. I wish she'd write *my* love story!'
Adib Khorram

'A welcome return from Sosa in a rom-com homage to *When Harry Met Sally* and *My Best Friend's Wedding*. Press into the hands of readers who love romances with past and present timelines'
Library Journal

'*When Javi Dumped Mari* is the friends-to-lovers romance of my dreams! Voicey and playful, sharp and sexy, this is Mia Sosa at her absolute best!'
Christina Lauren

'The Queen of Rom-Coms does it again! *When Javi Dumped Mari* is chock-full of the sorts of outrageous hijinks only Mia Sosa could pull off, along with the signature steaminess her readers know and love. Blending humor, spice, and drama, Sosa once again delivers romantic-comedy gold'
Alexis Daria

The Starter Ex

Mia Sosa

HEADLINE
ETERNAL

Copyright © Mia Sosa 2026

The right of Mia Sosa to be identified as the Author of the
Work has been asserted by her in accordance with the Copyright,
Designs and Patents Act 1988.

Published in agreement with G. P. Putnam's Sons
An imprint of Penguin Publishing Group
A division of Penguin Random House LLC

First published in the UK in 2026 by Headline Eternal
An imprint of Headline Publishing Group Limited

This paperback edition published in 2026

1

Apart from any use permitted under UK copyright law, this publication
may only be reproduced, stored, or transmitted, in any form, or by any
means, with prior permission in writing of the publishers or, in the case of
reprographic production, in accordance with the terms of licences
issued by the Copyright Licensing Agency.

All characters in this publication are fictitious and any resemblance
to real persons, living or dead, is purely coincidental.

Cataloguing in Publication Data is available from the British Library

Paperback ISBN 978 1 0354 4099 3

Offset in 9.8/15.48pt Guyot Headline by Six Red Marbles UK, Thetford, Norfolk

Printed and bound in Great Britain by Clays Ltd, Elcograf S.p.A.

Headline's policy is to use papers that are natural, renewable and recyclable
products and made from wood grown in well-managed forests and other
controlled sources. The logging and manufacturing processes are expected
to conform to the environmental regulations of the country of origin.

Headline Publishing Group Limited
An Hachette UK Company
Carmelite House
50 Victoria Embankment
London EC4Y 0DZ

The authorised representative in the EEA is Hachette Ireland,
8 Castlecourt Centre, Dublin 15, D15 XTP3, Ireland (email: info@hbgi.ie)

www.headlineeternal.com
www.headline.co.uk
www.hachette.co.uk

For the people in my neighborhood

author's note

Thank you for purchasing or borrowing *The Starter Ex*, a contemporary rom-com set in my hometown, New York City. This book was originally published as an Audible Original, and I'm delighted that the wonderful folks at Putnam have made it available in digital and print formats. Still, I'd like to take a moment to acknowledge the audiobook narrators, Noah B. Perez and Miranda Jay, who delivered spectacular performances as Jason and Vanessa, respectively. If this is your first time experiencing *TSE*, I hope you enjoy reading the story as much as I enjoyed writing it. Now grab your favorite orange drink from your local bodega (if you know, you know) and get ready for a ride!

The Starter Ex

prologue

VANESSA

It started out as a joke. During my junior year of college.

Red flags: 2. Vanessa: 0.

My roommate at UPenn's International House, Elena Fernández, a well-off Spaniard who was fluent in two languages but skilled at cussing in five, complained that she'd been unable to snag the attention of her latest boy crush. He seemed mildly interested, she explained, and they'd gone on a few dates, but she couldn't close the deal (her words, not mine). What she wanted was a boyfriend. What *he* wanted wasn't entirely clear.

One evening, Elena and I sat at the table in the living room of our two-bedroom campus-adjacent apartment, noshing on jamón, albóndigas, and patatas bravas. Elena was an excellent cook; many of the international students were. Indeed, the high probability that I could sponge off their scraps factored heavily into my decision to select International House as my top choice in the school's emergency housing lottery.

Minutes into stuffing our faces, Elena ventured into uncommon territory: asking for someone else's opinion. "What would you do if you were me, Vanessa?"

I took a sip of water before I spoke. "Honestly? I'd find another crush."

I didn't understand why this was such a big issue. Back then, college boys were as interchangeable and ubiquitous as off-brand iPhone chargers.

"But I like *him*," she said, her eyes pleading with me to come up with a solution.

"The thing is," I said between bites, "he needs a push in your direction."

"Get him jealous, you mean?" she asked, her eyes wide and creepily unblinking.

"Nah, that's not something you want to encourage."

"So what do you suggest?"

I thought about it for a second and casually dropped this gem: "You know what would be downright Machiavellian? If you could manufacture the world's worst girlfriend to date him for a while. Then, when she's made his life miserable and he's hit rock bottom, you can swoop in and save the day. Be the breath of fresh air he so desperately needs."

Blissfully unaware of the wheels turning in Elena's brain, I chomped on fried potatoes while she picked at her food.

Suddenly she straightened in her chair and set her plate aside. "It's a brilliant idea, actually."

"What?" I asked, my eyebrows snapping together. "No, it isn't. I was *joking*."

"Joking or not, I think you're absolutely right. And I want *you* to be the girlfriend."

I cackled. I wheezed. My eyes welled up with tears. Until I realized Elena wasn't joining in on my amusement. "Oh shit. You're serious?"

"Very."

I scoffed as I brought my dirty dish to the sink, the ratty sweatpants I adored sitting on my curvy hips. "Absolutely not."

"I'll pay you."

Insert the proverbial record scratch.

I'm ashamed to admit that the prospect of getting paid made me pause. After all, I was a scholarship student living off the wages from the work-study hours I'd been fitting into a jam-packed schedule of classes and frequent weekend trips to New York to help my overburdened parents run a bodega in East Harlem.

Not that Elena knew any of this.

Making sure to mask any eagerness in my voice, I asked, "How much are we talking about?"

She shrugged. "For two or three weeks of your time? Does a thousand dollars per week sound fair? We can see where we stand after that."

My heart galloped in my chest. Three thousand dollars. With the possibility of extra cash if the assignment proved to be more challenging than expected. Damn, I could do *so* much with that money. Buy books for next semester. Send most of it to my family. Not kiss my roommate's ass in order to eat a decent meal for a month or two. Which reminded me: "Kissing?"

She narrowed her eyes. "If you must. No fooling around, though, and *definitely* no sex."

"Oh, you don't have to worry about that."

But teasing was fair game, it seemed. And hey, I could be coy.

I certainly could be a bitch. Someone's worst nightmare? Sin duda. These were my personality traits in a nutshell, so the assignment wouldn't be a stretch by any means. In fact, this would be a cinch.

Well, that's what my overconfident and underdeveloped twenty-year-old brain reasoned, at least. So Elena and I shook hands, and thus began my lucrative college side gig.

By the time I graduated from Wharton with a degree in business, I'd served as the starter ex for ten struggling-to-solidify relationships. Bonus? I never had to explain why I wasn't interested in dating anyone—because I *was* dating. Sort of.

Yes, I should have kept this highly problematic venture firmly in my past. But I didn't. And now I'm screwed. What follows is my pathetic story. You're going to want to grab some popcorn for this one.

Sidenote (in case you were wondering): A few years ago, Elena and her boy crush got married in a lavish waterfront ceremony at Penn's Landing. They didn't invite me to the wedding.

chapter 1

VANESSA

Present Day

Let's get this out of the way: I'm a terrible person.

No, I'm not being self-deprecating in an effort to gain your sympathy; I truly am a terrible person. If you trust me on this now, whatever happens next will make a whole lot more sense. That said, I believe in seeking redemption, so after working as a financial planner in Chicago for eight years and accepting a job transfer over unemployment in a limp economy, I'm back in New York, licking my wounds and trying to make amends for my past transgressions. Judging by my younger sister's flat expression as she studies the menu in her hands, I have my work cut out for me.

We're sitting in Grenadine's Café on the Upper East Side of Manhattan. My treat, so my choice. I may have miscalculated on that front. Admittedly, it's a bad habit of mine—miscalculating things, that is.

"Is this supposed to be appealing?" Lisa asks, her dark brown eyes narrowing in confusion. "Pea foam and carrot puree? And how the hell does one deconstruct bread?" She sighs, her huff of breath ruffling her curly bangs, and tosses the menu on the table. "Get the hell out of here with this."

For as long as I can remember, this has been my life: straddling two worlds, the haves and the have-not-enoughs, neither of which fully embraced me. Or I suppose it's more accurate to say I never fully embraced them.

Jesus. It's as if the overwrought prose in my brain writes itself.

Get it together, Vanessa. You're here to atone for your mistakes.

"This isn't what I usually eat, but the place is close to the new office, and I'm trying to find lunch options so I'll be ready to entertain clients once we start accepting them."

She dismisses my explanation with a wave. "Ah, this is research. How convenient . . . for you."

Oof. Lisa's not in the mood for my bullshit. And I don't blame her. Still, it's hard to square the person in front of me with the fifteen-year-old who worshipped the ground I walked on when I left home for college more than a decade ago. Since then, she's always been polite whenever our paths cross—which, granted, hasn't been often—but civility between siblings is an embarrassingly low bar, and her attitude this afternoon suggests she's no longer interested in meeting even that. There's a "bite" to her personality I'm not used to, and it only underscores how far we've grown apart.

Promising to return for our orders "in a jiff," the server sets down our glasses of water and a basket of rolls, then rushes off.

"I'll let you choose next time," I say, leaning over to take Lisa's hand.

She dodges my effort and sits up straight. "Why am I here?"

I roll my shoulders and compose myself. This isn't going to be easy, but I want to lessen the tension between us once and for all. "I'm sorry."

The blanket apology gets her attention. She stares at me, and for the first time since we sat down, the furrow between her eyebrows disappears. "For what exactly?"

"For everything, Lisa. For leaving New York and never looking back. For saddling you with the job of looking out for Mami and Papi on the daily. For missing out on some really important moments in your life—prom, high school graduation, the celebration dinner when you got your master's degree. Hell, for limiting your opportunities because you felt you had to be the one to stick around and watch over our parents."

I didn't *want* to miss any of those milestones, but I couldn't face my family back then. Not Lisa. And certainly not my mother and father. So I pretended I was too busy managing other people's money and made myself scarce at home. In the end, I only managed to become even more estranged from the people who truly matter.

Her lips thin as she studies me, then she says, "So you've decided that my job as a school counselor is directly correlated to the fewer opportunities I had because I stayed in New York to keep an eye on Mom and Dad. Wow." She pulls in a so-help-me breath, then blows it out slowly. "You're a piece of work, sis."

See? Terrible.

"That sounded different in my head, Lili." I forge ahead, despite the side-eye she's giving me for using a nickname I lost the right to use years ago. "In my mind, it was ten times less condescending and a thousand times more graceful."

She sighs wearily. "Look, I'm not trying to be difficult. I

appreciate that you want to reconnect. It's just . . . I don't know you anymore, Vanessa. You want to pick up where we left off, but that's not going to happen overnight."

"I get it. I do. All I'm asking is that you let me in. Even if it's only a teeny bit. Now that I'm here, I'd like to spend time with you. Remember what Mami used to tell us? 'You two need to have each other's backs. It's you two against the world.'"

A hint of a smile battles her standoffish demeanor, and for the first time since we sat down at the table, a sense of hope takes root in my chest. Lisa's smile tells me the door to her heart is still open. Not *wide* open, mind you, but if a crack is all she'll give me, I'll gladly take it.

"We used to make fun of her when she told us that," she says, her expression suddenly wistful, as if she's remembering us giggling and sneakily rolling our eyes when Mami lectured us on the importance of sisterhood.

"We sure did."

In those days, Lisa and I were know-it-alls. Now I'm perfectly comfortable acknowledging I don't know shit about anything. Well, that's not entirely true. I know *a lot* about what makes men tick. As for everything else? Zip.

Lisa twists her lips, then angles her head. "Tell me about Chicago. Why'd you leave? What happened?"

My boss, David Warner, happened, I think to myself. For six months, I was happily dating a man who never asked me for more. Figuring we were on the same page about the obvious limits of our relationship, I foolishly overshared parts of me I'd never shared with anyone. Stuff about my goals and dreams, my strengths and weaknesses. My strained relationship with my family, and my fears about returning home someday. And then

I continued to disregard everything I know about men and did the unthinkable: I rejected his attempts to take us to, as he put it, "the next level." Worse, I told him I couldn't see myself being serious with anyone, let alone my boss.

In a tale as old as time, he lashed out when I rejected him, accusing me of using him to climb the corporate ladder. As if my disinterest in a lasting commitment couldn't possibly be genuine and had to be part of an elaborate ploy. He wouldn't be duped, he said, so he recommended me for the team that would help build the New York office. A relocation would be good for my career, he suggested—in the middle of a staff meeting. Wow, message received.

David Warner taught me another lesson: Give men what they claim to want, and they'll *still* find a way to screw you over.

Frankly, I wanted to shove that transfer up his ass. But I didn't have that luxury. Not when my parents are struggling to keep their business afloat until they can sell it. Not when my sister's working sixty hours a week and helping my parents at the store on weekends. How selfish would I be to put my needs before theirs? *Especially* after I cast them aside so easily years ago. No, the only answer was to grin and bear it.

"An opportunity to return to the city presented itself," I tell Lisa. "A promotion of sorts."

I'm not sharing the particulars with my sister. They're unimportant.

"So you're here for the foreseeable future?" she asks.

"Yeah."

"Then I'd like you to help us off-load the store," she says, picking at the sourdough carcass that passes for bread at Grenadine's. "Mami and Papi are procrastinating, but they need to slow down. Like, yesterday. They're exhausted. And they haven't taken a vacation in God knows how long. It's time."

La Flor Superette is my parents' bodega in East Harlem. Well, that's the name on the official paperwork, but to the neighborhood, it's the corner store. One of hundreds in the city. As for La Flor, though, my parents' blood, sweat, and tears are built into its foundation. Their life's work is situated at the intersection of 106th Street and Second Avenue. Getting them to give it up won't be easy.

"Whatever you need, I'll do it. I'd like to talk to them about their retirement funds too. I can help them make some strategic decisions. Do you happen to know if—"

"Vanessa?" a high-pitched voice behind me says, interrupting my inevitable barrage of bulldozing questions. "Is that you?"

I twist around in my seat and see one of my college roommates—and former clients. Yes, I'm using the latter term loosely here, but still. *Shit.*

"Charlotte," I singsong, recovering quickly and jumping to my feet. Unfortunately, she's not alone. The woman beside her could be her twin, though. "It's *so* good to see you."

"Get over here, woman." She steps forward and pulls me into a light hug. "It's totally bizarre that I'm seeing you after all these years. And today of all days."

"Oh, is it a special occasion?"

She swings her blond bob around and raises a thick, legal-sized accordion envelope in the air. "Receipts. The divorce is officially final."

"Oh no, you and Ian split up?"

I remember him well: Last name Thompson. White guy. A senior economics major from California. Straightlaced and serious. Biggest pet peeve: untidy people. Hence, the name of the assignment: Operation Messy. That one was fun.

"Sweetie, this is a *good* thing. I was in love with him. Truly. Then I discovered Ian doesn't have a loyal bone in his body. Short story: He's loaded. He cheated. No prenup. Cha-ching. We're visiting my parents to celebrate. In fact, I'd clink glasses with you if I had any champagne handy." Charlotte glances at her companion and furrows her brow. "Goodness, sorry. Julia, this is Vanessa Cordero. Vanessa, this is my bestie, Julia." Turning to Julia, she says, "Vanessa and I went to college together. She's the starter ex I told you about. The one who helped me land *the asshole* in the first place."

In the beginning, I'd considered asking my clients to sign a nondisclosure agreement, then felt mildly embarrassed at the thought of taking what I was doing so seriously. In this moment, however, I have regrets. Many, many regrets.

Her companion's eyes grow as wide as saucers. "Oh-em-gee, *this* is the genius who tortures men for a living?"

My face warms under her blunt appraisal. "That's not an accurate description of what I did. And anyway, it's all in the past." I wave away my and Charlotte's connection as if it's no big deal. "Misguided college stuff." Damn, it's hot in here. Is the restaurant's air-conditioning on the fritz?

"Well, past or not, I bow down to you, *girlfriend*."

Still seated at the table, Lisa clears her throat. Or maybe that's a snort. Yeah, considering this stranger unironically called me *girlfriend*, Lisa definitely just snorted.

I spin around as if my sister has appeared from nowhere. "Oh, right. Charlotte, this is Lisa. My younger sister. We were just heading out—"

"No, we weren't," my traitorous sister says. "We haven't even ordered." She motions to the empty chair next to hers. "Want to join us? I'd love to hear more about this torturing business from someone who has firsthand experience seeing my sister in action." Lisa pins me with a frosty stare, as if to say, *You have a lot of explaining to do, pendeja*.

I drop onto my chair and rub my temples. Damn, this is going to be painful.

× × ×

"Picture this," Charlotte tells my sister, as droplets from the second glass of champagne she ordered land on her place setting. "Vanessa knows Ian's a neat freak, so she comes over to his place after supposedly participating in a mud run—"

"A what?" Lisa asks, her forehead creased in confusion.

"It's like an obstacle course. Lots of running. Lots of mud. Think army training. Crawling on the ground. Climbing over a wall. Sprinting through a tire maze. Point is, there's no way you're finishing without getting absolutely filthy. So then *your sister* goes over to his place and asks if she can clean up there." Charlotte looks over at me. "Want to pick up the story from here?"

Not really, but they're all staring at me expectantly.

"Um, yeah, there isn't much to add. I stood outside his apartment, but he wouldn't let me through the door. He asked if mud runs were a hobby of mine, and I said yes. A once-a-month thing, in fact, I told him, which of course wasn't true. And I pointed out that if we got serious, I'd find a way to drag him along too. His face paled. He was already pale to begin with, by the way. I think the mud runs were the final straw. Before that, I'd rearranged his kitchen in a way that made no sense. Refused to take off my shoes at the door. Silly stuff, really, but I knew that wasn't enough for him to end things. The mud run, though? That was a deal-breaker. The key is to know your target's pressure points."

Lisa leans forward, setting aside her ridiculous "naked" pizza, which boasts no toppings and is the least offensive item on Grenadine's menu. "So how'd you smooth the way for Charlotte?"

"Well, he already knew Charlotte was my roommate. We met through her. So I started mentioning little things here and there. How she cleaned up after me. How she organized our apartment. How funny and engaging she was. Listen, it was all true. The thing is, he couldn't see or hear any of it until he needed a lifeline. It was like the juxtaposition of our personalities helped him realize she was better suited for him than I was."

"And you did this for multiple women?"

"Yes, and one guy. For that assignment, both the client and the target were bisexual men."

Lisa collapses back against her chair. She's peering at me as if she's looking at a stranger, as if everything she's ever understood about me has been upended. "Goodness. You're blowing my mind right now."

"You don't do it anymore?" Charlotte's friend Julia asks, a hopeful gleam in her eyes.

"No way. Can't imagine doing anything like that ever again. I'm not proud of what I did."

"Well, I'm grateful," Charlotte replies, her speech slurring just a touch.

"Okay, babe," Julia says, rising. "Time to get you to your

parents' place. Something tells me you're going to have a nasty hangover if you don't quit while you're ahead."

Charlotte allows Julia to help her stand. As Julia gathers their belongings, Charlotte slides over to me and squeezes my shoulder. "If you ever want to reopen your starter ex business, I have lots of friends who'd hire you."

"Thanks, but I'll pass. Those days are over."

She giggles. "Suit yourself." Then she blows kisses at us and trots away, Julia struggling behind her with their bags and that damn accordion file.

Lisa and I sit quietly for a moment, both of us absorbing the impact of Charlotte's revelations. I want to ask Lisa what she's thinking, even though I'm not sure I'd appreciate her answer.

After a minute, she blows out a breath. "I want you to do that for me."

"Do what?"

"Be a starter ex. For someone I'm interested in."

I cackle and wait for my sister to join in on my amusement. She doesn't. An eerie sense of déjà vu sets in. "Oh shit. You're serious about this?"

"I am."

"Absolutely not."

"Hear me out, Vanny."

Oh, we're back to nicknames, are we? How interesting. Still. "There's nothing to hear, Lili. The answer is no."

The light in her eyes dims, and her expression sours. "Fine. Let's just get the check."

Okay, I probably shouldn't have rejected the idea outright. This is an opportunity to connect with Lisa, and I squandered it. Mind you, I'd never agree to this kind of scheme again, but what's the harm in learning why she thinks she needs my help? Maybe I can use this as a chance to bond with her. "Tell me what's going on."

Lisa sits up, her expression softening. "His name is Jason Torres. He's my best friend's older brother. And I've had a thing for him since high school, but he doesn't see me in that way. I'm starting to think he never will."

"If he can't see how amazing you are on your own terms, then perhaps it's for the best."

Lisa slumps her shoulders. "I don't want to spend the rest of my life wondering *what if?*, though. All the men and women I've ever been interested in pale in comparison to him. When I'm with someone else, I'm thinking of him. And questioning if I'm with the wrong person. I just thought this starter ex stuff might kick Jason out of neutral. If he can see you as a potential girlfriend, it wouldn't be as much of a leap to see me as one too."

"It's a little more complicated than that, sweetie. The reason those other engagements worked was because I didn't have a hugely personal connection with the person asking for my help. Being your sister injects a fundamental flaw in the mix. If anything, he'd run in the opposite direction."

"That's assuming you two had some kind of grand love affair. But it wouldn't be anything heavy, right? It's not like you'd be dating him for years. You wouldn't even be having sex. And after the breakup, you'd sing my praises. Assure him you wouldn't be jealous and you're supportive of the relationship. Extra points if you were the one to suggest me as a replacement. Subtly, of course."

"Okay, but let's spin this out a bit: Let's say this works. Jason decides he'd prefer to date his ex-girlfriend's younger sister, and you two fall madly in love. There would always be this big lie of omission between you two. Honestly? I never understood why the people I worked with wanted that burden, but I was young and dumb and didn't care. As a grown-ass adult, though, I'm having a hard time understanding why you'd want to do this."

"Because I'm just not seeing it as a big deal. You're simply giving him a little push in my direction, that's all."

"It would be awkward as hell."

"Not really. It would be the kind of thing we'd laugh about one day. It doesn't have to be awkward if we don't make it awkward."

"For *him*, Lili. I meant for *him*."

She gives me a dismissive wave. "Guys are clueless about these things. They take their cues from us. Besides, if he thinks he's dodged a bullet by dating me instead of you, he won't care."

"So this guy, Jason, he means something to you?"

The faraway look in her eyes as she considers my question is answer enough, but I still want to hear what's going on in that head of hers.

"This isn't some silly crush. I've had real feelings—*strong* feelings—for Jason for a while now. I just don't know how to get him over that hump."

"Is he a lot older than you? Is that his hang-up?"

"No, he's twenty-nine. We're only three years apart."

This guy's my age, then. That's a relief.

"Is it because he thinks his sister would object?"

"She wouldn't. If anything, Camila would love for us to get together. It's him. He's jaded. Cynical about relationships. Not wary of women, per se. More like he's wary of people in general."

"Sounds like a charmer," I say under my breath.

"Don't get me wrong, he's a really great guy. It's just . . . he has his relationship walls up."

"Well then, he sounds like a challenge. And my usual antics probably won't fly with him."

"That's where I think you're wrong, actually. Remember, he's jaded. A terrible girlfriend is exactly what he'd expect. Nothing you do would ever surprise him. You'd just be playing into his preconceived notions."

"How does that help you?"

"I'll be the antithesis of a terrible girlfriend. The exception to the rule. The one person who wouldn't pull the bullshit you're doing. And if I can get his family—his mother especially—on my side, there's no way he wouldn't at least consider me."

I draw back and gawk at her. "Jesus. Who are you right now? When did my little sister become this scheming mastermind?"

"You've been gone a long time, sis. I've always been this way. It's just . . . you were never around to witness it."

A pang hits me deep in my chest. Well, she's right about that. But trying to reconnect with my sister shouldn't come at the expense of my efforts to be a better person, to make smarter decisions in my personal and professional lives. I'm *trying*. Agreeing to be a starter ex for her would set those efforts back several steps.

Lisa fidgets with the cloth napkin in her hands. "Let me ask you this: Has any person fallen for you despite whatever it is you do as a starter ex? Because that would be my only hesitation. I wouldn't want to toy with Jason's feelings. Not to the point that he'd actually get hurt."

"Good Lord, no. My tactics make that virtually impossible. Now, mind you, being a starter ex was a bit of a dance. These men wouldn't have continued to date me if I'd been terrible to them all the time. So there was flirting and fun. But then I was really good at making them miserable too. Seriously, Lili, my skills were unmatched. And my success rate stands at ninety percent. But again, that was a long time ago, and I have no interest in resurrecting that part of my past."

"*One more time*, Vanessa. That's all I'm asking. And it wouldn't be for long. Camila's getting married in July, and I'm her maid of honor. That'll give me plenty of opportunities to be around Jason. And just as many opportunities for you to be around the family if you two hit it off."

"There's a possibility we wouldn't hit it off at all. What then?"

"Then we'll forget about the idea altogether. I'll just act like Kathy Bates in *Misery* and chain him to my bed until he falls in love with me."

"Be serious for a minute."

"I *am* being serious," she says, shaking her head. "And I'm not doing this for shits and giggles. *Please*, Vanny. I *need* this."

There's a touch of urgency in her voice; it baffles me. "But *why*?"

"Because I don't have anything for myself, V. I work ridiculous hours, helping too many kids in an underfunded and understaffed education system, while my life remains stagnant. I'm tired all the time. My kids and their families take up most of my hours during the day, and when I get home, I continue thinking about their problems. And then when I'm not obsessing about my students, I'm helping *our* parents. I just want something for me. No, *someone* for me. Someone who'll put me first. I always put on a smile and tell people things will be okay, but I'd love to be able to lean on my partner when I'm worried that things might be as bad as they seem. Is that so much to ask?"

Turns out, Lisa also knows my pressure points. Reminding me that I've been absent in our parents' lives for most of my adult life—forcing her to fill the void—is an express ticket to the land of Guiltopia. And the feeling's multiplied by thousands when I remember *why* I made myself scarce. "Of course it's not too much to ask. But what's wrong with trying to get close to Jason the old-fashioned way?"

"I've been trying, but whatever I'm doing isn't working. He treats me like a sister, not a woman he could date. What he needs is a push. A *well-executed* push."

"I'm sorry, Lili," I say, avoiding her pained stare. "The answer is still no. It's a bad idea. And I bet if you give yourself time to think this through, you'll come to the same conclusion."

She leans back in her chair. "No, I don't think I will. Which isn't surprising. We're not as alike as I once thought." Then she digs into her purse and pulls out her wallet. Poking the inside of her cheek with her tongue, she flicks a few bills onto the table—for her share of the check, presumably—and leaves without a backward glance.

Lovely. This redemption tour is off to a *great* start.

chapter 2

JASON

Fact: I would take a bullet for my siblings if I had to.

Fact: If anyone ever hurt them, I'd track down the asshole and make him pay.

Fact: If my youngest sister begged me to take her place this very second, there isn't enough money in the world to convince me to say yes.

Right now, Camila Lorena Torres—or Cami as we call her—is slumped in a dining chair, her vacant gaze fixed on an old Easter family portrait hanging on the wall behind our mother. We're all wearing white in the photo. A cringe moment if ever there were one. To her credit, Cami's making a valiant effort to hold it together, but her usual tactic of mentally transporting herself to a different location doesn't appear to be working. A part of me feels sorry for her; the older brother in me thinks this shit is hilarious.

"Are you listening to me, Camila Lorena?"

Ooh, my mother invoked Cami's middle name; she's not playing around.

Cami shakes her head as if to clear it and rejoins the conversation. "Yeah, I'm listening, Mami."

"What's going on with your headpiece? The wedding is just weeks away, mija. It should have been here months ago."

"Oh, right. I think it came in, actually. A few boxes arrived yesterday, but I haven't had a chance to check. I've been busy with other ... stuff."

That pretty much sums up Cami's interest in wedding planning. She loves her fiancé, but she's not in love with anything about the run-up to saying I do.

Hearing Cami's dull response, my mother's lips flatten into a thin line. "Camila, I'm not going to plan this wedding by myself. It's bad enough that we had to do all this rush, rush, rush. You need to participate too."

Cami and her fiancé, both teachers, are moving to Chile as part of a two-year program to teach English abroad. Their marriage will guarantee they're placed in the same school district.

"I know, Mami. Perdón. I'll check tonight and let you know."

My mother's lips relax. Seconds later, though, her eyes widen in concern. "What about the ribbon and bells for the capias? Did you order them yet?"

Ah, the capias. A shudder runs through me when I remember my introduction to them as a kid. They were everywhere. Birthdays, graduation parties, and, yes, weddings. Somehow, Latinx people took the equivalent of a festive button covered in tulle and plastic charms and made it a thing. As a thank-you to their guests, supposedly. The plastic naked baby they put on the capia for baby showers was the worst. It was hot pink, had no eyes, and gave me nightmares for days. To top all that off, the hosts would pin it to your clothes but it never stayed in place, so whenever you touched your chest, it stabbed you.

"Umm, about that," Cami says. "I don't want to worry about poking people with those pins. Plus, the capia eventually falls apart anyway. And no one saves them anymore. So, yeah, Bryan and I don't think they're necessary."

No one stirs, not even a mouse, as we wait for my mother's reaction. I chance a glance at her face. Mom's eyes are as round in surprise as they were the day my other sister, Denise, told us she's a lesbian. Honestly, I bet in my mother's mind, this announcement is equally momentous.

Cami rushes on. "We were thinking about chocolate coins or dragées instead?"

My mother raises an eyebrow. "¿Qué, qué? What's a dragée?"

"A French drag queen," I say.

Cami laughs, then affectionately drops her forehead on my shoulder. After she regains her composure, we share a conspiratorial smile.

My mother's husband, Nelson, peeks his head around the Sunday paper he's reading and grins. "Good one," he says.

"Good one," my mother echoes, her mouth twisted in distaste. "Is this a joke to everyone? Is no one else seeing the problem? Aside from a few salsa and merengue songs, where will the *cultura* be in this wedding?"

Cami expels an exasperated breath and slaps a hand on her chest. "*Me*. I'm the cultura. I'm literally Latina. *You*. You're literally Latina too. Nelson, Denise, Jason. Well, how about that? They're also Latine. What more do you want, Mami?"

"Ca-pi-as," my mother says, exaggerating every syllable.

"Will that make you happy?" Cami says, her mouth twitching as she tries to hold back a smile.

"It will."

"Let's compromise, then. We'll order capias for the couples shower. How's that?"

My mother pouts, then asks, "Speaking of, are you sure Bryan and his family need to be there? Can't we throw a party just for you?"

"No, Mami. We want to celebrate our new life together. It's not *just* about me."

My mother sighs. "Okay, then capias at the couples shower would be nice."

"Great. It's settled."

"Thank you."

"You're welcome."

My mother always gets her way, but she does it with love. Or so she claims.

Denise, who's studying her phone with the focus of a brain surgeon in the operating room, raises her head and sweeps her disinterested gaze around the room. Satisfied she isn't missing anything, she returns her attention to the screen. Honestly, I suspect she uses that device for only two things: TikTok and sexting. She's licking her lips, so I'm guessing she's engaged in the latter. Then again, some of the shit that pops up on that app has made me want to bleach my eyes, so who knows. Why didn't I think to bring something to distract me from this conversation?

"Listen up, everyone," my mother says.

Oh yes. That's why.

My mother's voice is loud and firm, alerting us that she's not pleased. Nelson drops the paper, and Denise whips her head in our mother's direction. Elba Graciela Guzmán Colón might look like the quintessential suburban housewife, but I'm almost certain she has a shank in that humongous bag she's always carrying, and if you gave her a couple of cocktails, my mother could be the central figure on *The Real Housewives of Spanish Harlem*. Be afraid. Be *very* afraid.

"No one should be reading at the table," she says. "This is family time. All I ask is that we have one Sunday a month to catch up. Can we do that, please?" She spares me the evil eye.

"Sorry, cielito," Nelson says. "You're absolutely right." Hearing the appeasing tone of his voice, I can't help but grin. Nelson's a tall, imposing figure, with a head full of salt-and-pepper curls and smooth, dark skin; he's not the kind of man to back down from anyone. But my mother's not just anyone, and he chooses his battles wisely. In an effort to deflect any punishment for his minor infraction, Nelson turns to Denise. "Mija, put that phone away."

Denise smirks at him. "Sure, Papi." Then she turns to me. "So, bro, are you bringing a date to the wedding?"

I should have known this would come up. My mother's single-minded focus on the wedding supplies Denise with more than enough material to torment me. Being the oldest child and only son in a Puerto Rican family comes with many privileges—it also comes with several burdens. I'm twenty-nine, single, and uninterested in dating anyone seriously. In other words, my very existence is breaking my mother's heart.

"What single man in his right mind brings a woman to a wedding? I intend to show up unattached and ready to calm the fears of the unmarried ladies in distress."

"What exactly will they be distressed about?" Denise asks.

"Their unmarried status, of course. Everyone knows single women fall apart when their girlfriends get married. I'll be there to pick up the pieces."

Truth: I don't believe this at all. But someone has to annoy Denise, and I consider it my side hustle.

"You do realize you're almost thirty, right? Isn't it time for you to finally grow up?"

"You're pot, I'm kettle. We've already met." Denise flings a piece of bread at me, and I swat it away like a martial arts expert. I own a business. Denise is a second-year law student at NYU. We're adults with respectable prospects. But when we're together, we each chisel away at the other's maturity until we both resemble teenagers.

"Para con eso," my mother says. "In what world is it okay to throw food at the dining table? Not in this world, that's for sure."

"Sorry," I say.

My mom points a fork in my direction. "Now, I'm only going to say this once. There will be no hookups at the wedding. Jason, find a date. A *suitable* date."

"What about Denise?" I counter.

"Too busy with school," my lying sister says with a wink.

"Well, how am I supposed to find a date on such short notice?"

My mother's unmoved. "Use your resources... wisely. And *don't* bring a woman who thinks one of those spandex tube dresses is an appropriate outfit for a wedding."

"Now you're just expecting the impossible," Denise says.

Gesturing with her fingers, my mother tells Denise to *zip it*. Then she juts her ear out toward me, as if she's daring me to say anything. "In fact," she continues, "try something new: Bring someone you could see yourself dating seriously. Maybe even marrying. Isn't it about time you start thinking about a wife and kids?"

Shit, she's going for the jugular today. I thought about a wife and kids a few years ago, but as my mother damn well knows, it didn't work out the way I wanted it to.

"What about Lisa?" Denise asks me. "You already know her, and she's a do-gooder. The kind of person I could see you tolerating enough to settle down with one day."

"Ooh, yes," my mother says, detecting none of Denise's sarcasm. "She's a wonderful girl. Helps kids for a living. Good head on her shoulders. Respectful. Sweet. Doesn't try to be the center of attention all the time."

"All true, but I'm not dating my younger sister's best friend. Ever."

"Why not?" Denise asks. "She may not be my type, but even I can admit she's hot as hell."

Seriously, if Neanderthal were a language, Denise would be its most fluent speaker. To them, I say, "Because dating someone close to the family is a recipe for arroz y being all up in my business. Change of subject, please."

Besides, I'd prefer not to date, period. It's all bullshit anyway. People put on their best selves when they're dating, and then when things get serious, they drop the mask like it's the day after Halloween. Just ask my birth father. So no, thank you. I've learned my lessons, and I'm not interested in repeating them.

My mother peers at me; the gears in her head spinning, I'm sure. "Well, if you're not interested in bringing a date, you won't mind if I tell a few of my friends that you're available, right? Let's see if you enjoy having a bunch of women and their mothers trying to get your attention."

Denise chuckles. "What is this? Regency England? Planning to present Jason to the Latinx ton? Is he this season's diamond of the last water?"

I don't even know what that means, but I think there's an insult in there somewhere, so I pointedly stare at Denise as I scratch my nose with my middle finger. Childish, yes. Typical? Also yes.

"Well, if he wants to be single for the rest of his life, he shouldn't have a problem being the most eligible bachelor in the room."

"Sounds like a threat," I say.

"Sounds like you're scared," my mother replies.

The gleam in her eyes is a little frightening, but I school my expression. "Hardly. Give it your best shot."

"Oh, I will. Don't you worry about that."

I may not be interested in dating, but I'll never say no to a little fun, and if I'm understanding my mother correctly, she's planning to throw a bunch of women my way. Sounds like heaven.

chapter 3

JASON

I'm officially in hell.

"Open your legs a little," Manolo, an old family friend and top-notch tailor, tells me as he measures my inseam for the suit I'll be wearing to Cami's wedding.

"No foreplay?" I whisper.

He playfully smacks my thigh and continues to whip through the process.

We're in Xiomara's Bridal & Tux Shop, a small boutique located on the second floor of a three-story walk-up on Lexington Avenue. A few feet away, my mother talks with her older sister, Titi Lourdes, and another longtime friend as everyone waits for Cami to try on a different gown. Across from me, Denise and Lisa are being measured for their bridesmaid attire; consistent with her blunt personality, Denise is complaining about having to wear a "froufrou" dress.

"Get over it," Lisa snaps.

"Bite me," Denise counters.

Their squabbling isn't even the hellish part. No, the hellish part is that virtual strangers (to me) are stopping by to congratulate my mother on the upcoming nuptials—as if the day is all about her—and *every* single one of them thinks it's okay to interrogate me about my bachelor status. There are no boundaries among Latinx folks.

"What are you looking for in a wife?" my mother's friend asks. "A stay-at-home mom, or does she need to work outside the home too?"

As if I'm choosing my partner from a list of options on a touch screen. Jesus. "I'm not looking for a wife, so neither, I guess."

Giving me something to do, Manolo grabs a jacket off a wardrobe rack and hands it to me. "Try this one first."

As I slip on the jacket, another "visitor" pokes her head through the drapes separating the dressing area from the sales floor.

"Elba, ¿cómo estás, mi amor?"

"Ay, querida, estoy tan cansada. Esta boda me va a matar."

Being dramatic is my mother's full-time job. Is this wedding really going to kill her? Really?

"Jason, say hello to Maria. You remember her from the neighborhood, right? Her daughter was a year behind you at Mount Carmel."

"Sure, yeah. Nice to see you again."

Maria clasps her hands together and gives me heart eyes. "You're so tall and strong now! I can't believe some woman hasn't snapped you up yet. What are you waiting for?"

"That's the issue," my mother mutters. "He's not waiting for anyone or anything."

"I guess I just haven't found 'the one' yet," I say, narrowing my eyes at my mother.

"Do you want kids?" Maria asks.

"Um, I'm not at the stage of my life that kids are even in my head."

"But what about in the future? How many would you say is good? I hope my daughter is blessed with five. Three girls and two boys."

"Five?" I bark out. "¡¿En esta economía?!"

"Recession or not, we always find a way to care for our children."

What the hell is happening? I expected my mother to trot out a few women to make her point, but this is more than that. *Way* more than that. I'm being sized up like a prize horse. By random people whose daughters aren't even here.

Suddenly a younger version of Maria separates the drapes and strides inside. I spoke too soon. This is Maria's daughter, I presume. Can't remember her name, though. She gives the elders air-kisses, then sidles up to me. "I hear you're looking for a wife."

"Definitely not."

She gives me a shaky laugh. "Oh, good. Because I'm not interested in a husband. Way too busy with my career." Then she looks me up and down. "But a hookup would be nice. As long as you're not looking to stay the night. I'm way too—"

"Busy with your career," I finish for her. "Yeah, I get it. Uh, thanks for the offer, but I'm not really looking for a hookup, either, um . . . What's your name?"

"Does it matter?" she asks glumly.

Well, damn. "I'd like to think so, but if you don't want to give it to me, that's fine too. Good to see you anyway."

"Is it?"

I want to melt into the floor. Anything to get me out of this excruciating experience. My mother has really outdone herself.

Just when I think I won't be able to take any more, Cami reappears, her eyes glistening as she lets everyone take in the full effect of what I assume is "the dress." Damn, my baby sister is a vision. I remember when she and Denise would trail after me, wanting to play with their big brother. And I always would. Ditched my friends any chance I got. Because my sisters were kind and curious and looked up to me. I didn't deserve their adoration, but they gave it to me just the same. Now look at Cami. She's all grown up and ready to change the world.

"¡Dios mío, te ves hermosa, mija! ¡Como una princesa!" my mother exclaims.

Everyone gathers around Cami, oohing and aahing as they should. Behind her, Denise and Lisa look just as happy that this dress appears to be the winner. I glance at Lisa but quickly turn away when she meets my gaze shyly. I don't know for sure that she's interested in me, but sometimes I catch a look from her that can best be described as longing. She's been Cami's friend since they were teenagers, so I think of her as family. *Of course* my sister thinks Lisa and I would make the perfect couple, but I'm way too jaded for someone like her. She's butterflies and rainbows. I'm moths and cloudy skies. She's a love-can-conquer-anything kind of woman. I'm a love-is-never-gonna-happen type of guy.

I can already see how it all would go down too: I'd tell her that I'm not interested in anything serious. That I'm not sure I'll ever want to get married or have children. And she'll play along, claiming she's not sure about any of that stuff either. Because that's what people do. They bend. They reinvent themselves. Or they pretend so they can get their foot in the door, figuratively speaking. We're never our true selves when we're trying to impress someone. Not even me. No one really knows the person they're with. It's no surprise, then, that relationships inevitably sour. When intentions are revealed. Or indiscretions are discovered.

Maria subtly makes her way over to me. "Ask my daughter on a date. I bet she would say yes."

"Did my mother put you up to this?"

Maria shrugs. "She just mentioned that you need a woman to help you settle down."

"Your daughter isn't interested in settling down either."

"Danielle doesn't know what she wants. Maybe you two would be good for each other."

"If we are, I'm sure we could find that out on our own. Without our mothers being involved."

Maria backs away. "Okay, okay. I can take a hint. But what about—"

My phone rings, and Maria swallows whatever she was going to say. Yes. Finally. A reprieve. Based on the tone, I already know the call's from Eric, my best friend and business partner. Feigning a pressing need to answer, I excuse myself and walk out to the sales floor.

"What's up, man?" I say.

"Hey, just a heads-up that the cabinets the designer wanted are back-ordered..."

Okay, *this* issue I can handle. Mothers trying to convince me to date their daughters? Not so much.

VANESSA

"C'mon, c'mon. Where *is* she?"

I'm double-parked near the door to Xiomara's Bridal & Tux Shop, and my sister isn't answering my texts. Of course. This is what I get for trying to warm Lisa up with small favors and offering her a ride to her place in the Bronx. What are the odds I'll be able to run upstairs and let her know I'm here without getting a ticket or pissing off the person I'm blocking with my car? With my luck? The odds are definitely *not* in my favor, but I'm going to risk it anyway. So I take one last look at my phone, willing Lisa to respond, and when she doesn't, I dart out of the car.

After huffing and puffing up the stairs, I dash inside the shop, the chime above the door summoning absolutely no one.

"Hello?"

I spin around uselessly, trying to figure out where everyone could be, until I register people laughing in the back. I'm looking down at my phone again to see if Lisa received my messages as I make my way in that direction, when suddenly I'm tumbling into a clothing rack and grasping at air to avert a catastrophe. "Shit!"

Someone helps to keep me upright, and before I can get my bearings, the person is chuckling.

"Sorry," I say as I unhook my shorts from the steel rod holding a mishmash of glittery miniskirts. Looking back, I immediately spot the culprit that caused my graceless entrance: a piece of worn and buckling carpet. "That was a close one."

"I'll give you points for creativity, but if you wanted to meet me, all you had to do is shake my hand and say hello."

The arrogance in the person's voice causes me to whip my head in their direction. Wow, he's a cutie—but his mouth is ruining the view. He's tall, broad shouldered, and boy-next-door handsome. Inky black hair, dark eyes, and thick brows. A jaw so sharp I can picture the points of a triangle mapped onto it. His lips curve into a smile that sends my brain to dangerous places. It's telling me he can sweet-talk my mother and dirty-talk his way into my pants. I'm unreasonably annoyed by his presence. "Sorry to burst your bubble, but that was *not* an attempt to flirt. I literally tripped."

"Sure you did," the guy says, his knowing smile widening.

Whatever. I dismiss him with a wave and bend to pick up my phone, feeling a twinge in my lower back as I do. Ouch. Must have strained a muscle as I attempted to break my fall.

When I straighten, the guy's still standing there, a smug expression firmly in place. "I'm looking for the Torres wedding party." I point behind him. "Are they back there?"

"The person you're actually looking for is right here. Did my mother invite you?"

"What? Why would she?"

"Look, I know what's going on," he says wearily as he flips his baseball cap backward and places it on his head. "And although I'm sure you're a lovely woman, I'm not interested in dating someone handpicked by my mother."

Oh, this is hilarious. This guy doesn't have a clue. "I'm not sure what's sadder: that your mother handpicks potential dates for you or that you're presumptuous enough to think I'm one of them. Either way, you're acting like an overgrown toddler."

His smile slips, then he winces, his face scrunched up in embarrassment. When he tries to speak, his words get swallowed by a coughing fit. Bending at the waist, he walks in a circle as he tries to clear his throat.

"There, there. Do you need me to burp you? Or is it time to go potty?"

"Haha," he says, returning to his full height. "I'm fine, thank you. And yeah, I deserved that. My apologies. I completely misread the situation."

"You certainly did. Now, can you tell me if the Torres family is back there?"

"They are." He puts out a hand. "I'm Jason Torres, older brother of the bride."

I take it—grudgingly. "I'm Vanessa Cordero, older sister of one of the bridesmaids."

His eyes widen. "You're Lisa's sister."

"Yes."

Then it hits me: This is the guy Lisa's infatuated with. Yikes. I couldn't be more underwhelmed. Well, okay, I get the surface appeal. He's good-looking, sure. Still, I've only been in his presence for a minute, and his personality not only leaves a lot to be desired but also extinguishes any desire altogether. He's a molten chocolate lava cake that doesn't erupt when you sink your spoon into it: a beauty on the outside that doesn't deliver the goods as advertised. My gut's telling me this isn't Lisa's person, but if I tell her so, she'll only convince herself I'm wrong.

"Your sister's a sweetheart," he says. "And it's nice to meet you."

"It's interesting to meet you too."

"Interesting?"

"I'm trying to be polite."

"Right," he says, dragging out the word to underscore that I'm not being polite at all.

"So," I say, pointing behind him. "Can I head back there? I'm double-parked."

He slides out of my way and gestures grandly. "Be my guest."

I shuffle past him and poke my head through the drapes, spotting my sister next to the bride-to-be. Wait a minute. Something's not right. I reach behind me and make direct contact with my ... underwear. Because I ripped my goddamn shorts when I collided with the damn clothing rack. What in the nineties-rom-com nonsense is this? I squeeze my eyes shut and count to five. I am never doing anyone a favor ever again.

"You can go right in," Jason says.

Hoping he hasn't noticed my white cotton bloomers, I turn to the side. "Um, no. I don't want to interrupt." I wave frantically at my sister, but she refuses to look in my direction. "Psst, Lisa. Psst."

Jason gives me a quizzical once-over, then pushes back the drapes and enters the dressing area. "Lisa, your sister's here!"

"She is?" Wearing an I-don't-give-a-single-fuck expression, Lisa finally meets my gaze. She's been blowing hot and cold ever since I told her I wouldn't be her starter ex. "Sorry, Vanessa. I was supposed to be outside at three, wasn't I?"

She knows for a fact she was supposed to be outside. I'm tempted to snatch a chunk of hair from her head to jog her memory. *Breathe, Vanessa, breathe. Patience, serenity, lead with love.* "It's okay, but we do have to go. I'm going to get a ticket if we don't leave soon."

"No problem. We're done here. But let me introduce you to everyone before we take off."

"Um, sure," I say, scooting just inside the room.

As Lisa goes through the introductions, I wave at everyone,

making sure to keep my backside hidden from view. "Congrats on the wedding. I'm sure it's going to be lovely. So happy for you, Cami. Okay, bye now!"

Lisa trots after me as I scurry through the sales floor. "What's going on? You were so standoffish. You couldn't even come inside and shake their hands? Give their mom a hug?"

"No. I couldn't. Not with my ass hanging out," I say, pointing to my torn shorts.

Lisa inspects my bottom half and bursts out laughing.

"It's not funny."

"Oh, yes it is."

"Ugh, just ... let's go."

Before we exit the shop, a voice behind us says, "Good to meet you, Vanessa. I'm sure meeting us was a *breath of fresh air*."

I turn around. Jason gives my shorts a once-over, then his mouth twitches.

That. *Asshole*. He couldn't even let me leave with a fraction of my dignity intact. I hope he sleeps in his skivvies tonight and gets attacked by a swarm of mosquitos.

Once we're inside the car, I turn to Lisa. "So that's Jason, huh?"

"Yeah," she says, her expression dreamy. "And his mom was in there, throwing the possibility of women at him left and right. A lady even propositioned him for a hookup, and I was literally standing three feet away from them. It was torture."

Lisa looks so forlorn at this, my heart hurts for her. But there's something sinister stirring in me too: Lisa wants Jason. Jason needs to be humbled. And isn't it lovely that I know exactly how to accomplish both?

"I'll do it," I blurt out.

Lisa tilts her head and squints at me. "Do what?"

"Be your starter ex."

Her eyes flicker with hope. "You will?"

"I will."

"Shit, V. I'm so damn grateful." She leans over and hugs me tightly. We haven't had a moment like this in ages; it's promising and gives me the mental push to commit to this farce.

After we separate, she grabs on to my arm. "Ooh, I have an idea. Let's have a sleepover. Like when we were young. We can order some food from La Fonda, get in our jammies, and chat about how we're going to do this. What do you think?"

"But I don't have any clothes," I say with a chuckle.

The thing is, I'm playing it cool, but I'm actually giddy inside. This is precisely what I wanted: a chance to reconnect with my sister. It's almost as if the incident we never speak about has been wiped from her brain. I'm not so arrogant to think that's actually true, but her enthusiasm gives me hope that we can get beyond it someday.

"Pfft, that's not a big deal," she says. "I can let you borrow something."

"Okay, let's do it."

Lisa dives back in for another hug. "Ahh, this is going to be great. You're the best, Vanny."

No, in reality, I'm the worst. And Jason's going to discover that fact soon enough.

chapter 4

VANESSA

"¿Quieres un poco de mi bistec encebollado?" Lisa asks.

"What?"

"My steak and onions, Vanny. Goodness. Do you want some?"

"Oh, sure. I didn't hear you."

"More like your command of the Spanish language is limited to hola, adiós, tengo hambre, and ¿dónde está el baño?"

She's not wrong, but I'll never tell her how much that fact bothers me, so I pretend to be unfazed. "Shut up, pendeja. I know more than that. You forgot cabrón, puñeta, coño, hijo de la gran puta, bicho, chocha, and arranca pa'l carajo."

"Impressive. You can have sex with a guy and insult him *and* his mother when he turns out to be bad in bed."

"Exactly. Got *all* of my important bases covered."

Lisa reaches over and sticks her fork in my pollo guisado, swiping a potato before I can even object. We're facing each other on a sumptuous midnight-blue velvet couch, our lower halves tucked under chenille throws.

"Okay, so what's the plan?" she asks. "How does this usually work?"

I set down my plate and take her through the basics: "Think of it as a roller-coaster ride. The relationship starts with the initial climb. There's anticipation. Excitement. A little trepidation. This is when I'm flirty and giving good banter. Then we reach the top of the hill. Things are good. He's truly starting to see the possibilities. In reality, it's the high point, and he's about to experience a nightmare of a drop."

"How do you keep him coming back after the drop?"

"That's when we enter the loop-the-loop phase. A little good here. A little confusion there. Just enough to make him feel like he doesn't know up from down. He starts to wonder whether I'm right for him. And then I do something that pulls him back in."

"Girl, this is diabolical."

"I know."

"And then what?"

"And then we settle into the brake run."

"What's that?"

"That's the section of track that slows down the ride before it ends. So to continue with the analogy, this is when the writing's on the wall and the breakup is close."

"And this works for you?"

I pick up my plate and dig in to my food again. "Not every time, but it's worked way more often than it's failed."

"So how do we get started? Setting this in motion with Jason, I mean."

"Well, we need a reason for us to be in the same place. That's the first step. It's probably too soon to get an invite to anything related to his sister's wedding. And since I can't guarantee that

I'll be able to charm him quickly, we need a nonobvious reason to put me in his orbit on more than one occasion."

Lisa ponders this for a moment, her head tilted to the side. "What about the store? Jason's in construction, and La Flor needs some updating before Mami and Papi can put it on the market, right? I already talked to Papi about the idea of getting someone to stage the place, so he won't mind or ask too many questions. I'm thinking it wouldn't be suspicious at all to ask for Jason's advice. See if he would be willing to stop by and take a look. Maybe he'd agree to help."

"That could work, actually. I'm on vacation until the satellite office opens in August, so I can help at the store until then and be the go-between if he comes around. If that doesn't pan out, we can always regroup and think up a different plan."

"Okay, great. I'll call him and see if he's free next week."

"Perfect. The next step is target reconnaissance."

"Which means?"

"I need as much information about Jason as you can give me. I'll do my own search of his social media accounts, but why don't you share what you know firsthand. Likes, dislikes, past relationships, whatever else might be helpful. I'm looking for things I can use to my advantage. Either to hook him or to sink him."

She places her finished plate on the coffee table and snuggles into her throw. "Okay, he's twenty-nine like you, grew up Catholic, has two sisters, Cami—she's the one getting married, obviously—and Denise, the law student who swears she's a lawyer already. She's scarily brilliant and also irritating as fuck."

"What's the irritating one's deal?" I ask between forkfuls of stewed chicken.

Lisa shrugs. "She doesn't like me. Never has. I think she's

jealous of my relationship with Cami. Whatever. I try to avoid her as much as possible. I suggest you steer clear of her too."

"Got it. What else?"

"He's an excellent cook. Always brings the most amazing food to family get-togethers."

"Are you sure it's not store-bought?"

"I'm sure. He's using his mother's recipes, and she's damn proud of it."

"That's good. I'll try to make use of that somehow. So he's close to his mom?"

"He's the oldest, and he's the only boy. I don't think he has a choice in the matter."

"True," I say, my lips twisted in a half smile. "What about hobbies?"

"He's a Mets fan. Or is it the Yankees? ¿Qué sé yo?"

"Lili, that's not even funny. There's a huge difference between being a Yankees fan and a Mets fan."

"He's a Mets fan, all right?" Under her breath, she adds, "I'm pretty sure."

"Never mind. It'll be easy enough to get that info on my own."

"Oh," she says, her eyes widening, "and he likes to go thrifting. Also, flea markets. It's a running joke in the family that all of his gifts are secondhand items. I don't think that's true, but they kid him about it anyway."

"That's . . . enlightening. Do *you* enjoy any of his interests?"

She frowns at my question, as if it never occurred to her that she should. "Not sure. Which is why I need the opportunity to figure that out."

Okay then. I'm going to hold my tongue here. No sense in

making her defensive when she's only now warming up to me. "How about past relationships?"

"He's tight-lipped about anyone he's ever dated, but I know he had a serious girlfriend a few years ago. They were talking about an engagement. Cami said they just drifted apart, but I don't think she's telling me the whole story."

"Okay, I'll try to probe him on that topic at some point. It might give you some insight into what he's like as a romantic partner, what issues might come up. How about dislikes? Is he a germophobe? Does he hate dancing in public? Anything I can exploit as a weakness?"

"Ooh, I know he's not big on public displays of affection."

"And how do you know this?" I say, raising an eyebrow.

"Ha, I wish. We've never done anything remotely intimate. But I remember that when Cami first started seeing Bryan, she was confused about his lack of affection on dates, so she asked Jason about it. He said he understood where Bryan was coming from because not all guys are into PDA, including him. He told her this might be something she would have to compromise on. That she couldn't expect Bryan to go beyond his own comfort zone if he didn't want to, but also that Bryan should try to bend a bit as well."

That's surprisingly decent advice. Maybe Jason isn't a complete asshole; maybe it's a three-quarters deal. "And you said he's in construction?"

"Yeah, he runs his own construction management firm. I don't think he gets his hands all that dirty anymore. Mostly supervises projects around the city. Brings subcontractors together. Orders in bulk to get discounts for all of his subs."

"What's the name of the firm?"

"TAG Building Group."

I immediately think of the talented and gifted program I attended before I was whisked away to private school. "Does TAG stand for something?"

"Torres and Gibson. Eric Gibson is his friend and partner."

"So he's handsome, he cooks, he owns a business, and he loves his family. I'm beginning to see the appeal."

Lisa's eyes spark with admiration. "Told you he's a catch. And he's my best friend's brother, which is just the icing on the cake."

Any minute now, my internal eye roll is going to dislodge a critical part of my brain. "Do you have any clue what he's like as a boss?"

"I know from Cami that he's self-conscious about his age relative to his employees. A number of them have been working in construction for decades, and here comes this kid, telling them what to do. He's a bit withdrawn around them, according to her."

Lovingly patting my food baby, I stand and take my plate to the sink, where I wash and rinse it before placing it in the dish rack. "I think that's enough to get me going. If you remember anything else that might be useful, just let me know."

"Sounds good. I'm going to check in with him about visiting the store." She waggles her eyebrows. "Now I have an excuse to contact him."

She picks up her phone.

"You're calling him *this minute*?"

"No time like the present!"

Seeing her so enthusiastic about our joint project confirms that I made the right choice. She's brimming with the kind of good energy I haven't seen in her since I came home.

I chew on a hangnail as I wait for the call to connect. Judging by the way she jumps up from the couch, it does.

"Hey, Jason. It's Lisa. How are you?"

There's a pause on Lisa's end, and then she lets out a torrent of words: "Oh no, everything's fine. It's just . . . I wanted to ask a favor. See, my parents are trying to get a buyer to take over their business, and my sister and I think it's going to need some updating before anyone will even look at it. We don't want to get fleeced by anyone, so I was wondering if you would be willing to check out the store and give us your recommendations. Maybe give us a sense of how much we should pay for the changes . . . You will? That's amazing, thank you! Oh, tomorrow? That soon?"

Lisa gives me a questioning look, and I give her a thumbs-up.

"Yeah, tomorrow works. Eleven?"

She stares at me, her head tilted to indicate that she's asking the question to us both. I nod.

"Yeah, eleven's good," she says. "Sure, great. We'll see you then. And thanks again!" After the call ends, she blows out her cheeks. "He'll drop by tomorrow."

"Excellent. I'm going to tell Mami I'll cover for her so she can sleep in. Otherwise, she's going to be nosy and wonder if we're up to something. Why don't you plan to show up after eleven? That way, he'll be forced to talk to me before you get there. Sound good?"

"Yeah." Then she shakes her head.

"What? Second thoughts already?"

"No, it's just . . . it's exciting and nerve-racking at the same time. And holy shit, this might work."

"Of course it'll work. But Lili, you need to be sure about this.

Because once we go down this road, you can't just take it back. It'll always be a thing between you two. And you can never tell him. Not unless you want to undo everything you accomplished."

She nods decisively. "I know. And I'm sure. He's worth it."

Now *that* remains to be seen, but if she truly wants to go through with this scheme, I promise to be the best worst girlfriend Jason Torres has ever had.

"Good. Let's shake on it."

She takes my hand, her eyes overly bright. Okay, then. Ill-advised or not, we're doing this. Let Operation Best Friend's Older Brother begin.

chapter 5

JASON

The outside of the Corderos' store reminds me of American Deli Market, a bodega in my Greenpoint, Brooklyn, neighborhood that was forced to close a few years ago. A weathered yellow-and-red sign tells me I'll find beer, vegetables, and an ATM behind its doors. Faded dollar bills with the words *Buena suerte* and *Good luck* are taped to the window, a tribute to the customers who wished the Corderos well when they first opened the place. And yeah, there's a cat sitting by the entrance, but that cat has a purpose, like it will fuck you up if you mess with the stacks of Deer Park water bottles it naps on every afternoon.

To the people in this community, like in my own, a convenience store isn't just the spot to grab a loose cigarette, a half gallon of milk, or a lottery ticket. No, it's an institution, the local watercooler, and the best spot to get a cheap and delicious sandwich. For the folks who grew up here, it signifies home.

Wanting to get a feel for the environment before announcing my arrival, I slip inside behind a group of teenagers and try to blend in as best I can. The sounds of Mega 97.9 play from speakers hidden somewhere above the white drop tile ceiling, and people are conversing while they shop, as if the middle of an aisle is the perfect location to catch up or ask about Doña Isabel's arthritis. There's a middle-aged guy making sandwiches on the grill, and Lisa's older sister, Vanessa, is manning the register. She's a live wire, that one. When I saved her from face-planting yesterday afternoon, the restless energy crackled off her in waves. Now she looks chill. In her element. And she's actually smiling, a thing I wasn't sure she knew how to do. Her testy attitude amuses me. Makes me want to burrow under her skin and remain there, just to spite her. It's an immature reaction, sure, but I have to acknowledge my flaws if I want to try to get rid of them.

There's a long line to place deli orders, so it's easy to escape everyone's notice. I walk through the aisles, relieved to see enough space for two people to pass each other—that's a luxury in Manhattan. I can picture the necessary improvements already: better lighting, dedicated and easier-to-reach shelves for fruits and vegetables, a different style of tile flooring than the psychedelic black-and-white diamond pattern that's making my head spin. I assume they're looking for easy fixes, updates that will increase the attractiveness of the property instead of eating into the profits from the sale. The work wouldn't take too long—a few weekends at most—and I could get it done myself with the help of one or two of my men. But I won't offer my time just yet. I need to get a sense of the dynamic I'd be signing up for first.

Seconds after the door chime rings, a booming voice grabs my attention. "Yo, Papito, can I get a medium coffee with cream and sugar and a bacon, egg, and cheese on a roll? Don't skimp on the butter when you toast that roll, okay?"

The person, probably in his twenties, walks into the store like it's his regular hangout spot and the long line of customers isn't his concern. Judging by the smiles and waves thrown his way, everyone seems to know him too. Each neighborhood has at least one larger-than-life character; this guy looks to be theirs.

With his back turned, the guy at the grill raises his hand in the air, then continues flipping items.

"My shift starts soon, so make it snappy!" the new customer says, laughter in his voice.

"Snappy, my ass," the cook replies, his spatula swinging in the air.

"Why you gotta be like that, Papito?"

"Because you're a pain."

"But you love me, too, right?"

The cook grunts.

The new guy's eyes shift to Vanessa and go wide. "Ey-yo! Is that little Vanny I see?"

"Yup, it's me, Chito," she says, smiling.

Vanny. I like the nickname. Makes her seem more approachable.

"Look at you, mama," Chito says. "All grown up. Your mom said you were in Chicago. Just visiting, I hope?"

My ears perk up. I'm curious to know her deal, and I don't really have a good reason to ask her these questions myself, so I eavesdrop on their conversation.

"I'm here for a while, actually," she tells Chito. "My firm's opening an office in Midtown and asked me to be a part of the launch. Taking some time off until I start in August."

"It's a promotion," the older guy proudly says from his spot at the grill.

"Living with your parents?" Chito asks Vanessa.

"No, I'm renting a place in the Village."

"Nice. I always knew you would do big things. I'm glad you got out. This neighborhood was never good enough for you anyway."

I think Chito means it as a compliment, but Vanessa's face falls, leading me to believe she didn't take it as one.

"What about you?" she asks, apparently shaking off whatever bothered her about his statement. "How's your mom? Your little sister?"

"We're all fine. Can't complain. I work for the MTA now. Driving buses, mostly the M15 line."

"You like it?"

"It's all right. Pays the bills."

"Order up, *Papito*," the guy at the grill says, sarcastically mimicking the nickname Chito used for him earlier. Now that the cook's facing the sales floor, I realize he bears a striking resemblance to Vanessa. Must be her father.

Chito grabs the bag and the to-go cup of coffee, places a few bills on the counter, and heads for the door. "Take care, Vanny. Be good, okay?"

"Where's the fun in that?" Vanessa says with a wink and a wave.

Huh. She's a flirty one too. I'm learning a lot about Ms. Cordero this morning.

Her eyes scan the store, then she does a double take when she notices me standing among the other customers. "Oh, you're here."

"Wanted to grab something to drink first," I say, raising the bottle of iced tea I grabbed for cover. "How much?"

"It's on us. Lisa mentioned that you'd be stopping by to make some recommendations for the store. That was . . . nice of you."

I tilt my head and grin at her. "Was that hard? Speaking about me in positive terms?"

"Yes," she says, her eyes twinkling. "Considering how you acted when we met, I made all kinds of assumptions. I can admit some of them may have been too harsh."

"You're forgiven."

"Oh, I wasn't apologizing."

"Of course not. Let me guess, you operate without a filter."

"Ha, this *is* the filtered version. If you knew my real thoughts, you'd probably cry."

"Too late. I'm already crying on the inside."

Her smile fades. "Yes, well, I seem to have that effect on people."

"That's not what I . . ." I cut myself off and rake a hand through my freshly cut hair. We don't know each other well enough for me to dig into whatever *that* was. "Is Lisa around?"

"She's running a little late, but she'll be here soon. Let me check these folks out, and then I'll introduce you to my dad."

"Sounds good," I say, opening the bottle.

After she sorts out the customers, and there's no one else in line, she rounds the counter and motions for me to follow her. She raps on the top of the deli display case. "Papi, let me introduce you to someone."

"Coming, nena," he says as he removes his plastic gloves. When he sees me, he smiles.

Vanessa points to me as if she's Vanna White presenting a prize package. "Papi, this is Jason. He's Camila's older brother. Jason, this is my father, Cándido."

"Mucho gusto," her father says. "Your sister's an angel."

"El gusto es mío. And yeah, that's what we call her sometimes."

"Jason works in construction," Vanessa says.

"I'm a home builder."

"He owns his own business too," Vanessa adds.

"I do commercial and residential remodeling as well."

Cándido looks between Vanessa and me. "You two should take this show on the road."

The wisecrack breaks the ice, and we all laugh.

"Lisa told me you could give us some pointers," he continues. "But I want to be clear: I don't have a lot of money to make all kinds of changes. This one"—he points at Vanessa—"wants to make this a place for the gringos."

My gaze darts to Vanessa, and her chin dips. I'm interested in knowing why it does, but I'm also unsure why it matters.

"All I want is for La Flor to stay the same," Cándido says, his hands gesturing wildly. "We're in Harlem. This is El Ba-rri-o. Spanish Harlem. Not SpaHa or whatever the hell the kids are calling it now. I want someone to take over the lease and make bacon, egg, and cheese sandwiches all day."

"Understood," I say. "I have only one question."

"Dímelo," he says, stepping forward and crossing his arms.

"Does the cat come with the store?"

Cándido's stance relaxes, and he wags a finger at me. "You're a good kid. I can tell." Then he slaps me on the back. "Come by anytime."

Behind him, Vanessa rolls her eyes. And because I know she'll hate it, I wink at her. She flicks her gaze at the ceiling and walks away. Yeah, this is going to be fun.

✕ ✕ ✕

"So that's it," I say after walking through the suggested improvements with Cándido and Vanessa. "Not a complete overhaul. Just small fixes here and there."

"Sounds reasonable," Cándido says. "I can picture everything. Would look real nice. I can even see myself hanging on to the store a few more years with those kinds of changes."

Vanessa grumbles. "That's definitely not the point, Papi."

He grimaces in embarrassment. "I know, I know." To me, he says, "Do you have someone you could recommend for this kind of job?"

This is clearly in my wheelhouse, and he's already mentioned that money's tight. Plus, I like that he's trying to preserve the neighborhood's vibe. It's an easy decision. "I can do it. Not by myself. But I have a couple of work friends who owe me a favor anyway."

"How much would it cost?" he asks, his eyes narrowing as though he expects me to hoodwink him.

"Free of charge," I say easily.

"What?" he replies, placing his hands on his chest. "That's too much."

"I can pay you," Vanessa adds. "Assuming your fees are reasonable."

"No, you can't, mija," her father says. "I won't allow it. This is *our* business, your mother's and mine. We're responsible for the expenses."

"But Papi—"

"I'm not charging anything, so there's no need for you two to get into it," I interject. "Please. Lisa's like family to me, so that makes you family too. And it would be my pleasure to help keep a Latinx business in the community. I'll get the materials from the leftovers of past jobs. All in top condition, so I won't be cutting corners. The only thing I ask is that you give us some of those amazing sandwiches when we're hungry."

"That's no problem at all. We'll take good care of you." Cándido's eyes grow wide, then he scurries away, shouting over his shoulder, "Hold on a minute. I might have something you'd like." He returns with two tickets in his hand. "You're a fan of the Mets?"

"Damn right I am. They're my team."

"Eh, we can't all be perfect. A customer gave them to me, but if they're your team, I want you to have them. Consider it a small gift for agreeing to help with the store."

I glance at the tickets as he hands them to me. "The Mets versus the Cincinnati Reds. That's very generous. Why don't you want them?"

Cándido rolls up his sleeve and points to his forearm. "Do you see that?"

"Um, what I am looking for? Your veins?"

"Exactly," he says. "That's Yankees blood running through them. I will never step foot in Citi Field. Not as long as it's where the Mets play."

"The theater called; it wants the drama back," Vanessa says. "And if I'm recalling correctly, you promised those tickets to me. So I could finally get to experience Citi Field in person."

"I did?"

"You did, Papi," Lisa says, appearing at the end of an aisle like a jack-in-the-box. "And sorry I'm late, but I did hear you say you'd give them to Vanny."

Cándido frowns. "Maybe I did." He shrugs. "I don't remember."

"She can have them," I say to Cándido. "I don't want you to have to go back on your promise."

Lisa looks between Vanessa and me, her eyes brightening as if an idea has just popped into her head. "Why don't you two go together? That way, Papi gets to keep his promise and Jason gets his gift." She claps once. "Done."

"Great idea," Cándido says.

"Why do you two assume I don't already have plans to take someone?" Vanessa asks.

"Do you?" her father and Lisa ask in unison.

"No," she mutters.

"See?" her father says. "And it doesn't have to be a date or anything. But you're never going to find someone if you stay in your apartment all day."

Vanessa snaps her eyes shut. "Oh my God."

"I feel your pain," I offer.

She opens her eyes. "Do you? Is your pain named Cándido too?"

We all laugh, and then Vanessa lets out a sigh of defeat.

"I'm game," she says, her head tilted as she studies me. "How about you?"

"I'm game too."

"It's settled," Lisa says, rushing over to the register to help a customer who's starting to look annoyed by the wait.

"I'm going to get out of here, then," Vanessa tells us. "I need to hit the GreenFlea Market"—she narrows her eyes at her father—"so the *apartment I stay in all day* doesn't look so empty."

"It's called the Grand Bazaar NYC now," I say.

"Thanks, Wikipedia, but it'll always be GreenFlea to me."

"What are you looking for?" Lisa asks.

"A dresser."

Lisa's brows snap together. "How are you going to fit it into your tiny-ass car?"

Vanessa waves away her sister's question. "I'll figure it out. I always do."

This, too, is an easy decision. I want to be around this woman—if only to get a better sense of who she is—so I'm going to offer her a ride. "I have my truck. Want me to take you?"

Her eyes round in surprise. "The better question is, do *you* want to take me?"

"I do."

"You'd wait around as I shop?"

"I, uh, I wouldn't mind picking up a few things for myself. Flea market shopping is kind of my thing."

She blinks at me. "Come again?"

"I said flea market shopping is kind of my thing," I repeat with a chuckle.

"Let's do it, then," Vanessa says, giving me a wink.

She's so damn beautiful I can't think straight. Makeup-free and glowing, she's a sight to behold. The bronze curls that dance across her shoulders and appear soft to the touch only add to her allure. Tanned skin. Golden-brown eyes. A dusting of freckles on her nose and cheeks. Looking at her is like facing the sun and letting its warmth settle into your skin. I stare at her—for too long, apparently.

"Jason."

"What?"

"Your offer. I'm taking you up on it...unless you've changed your mind?"

I step back, shaking my head. "Right. The flea market. Yeah, let's do it."

"Are you okay?"

"I'm fine. Not enough sugar today. Probably hypoglycemic."

"The iced tea in your hand might help."

"Right," I say, then guzzle said tea like the thirsty man I am.

Damn, why do I feel like a kid around her? Awkward and shy. No game to be found anywhere. Maybe it's because, for the first time in a long while, I'm not looking for red flags. Vanessa isn't concerned about impressing me. She's comfortable in her own skin, and if you don't like the skin she's in, she doesn't care. I admire that about her. A lot. For once, I'm open to going with the flow and seeing where this goes. Hopefully my instincts won't steer me wrong.

chapter 6

VANESSA

This is going to be a ridiculously easy assignment.

I mean, the guy can't even resist going to a flea market with a woman who's obviously not impressed with him. It's kind of adorable, actually. Maybe Jason *could* be Lisa's person someday. So yeah, it's all working out beautifully. And my dad coming through in the clutch by offering him Mets tickets? Perfection.

Jason's handling the city streets as if he's on a Sunday drive in the suburbs. He's not even bothered by the people rudely honking before they cut him off. He's relaxed. Unwary and unsuspecting. Which means it's time to hook him with my patented tease-him-until-it-hurts-so-good approach. I groan dramatically. "At this rate, the market will be closed when we get there."

"Are you criticizing my driving?"

"Yeah. Isn't that obvious?"

He lifts his foot off the accelerator, and the truck slows to a crawl. "Better?"

"No. Do you need me to get out and push?"

"Cute."

"Not as cute as the dresser I can't buy because I'm stuck in this turtle you call a pickup."

Jason doesn't say anything, but the moment there's a break in traffic, he pulls over and stops the vehicle.

"Oh no, what's wrong with it? A flat?"

"Nothing's wrong with it," he says as he unfastens his seat belt. "I'm letting you take over."

"I'm not driving this behemoth! And who owns an F-150 in the city anyway?"

"A person who does construction for a living. Now, if you don't want to drive, I suggest you sit quietly and enjoy the ride. I'm doing you a favor, remember?"

"Testy, testy," I say, crossing my arms over my chest.

"Whiny, whiny," Jason replies.

He. Did. Not. But okay, considering that's the reaction I was going for, I'll give him that one. "Since you're a flea market regular, and we'll be in this turtle-mobile for fourscore and seven years, do you have any tips for getting good deals?"

He makes a low rumbling sound.

"What?" I ask. "You didn't think that little performance was going to change my behavior, did you?"

"I'm slowly learning what to expect from you," he mutters.

"All good, I hope," I say, batting my eyes.

"All interesting, that's for sure."

"And the answer to my question is?"

"I don't even remember the question."

"Tips. I asked if you had any tips for how to get a good deal."

"Ah, right. That's simple: Use me as your secret weapon."

"How?"

"Simple. Pretend that I'm your boyfriend and we need to agree on the sale. If you're trying to cut a deal, ask for my opinion. I'll say the price is too high and walk away. Then you can drag me back and reopen the negotiations. Works every time."

"Look at you," I say, shifting in my seat to give him a once-over. "Undercutting small businesses trying to make ends meet in a struggling economy. You must be so proud."

"Hold up, that's not fair. This is New York. Everyone knows the first price is too high, and they can always be talked down."

"Is that what you tell yourself so you can sleep at night?"

"Damn, I can't win with you."

I give him a lopsided smile. "And there's no point even trying."

In a once-in-a-lifetime maneuver, Jason slips into a parking spot on Columbus Avenue, just as another car abandons it. "This is a good sign. It means we were meant to be here today."

"Maybe it means the dresser of my dreams is in there somewhere," I say as I unfasten my seat belt. "Assuming someone hasn't purchased it already because you drive like you're manning a parade float."

"I'm ignoring you."

"Believe me, others have tried. It can't be done."

He flops his head back against the headrest. "Jesus."

"He's too busy to help you today."

"Lucifer's got *all* the time, I see."

My mouth twitches. Dammit, I'm charmed. *Focus, Vanessa.* "Okay, enough dillydallying. Ready to show me your flea-marketing skills?"

He throws on a fitted Mets cap and surveys the crowd as

though he's preparing for battle. "Let's do this," he says, slipping on a pair of sunglasses.

Oh shit. He truly *is* a flea market aficionado. Why is that so hot?

× × ×

There it is.

With only a few nicks here and there, the double dresser of my dreams is calling to me. A coat of paint and some new hardware will do wonders to make it fit my bedroom aesthetic.

"How much—"

"Keep moving," Jason whispers behind me. "Don't ask about it yet."

"What? Why not?"

He doesn't answer; instead, he takes my hand and pulls me past the vendor's tent.

When we're several feet away, Jason says, "You need to assess the situation first. See if it's a popular item or not."

"But if it's in demand, don't I risk losing out on the chance to buy it?"

"If it's in demand, you're going to end up paying too much for it. Better to focus on the items that aren't getting as much attention."

"But aren't they getting less attention because they're less desirable?"

"Desirability is in the eye of the beholder. The key here is to focus on the diamonds in the rough. The items *you* have a vision for. Don't focus on anyone else. Focus on how *you* feel about it."

"I want to paint the dresser cobalt blue and replace the hardware with glass knobs. I can already picture it in my bedroom."

"Now we're talking," he says, rubbing his hands together. "And in the time we've been standing here, no one's asked about it. See? We're gathering data. Ready to pretend to be my girlfriend?"

"Oh, we're doing that now?"

"Yeah. Would it be okay if I hug you as part of the act?"

"Sure."

"All right," he says. "I'll be there in a few minutes."

"If this works, I'll buy you a shish kebab from that stand over there."

"Make it two, and I'll deliver an Oscar-worthy performance."

"You're on."

We go our separate ways, and then I stroll past the vendor's tent and take a spin around the dresser. "How much are you asking for this one?"

The middle-aged white woman selling it stops reading the book in her hands and grins at me. "One hundred and twenty-five dollars. Just needs a coat of paint and some drawer pulls, and it'll be good as new."

"Nice, isn't it?" a voice behind me says.

I turn and look up at a handsome white man with thick-framed glasses who's giving me a friendly smile. "It is. Calling dibs right now."

He puts up his hands in mock surrender. "It's all yours. I'm interested in something else anyway."

"What?"

"Your number."

I groan. "Wow, does that really work—"

Before I can finish my sentence, Jason wraps his arm around my middle and pulls me toward the front of his body. Whoa. I'm *surrounded* by him. And he smells phenomenal. So much so that I'm tempted to curve into his neck and sniff him. Listen, I'm not a dainty person. I take up space and own it. But I'll confess to enjoying the way I disappear in his arms. This is more than a hug; it's an intimacy that appears grounded in familiarity, even though Jason and I know it's just for show. What's more troubling is that I desperately want to forget all the reasons I should be objecting to the way he's embracing me.

"Find anything you like?" he asks against my ear, his voice silky and low.

The flirty stranger by my side silently slinks away, and I'm left to focus on nothing but my brain's reaction to the man at my back. *This is a superb way to spend a Sunday*, the right side of my brain thinks. *No, it isn't, you disloyal tramp*, thinks the left side.

"Baby, you okay?" he prompts.

Oh, right. We're pretending to be a couple, and I'm messing up my part. Worse, for whatever reason, I go off our nonexistent script and settle my hand over his, essentially encouraging him to remain in place. "Got my eye on this dresser for our bedroom. It's a hundred and twenty-five dollars. What do you think?"

"Eh, it's okay, but I think we should keep looking. I saw another one a few rows down. Want to check that one out before you make any decisions?"

"Ooh, yes. This one isn't *quite* what I was looking for."

"I could do a hundred," the vendor calls out as we're walking away.

"I'll keep that in mind," I say over my shoulder. "Just want to see what else is available."

She gives us a curt nod and returns to her book.

"So what do you think?" I ask Jason. "I want a deal, but I also want to be fair."

"A hundred seems fair to me."

"So let's head back in a few minutes. I don't really need to see anything else."

As we're strolling through the market, Jason occasionally stops at the most random tents.

"Are you looking for something in particular?" I ask him.

"Possibly. Was thinking about a wedding gift for Cami and Bryan. Something unique. Maybe something they could use in Chile."

"I take it you like your sister's fiancé."

"He seems like a good guy. She adores him, and he seems to adore her. Seems like they're a good match."

"Those 'seems' are doing a lot of heavy lifting. He *seems* like a good guy. He *seems* to adore her. They *seem* to be a good match."

"Well, shit. I didn't even realize what I was saying. They *are* a good match."

He bites on his lip as he stares at an item, but I don't think he's actually considering it.

I place a hand on his arm. "Lisa thinks they were made for each other, and she's an excellent judge of character."

"That's comforting."

Why does he need to be comforted, though? Wait. Forget I asked. The answer is for Lisa to know and for me *not* to find out. That's true couple shit and definitely not what we're doing here. Diving into Jason's interior and learning what makes him, well, *him*, is *not* part of the plan.

"Ready to head back?" I ask, snapping us both out of our thoughts.

"Yeah, as soon as you admit that my tactics worked like a charm."

"They did," I say, giving him a lopsided grin. "And I owe you two shish kebabs."

A woman passes us and hands us brochures. I glance at mine and read aloud the market's mission, which says "a portion of the profits benefits four local public schools."

I look up at Jason. "Did you remember this part?"

"I didn't," he says sheepishly.

"Are you thinking what I'm thinking?"

"That you're going to pay full price for the dresser? Yeah."

We smile at each other, then he says, "She *does* have a heart."

"Don't tell anyone, though," I whisper. "It's a closely guarded secret."

Honestly, it's one of the nicest things anyone's ever said to me. The sad part is, I'm not exactly sure it's true.

× × ×

"It's perfect," I say, staring at the latest addition to my tiny one-bedroom apartment in the East Village. Never mind that the dresser consumes enough space to be considered my roommate.

Jason wipes his brow. "Doesn't matter. Those damn stairs were a nightmare, so you're stuck with it."

I lightly shove him to the side and hand him a water bottle. "Seriously, though, thanks for helping me get it up here. I couldn't have done it without you."

He waves me off. "No biggie. Happy to lend a hand."

"Okay, then," I say, swinging my arms awkwardly. "This has been great, and now I'm letting you off the hook so you can enjoy the rest of your Sunday."

"Right. Of course. Wouldn't want to overstay my welcome."

I laugh. "That's not what I meant."

A smile dances on his lips as he walks to the door. "But that's what I heard."

"Take care," I say, rolling my eyes. "And thanks again for agreeing to update the store."

"It's my pleasure. Your father's good people. And playing a part in keeping a bodega in East Harlem open is exactly what I'd want to do with my free time anyway."

Great. I feel like shit. This guy isn't even half as bad as I initially thought. As usual, I went off half-cocked, led astray by my need to come out on top in any given situation, and now I'm stuck in a scheme with him at the center. My only consolation is that he and Lisa might embark on a lasting relationship as a result of my meddling. I suppose I'll gain a decent brother-in-law too. Squaring my shoulders, I resolve to set aside my misgivings and finish what I started.

With all that in mind, I muster a friendly smile, open the door, and lean against the frame. "I'll see you around, then."

"Yeah, take care," he says, throwing up a hand as he passes me.

After closing the door, I fall against it and let out a deep breath. Next time I see him at the store, I'll try to finagle an invite to dinner or something. Then I can *really* begin my campaign.

Seconds later, a soft knock at the door startles me, and when I look through the peephole, I see Jason clutching his baseball cap against his chest. I open the door wide. "Back so soon?"

"Yeah," he says, then swallows hard. "I, uh . . . I forgot to mention that Camila and Bryan are having a couples shower two weeks from now. They're not into a lot of the traditional wedding stuff most people do, so they're hosting it together. Anyway, I was thinking, since you're just getting back into the swing of being in New York, it might be nice to hang out with some cool people. My family. Some friends. Your sister will be there, too, I'm sure." He shrugs. "I don't know. I just thought you might like to tell your parents you're being social."

"Thanks for the invitation, but a couples shower seems like something for close friends and family. I wouldn't want to impose."

"We're Puerto Rican, and it's a party. There's no such thing as imposing."

I laugh. "Okay, okay. When and what time?"

"Saturday, the eighth. Starts at three."

"You'll send me the details?"

"I'll need your digits for that."

"Come inside, then." I grab my phone off the kitchen counter. "What's your number? I'll call you so you can save mine in your phone."

After we exchange numbers, I walk him to the door again.

"I'm leaving for real this time," he says. "Bye."

"Bye, Jason."

I close the door and grin at this minor victory: an invite and his cell phone number. Now I can send him text messages. Sweet ones at first. Annoyingly detailed ones later. Oh, Jason, you have no idea who you're dealing with.

Yeah, this is going to be a ridiculously easy assignment. For Lisa's sake, I hope he's worth it.

chapter 7

JASON

Vanessa: Hey, Jason. This is Vanessa. How are you?

Me: Hey, Vanessa. I'm good. You?

Vanessa: I'm doing great. Just had a quick question about the work you're planning to do at the store. Do we need permits? Because I'd like to be sure the work won't affect my parents' insurance coverage or the sale. Everything needs to be on the up-and-up.

Me: No permits necessary. The code considers the projects I'm doing minor alterations. You only need someone licensed to do the work, which I am.

Vanessa: Excellent. Thanks!

Vanessa: One more thing: behold the refurbished dresser. I think it was worth the back strain. If you disagree, don't tell me. ☺

I tap on the photograph Vanessa sent and zoom in on the dresser, which is now painted cobalt blue and has glass knobs, just as she envisioned.

Me: It's perfect. Definitely worth the back strain.

Vanessa: I bet you say that to all the girls...

Me: *searches for a scandalized GIF*

"What the hell is on your face?"

My business partner Eric's wide-eyed stare causes me to swipe at my cheeks. "What? What is it?"

"A smile, man. Haven't seen one of those in a while."

"Shit. I thought there was a damn bug on me."

"No, but that smile is just as scary. Can't remember the last time I saw your mouth do anything other than frown at work."

"I'm not *that* bad."

"Tell that to your crew. They jump to attention whenever you show up on-site."

"I'm their boss. It's the nature of the beast."

"You're the beast in this scenario, right?"

"Yeah, yeah, whatever."

He leans over and tries to steal a glance at my phone screen. "Seriously, what—or should I say *who's*—got you looking whipped?"

"I'm not whipped, but I *am* smiling at something that was sent to me."

"A dick pic?"

"No, you asshole."

"A tit pic?"

"Now you're an even bigger asshole."

"Damn, the clues are right in front of me: an even bigger asshole pic than the one you got last week?"

"Fuck off," I say, putting my phone in my back pocket, then rising to gather my trash.

When Eric and I started TAG Building Group seven years ago, we instituted a standing Tuesday lunch appointment in our office's only conference room. This is our time to catch up, to focus on our lives beyond the business. In the last few months, it's become Eric's way to keep track of my love life. I don't have one, so he just uses this time to mess with me. I use it to ignore him. Mostly.

Unbothered by my response, Eric shakes his head and shoots a napkin into the garbage bin. "Listen, I know I kid around a lot, but I'm worried about you."

"Why would you be? I'm fine."

"That's exactly it, J. You're fine. Nothing more, nothing less. Save the mediocrity for middle-aged white dudes."

I drop back into my chair. "What else am I supposed to be doing?"

"You're supposed to be *living*, man. Filling your days with something other than your work. Finding things that make you happy. Connecting to something—or someone."

"Eric, chill. I'm good. I have my job; I have my family; I have you. That's enough for me."

"But when did we start using *enough* as our standard? It wasn't that long ago when we both decided finishing college and getting a regular nine-to-five wasn't for us. That we wanted to be our own bosses. That we wanted *more*." He makes a sweeping motion and gestures around the room. "We're sitting in a place that only came about because 'enough' was *never* our standard."

"All right, I'll bite. What do you want me to do?"

"Do whatever it is that will put a smile on your face. Not once a week but every day."

I immediately picture Vanessa flashing her underwear and struggle to keep from grinning.

"There it is!" Eric exclaims. "*That's* what I'm talking about. More of that, please."

"Well, I did meet someone."

Eric sits up and rubs his hands together. "Okay, okay. Now we're getting somewhere."

"It's probably nothing, but like you said, she makes me smile."

"That's a good start, man."

"Problem is, she's the older sister of Camila's best friend, Lisa."

"The one you described as the cutie with curly hair?"

"Yeah. And I think the cutie with curly hair has a crush on me."

"You're not interested?"

I shake my head. "Never have been. And I keep thinking about her older sister, Vanessa. Which is new for me."

"Is this the first time you've been interested in someone since you broke up with she-who-shall-not-be-named?"

I bark out a laugh. "You can say it. Not naming her gives her power over me."

"Elyse," he says, making a big show of shuddering.

Elyse doesn't take up too much real estate in my brain anymore, but I have her to thank for reinforcing one of my most important life lessons: Putting people high on pedestals just means they'll land harder than everyone else when they inevitably fall. "See? You didn't conjure her or anything. And yeah, Vanessa's the first person to spark my interest in years."

"Why?"

"I don't know, man. It's wild. She's prickly. Sarcastic. Funny. Definitely doesn't want to be perceived as sweet. That intrigues me. It's a shock to my system, I guess."

"Interesting. Sounds like your system needs shocking. Maybe it needs... *more*."

"You really thought you were doing something when you took those two psych classes our junior year, didn't you?"

He brushes off his shoulders. "Don't be jealous of my emotional intelligence. I'm using it to help you."

"I don't want to make too much of this thing with Vanessa, though. Kind of nice to just be around her. That's all I'm ready for."

"And she texted you?"

"Yeah. Their parents own a bodega uptown. I'm helping them with some renovations."

"Is that all she texted about?"

"She showed me the dresser we picked up at the flea market this weekend."

"So she's interested too."

"Hard to tell." I shrug. "Maybe."

"It's your move, then."

"I already invited her to Cami and Bryan's couples shower."

"But that's almost two weeks from now. You're going to lose momentum. Plus, she's going to be too nervous around your family to really enjoy herself. Why don't you take her out this weekend?"

"Can't. I'm working on that single-family in Queens."

"The one for Built to Excel?"

"Yeah."

"Invite her to volunteer with you."

I tilt my head and stare at him like he's gone bonkers. "You want me to invite her to a reno project?"

"Yeah, why not? It's for a good cause. If she's as great as you say she is, she'll enjoy the opportunity to help out."

"That's not a bad idea, actually. I'll think about it."

"Don't think too hard or too long. It's a chance to get to know her better. Without your family staring you down. Trust me, spend some more time with... what's her name again?"

"Vanessa."

"Right. Spend some more time with Vanessa before you throw her into the Torres family chaos. That way, she'll be less likely to run away."

"She doesn't strike me as a runner."

"Then she sounds like a keeper."

"Not looking for one, though."

"J, you're too old to be just vibing. Put in some effort for a change. I'm not saying you should marry this woman, but I *am* saying you need to put Elyse in your past and move on. Not everyone is like her."

Eric's right, of course: I *know* not everyone is like Elyse. Or my father. But sometimes I feel like I'm a magnet for individuals with ulterior motives, and it's made me wary of opening myself up to anyone. Still, Vanessa doesn't deserve to be lumped in with the people who've let me down. She hasn't done anything but be herself. "Fine. You've convinced me. I'll invite her to the reno."

"See there? Was that hard?"

"Actually, it was."

"Then I'm proud of you. And remember: When you two get married, I want to be the best man."

"I'm not sure marriage is in the cards for me, but if that ever happens, you better believe I'd want you there."

"Same, man. Same. And don't try to distract me. Whip out your phone and invite Vanessa to the reno."

"Okay, okay," I say, chuckling as I fish my phone out of my back pocket. "I'm on it."

Me: Hey, Vanessa. Can I give you a ring? Want to run something by you.

Vanessa: Sure.

Eric watches me make the call. I take a deep breath as the phone rings and let it out once Vanessa picks up.

"Hey, you," she says. "Everything okay?"

"Everything's fine. I just had an idea."

"Congratulations."

"Ha, yeah. Anyway, I, uh..."

Eric motions for me to keep going.

"You're doing great, sweetie," Vanessa says.

These two would get along so well. Confidence destroyers, the both of them.

"So, um, I volunteer with a community group called Built to Excel. It's meant to help people who've ditched high school find success in the construction industry. We renovate homes in the five boroughs. For low-income families. And BTE, that's the acronym, does seminars for the kids. On interviewing, résumés, time management, that kind of stuff."

"Sounds like an amazing group."

"Yeah, it is. The kids are great. I've even hired a couple of participants after they completed the program."

"And you're telling me this because...?"

"Damn, you're brutal."

Eric tilts his head, his eyebrows squished together in confusion. I turn around so he won't distract me.

"I'm just trying to help you out here," Vanessa says with a laugh.

"If this is help, I can't imagine what sabotaging looks like to you."

She clears her throat but remains silent.

"Kidding," I say.

"I gathered."

Is she teasing me? I *think* she is. "So, uh"—damn, I'm bombing this—"I was wondering if you'd be interested in joining me on a renovation project we're doing in Queens. This Saturday. I know it's not a glamorous date or anything, but I thought you might enjoy it. Giving back, I mean."

"I'm really flattered that you thought of me. And it sounds like the perfect date. Seriously. When and how do I get there, and what should I wear?"

"We start at ten o'clock and end at three in the afternoon. I can pick you up around nine fifteen and drive you back home. And whatever you'd wear to paint your apartment should be fine."

"Sounds great. I'll see you on Saturday, then."

"See you then. Bye, Vanessa."

"Bye, Jason."

I turn around and catch Eric looking at me with pride in his eyes. He bats his eyelashes, his lips curved into a sickeningly sweet smile. "My little boy is growing up."

I scrunch a napkin into a ball and ping him in the chin with it. "Shut up."

"It's progress, man. It counts for something."

He's right. It does. And Vanessa didn't object when I called it a date. Maybe this is the start of something. Maybe even the start of something good.

chapter 8

VANESSA

Oh dear God, he's dressed like a contestant on *FBoy Island*. I didn't get the full effect of his outfit when he picked me up, but now that he's climbing out of the car, I can't help noticing the straight-leg 501s and the super-snug black T-shirt.

Okay, forgive me, Lisa, but I'd have to be dead not to notice how my future brother-in-law fills out a pair of jeans. They're also faded, and now I'm crying in Spanglish.

"You good?" he asks.

I pull the cotton fluff out of my brain and nod. "Yeah, I'm good."

He walks over to my side of the car and shuts the door, then he gestures at a pale yellow single-family home across the street. "There it is. We call it Sueños."

"Dreams. That's nice. This house represents a family's dream, right?"

"Yeah. But not just theirs; ours too. It represents our dreams for them, our dreams for the people who come after them, and our dreams for the hands that touch this place. A common goal that brings joy to many."

My heart squeezes in my chest. This man. Is he a saint or something? It's bad enough that he's handsome, but he also has the nerve to be a good person? Ugh. Zero stars. Do not like. To him, I say, "It must be so satisfying to finish a project like this."

"It is. You know when people talk about refilling the well? Being involved in Built to Excel does that for me."

Honestly, I envy him. I don't have anything that refills my well, and I don't know what will. Unfortunately, the well is well and truly empty. "Ready to head inside?"

He stares at me a moment too long before he answers. "Yeah, let's go."

When he holds out his hand, I take it without hesitation. I'm supposed to charm him, after all. Only problem is, he's being more charming than I am.

We enter the home through the front door, and I immediately inhale an almost lethal dose of paint fumes. "Good God, that's strong."

"Sorry, I guess I'm used to it. I'll grab you a mask in the kitchen."

"Should I be wearing a hard hat?"

"Nah, all the structural stuff is done. We'll just be working on the finishing touches." He flicks one of my curls. "I bet you'd look cute, though. Maybe another time."

Oh, well, hey now. He's leveling up on his flirting game. And he's ahead of schedule too. Just as I predicted, *easy*.

In the kitchen, a small group of teens and a middle-aged Black man are shooting the shit as they drink coffee from paper cups.

"I brought our latest sacrifice," Jason says jokingly as he points at me over his shoulder.

"Wait, should I be worried?" I ask.

The man steps forward and puts out his hand. "Not at all. We're a nice bunch." He gives the teens behind him side-eye. "*Most* of the time. I'm Silas, the director of Built to Excel. And you are?"

"Vanessa. Jason's . . . friend."

The pause is purposeful, of course. The power of suggestion is a reliable tool in my arsenal, and my apparent equivocation suggests that I'm considering whether there's more to the relationship than I'm acknowledging.

"Thanks for joining us, Vanessa. Did Jason tell you what we're about?"

"He did. It's an impressive mission. I'm happy to be put to work for such an excellent cause."

The rest of the people in the group, seven Black and brown teenagers in all, introduce themselves as I struggle to remember everyone's names.

A Latine teen with a ball cap on backward—Benny, I think—grins at me. "So, are you Jason's girlfriend?"

One of the girls, Ivy, smacks Benny's shoulder. "She's the first person he's brought around here. What do *you* think?"

"We're getting to know each other," I clarify.

"Aaaand that ends the interview portion of the program," Jason says, grabbing a mask off the kitchen counter. "We're here to work." He looks over at Silas. "Where do you need us?"

Silas consults his clipboard. "We need to prep and paint the dining room. Think you can handle that?"

Jason turns to me. "Sound good to you?"

That small gesture, considering my wishes, means a lot. It's not as if he deserves brownie points for it—politeness is the floor—but it's a relief that he isn't the kind of guy who expects a woman to go along with whatever he wants.

Why do I care, though?

Oh, right. Because Lisa wants to date him. And I'm here to make that happen. And it's a good thing that Lisa's interested in a nice guy. Yes, that's *exactly* why it matters.

"Works for me," I say.

"Want a tour of the house first?"

"I was hoping you'd ask."

He smiles, and the brightness in his eyes twists my insides. I'm trying to remember the reasons for my initial reaction to him—my visceral need to take him down a peg—and I'm coming up empty. I'm *such* a hothead. All I can do now, though, is play matchmaker for him and my sister. That'll make the pettiness I'll eventually unleash on him worth it.

"We're still on for the Intro to the Construction Industry workshop at the end of the month?" Silas asks Jason.

"Yeah, I'll be there. Just remember, you promised to bring doughnuts."

"I won't forget," Silas replies. To me, he says, "Be sure to make Jason do most of the work."

"That's the plan," I say, waggling my eyebrows.

Silas salutes us with his baseball cap. "If you need anything, I'll be outside with the kids working on the yard. Thanks again."

"Our pleasure," we say in unison.

Jason rests a hand on my lower back and guides me out of the kitchen.

"Do you know anything about the family who's going to live here?"

"Not yet. There's an application process. And a training process too. The head of household commits to attending home-ownership workshops as part of the deal."

"The home's all paid up?"

"No, but the remaining mortgage payment is lower than the average rent in the area. Much lower, actually."

"That's fantastic. I can imagine it's a huge relief to the families who participate."

"Seems to be," he says. "Last year, we did a reno in Brooklyn and two women who'd been living in shelters scored this fantastic brownstone that had been given to the program by a former member of the board. The only requirement was that whoever the program chose had to be an abuse survivor. They both were, and they wrote letters to BTE explaining how this was going to change their lives."

"I can see why you'd want to be a part of this. It's inspiring."

"It is."

We walk up the stairs, and Jason points out the various rooms from the landing.

"Tell me there's a bathroom in the primary bedroom," I say. "That's my dream come true."

"There is," he says, chuckling. "And a Jack and Jill bathroom for the kids."

I'm in awe as we walk through the home's interior. It's modest but comfortable, and the upstairs rooms are already furnished with the basic necessities—beds, nightstands, and dressers. The craftsmanship appears to be top-notch, too, which I'm guessing Jason's partly responsible for. "Who pays for all of this?"

"Donors, mostly. Every couple of years, the program lands a

grant, but Silas doesn't have the time to chase down money constantly. We could probably do much more if he had a bigger staff."

"Yeah, nonprofits always seem to deal with staffing challenges."

"Exactly. Silas complains about it all the time, so I try to lighten his load in other ways. Ready to head down?"

"Let's do it. I'm excited to help."

"I had a feeling you would be."

The dining area is small and has just enough space to fit a table set and a sideboard. The walls are adorned with crown molding and feature a chair rail along the perimeter of the room. I picture a family spending their first holiday here, sharing a meal, with the falling snow visible through the arched windows. The vision energizes me, makes me want to be part of bringing it to fruition.

"I'm your apprentice today, so I'm following your orders. What do you need me to do?"

"Hang on a minute," he says, fishing something from his pocket, then pulling out his phone. "Say that again. I want to record it."

I roll my eyes at him. "And just like that, the truce is over."

He gives me a half smile, one I'm starting to get used to. "I knew it wouldn't last." He hands me painter's tape and a putty knife.

"What do I do with the knife?"

"We should start by masking off the trim and chair rails, then we use the putty knife to make sure we get a good seal. We don't want the paint to bleed through."

"That's a great tip. It's almost as if you're a pro or something."

"No more lip, woman. Get to work."

"Okay, okay," I say, heading to the wall opposite Jason's and putting on my mask.

We work in companionable silence most of the time, occasionally checking in with each other's progress. The mask is stifling, though, so after a few minutes I remove it and slowly grow accustomed to the paint smell. "Do we have to sand the walls after this?"

"Yeah, that's next."

"How'd you end up volunteering here anyway?"

"One of my former employees told me about it. He moved to Pennsylvania, but before that, he participated in BTE's program. Considering he was one of my best workers, I became curious about the training. I visited the home base in Manhattan, met Silas, and decided I wanted to be a part of it. He's a friend now. Silas, I mean."

"Kind of like a father figure?"

"Exactly."

"This isn't a conventional place to take someone on a date, but I'm glad you invited me. Makes me feel like I'm part of something important."

"Because you don't feel that way now?"

"Not really," I say, shrugging. "I have a good job, but I'm not really tied to anything. Basically, I grind, I sleep, I wake up, I grind some more. It's been that way since I graduated from college."

"What about fun?" he asks, his forehead furrowed.

"What's that?"

"But you're so young. Why is work your only focus? What about friends? Spending time with family? I mean, I'm not a party animal, but even I know it's important to connect with other people."

"I get it, I do. But I don't make friends easily, and before you say anything, yes, I know that's a red flag. And my family... well, let's just say they have every reason to be wary of me."

"There's a story there."

"There is."

"You don't want to share it, though."

"Hell no. Not on the first date."

In fact, I'm not even sure how he got *this* much out of me. I need to be careful around this one. Usually my lips are sealed so tightly you'd have to pry them open with a crowbar, but Jason has a way of disarming me.

"Ah, so you're expecting a second date," Jason says.

"You invited me to your sister and brother-in-law's shower. It's already in the bag, baby." I jump off the stepladder and point at my work. "Ta-da. All done."

Jason surveys my side of the room. "Passable."

I grab a rag off the stepladder and fling it at his chest. "That's better than passable."

"And just for that, you're going to use sandpaper."

"As opposed to what?"

He digs in a tool kit and lifts out a sander. "As opposed to this. Makes sanding a breeze."

"That's for people who can't handle a little hard labor."

"She says to the person who does hard labor for a living."

"That's debatable. I hear you mostly push pencils these days."

"Does this look like I push pencils all day?" he asks, lifting his T-shirt a fraction so I can get a peek at his stomach.

It's a phenomenal stomach. With enough squares that I could play checkers on it. Da-yum. Still, I burst out laughing. And the more I think about it, the harder I laugh, until I'm weeping in amusement.

"What's so funny?" he asks, his eyebrows snapping together.

"You. You're what's funny. Were you waiting for the perfect opening to show me your abs? Who *does* that?"

"Apparently I do," he mutters.

I lift my shirt a fraction, mimicking what he just did. "'Does this look like I push pencils all day?' Seriously, Jason? You're adorable."

Jason strides across the room before I can even catch my breath. "Make fun of me all you want. I can take it."

I snap my mouth shut, cutting off my laughter, then open it when I regain my composure. "Because you're a glutton for punishment?"

He pins me with an intense gaze, crowding me, enveloping us in a bubble that's poised to pop. He's close. *Too* close. "Because I'm a glutton for whatever you're willing to dish out. And yeah, I'm not the smoothest guy in the world, but I like you, Vanessa. A lot. And I don't give a shit if I look silly proving that to you."

Oh. I don't know what to say to that, so I swallow, drawing his gaze to my throat. Then he licks his lips as he stares at mine, and my heart gallops in my chest. I knew this was coming. Eventually. It's a part of the ruse. So why am I seconds away from swaying on my feet?

"May I kiss you?" he asks.

"I'd like that," I say, an unrecognizable shyness in my voice.

Get yourself together, Vanessa. Treat this as a clinical exercise. You're fulfilling the terms of the assignment, and this is not *the time to go mushy.*

Jason doesn't place his lips on mine like I expect him to. Instead, he pulls me flush against him, then slides his nose along my jaw, humming when he feels my skin.

"So soft," he murmurs. "Just as I imagined."

"You imagined this?"

"Many, many times."

I breathe him in and literally swoon. Good God, he smells like a heady combination of barrel-aged cognac and evergreens after a light rain. As if Paul Bunyan decided to quit his job as a lumberjack and opened a distillery instead.

Jason presses his mouth against my jaw, then inches his lips closer and closer to mine. "I'm trying to prolong this," he whispers against my cheek. "Because I know the moment I touch those gorgeous lips, I'm going to taste heaven. The anticipation is killing me."

It's killing me, too, honestly. And he thinks he isn't smooth? Wow, he couldn't be more wrong. Because everything he's doing right now is working for me on multiple levels.

Finally, *finally*, he places his lips on mine and slides his tongue inside my mouth as he runs a hand over the back of my neck. Oh. Oh, this . . . Oh, this is scrambling my brain. Every aspect of this kiss strikes the perfect balance between precise and frenzied. Sloppy with lust isn't his style, but he's ravenous—the way he breathes into me, the way he draws me tightly against him, the way he peppers me with tiny bites in between the tangling of our tongues. He's fully immersed in this kiss, which leaves me fully immersed in him. His scent, his five-o'clock shadow grazing my skin, his strong fingers clutching my waist.

This is Jason's version of foreplay, and oh my God, judging by the way my nipples are hardening to uncomfortably rigid peaks under my thin top, it's working. I squeeze my eyes shut so I can concentrate and mentally confirm that what I'm doing with him is okay. That I'm not crossing any preestablished boundaries. The rules of this scheme are simple: no fooling around and absolutely no sex. Kisses are fine, though. And that's all we'd be able to do in our current environment anyway. Nevertheless, this kiss *feels* like a road map for what he'd do to me in the privacy of a bedroom: It's the tongue-twirling equivalent of frantic and sweaty sex with an earth-shattering orgasm as its finale. Lisa would *not* approve.

With a hand against his chest, I step back and gently push him away.

"Too much?" he asks, his eyes dark and hooded.

"Too good," I whisper honestly. "We need to slow this down."

He wraps one of my curls around his index finger. "I'm willing to slow this down to a snail's pace if it means we get to do that again. Whenever you're ready."

"Thanks for being patient with me."

"I'm not being patient. That makes it seem like there's a right and a wrong speed. I'm slowing down because that's what you need. Nothing more, nothing less."

"Well, thanks for being you, then."

"You're welcome," he says, reaching over and using his thumb to caress my top lip.

"Time to sand the walls?" I ask, dropping my chin to escape his touch.

"Sure." Then he clears his throat. "Why don't we grab a drink in the kitchen first?"

"Okay."

But nothing's truly okay. Because that kiss ranks among the best I've ever experienced. I'll be thinking about it tonight, tomorrow, and next week. Shit, this is not good. Not good at all.

chapter 9

VANESSA

I video-call Lisa as soon as I get home. Yes, we need to debrief, but my date with Jason has also shaken me to my core, and I'm desperate for the reminder that I can never view him as anything more than a means to an end.

She answers immediately, greeting me with a genuine smile. Her friendly expression is a timely reminder that *this* is what I wanted: an authentic connection with my younger sister. Sure, it's based on my ability to help her land a man, but I'm hopeful we'll blossom from there.

Her hair's up in a doobie—a telltale sign she visited a Dominican hair salon for a blowout—and she's holding a large white bowl.

"Ice cream," she explains, raising a spoon in the air. "And my DVR's getting a workout."

"What are you watching?"

"Old episodes of *Project Runway*. When Heidi and Tim were still around."

This isn't surprising. Before I left home, Lisa was designing the clothes she wore in high school. "Are you still making your own stuff?"

She shakes her head. "No time. Whenever I get home, I'm too mentally exhausted to do anything other than watch mindless TV."

"Maybe now that I'm back, you'll have more freedom to do what you want. Start a new design project. Or take dance classes again."

"I haven't danced in ages, Vanny." When she sees my face fall, she adds, "But yeah, that could be nice."

And she sounds sincere, which is a relief. *Baby steps, Vanessa. Baby steps.*

"Anyway, enough about me," she says. "How did it go today?"

"It went well, I think. It's progressing exactly the way it's supposed to."

"Did you do any work on the house?"

"Hell yes, and you owe me. I had to tape, sand, and paint a dining room."

"Ugh, I'll make it up to you somehow."

"I'm expecting you to," I say with a smile.

A niggling thought lingers at the back of my mind: Why can't I tell Lisa that I actually enjoyed it? That I felt like I was doing something meaningful for a change? That working on that home temporarily filled a void? Probably because I hate admitting to anyone that I'm not perfectly happy just as I am. Because doing so begets questions. And questions require answers. It's always safer to say nothing. No one teases you for saying nothing. No one *judges* you for saying nothing. I mean, what the hell do I have to be unhappy about anyway? Would

Lisa even care? She deals with students with *real* problems, day in and day out. My bullshit can't possibly be worth her time.

You admitted your feelings to Jason, though, my inner critic reminds me. *Why's that, huh?* Screw you, brain. You're not helping.

To Lisa, I say, "Seriously, though, don't worry about it. Consider it my one and only good deed for the year."

"Well, now I *definitely* need to repay you. Especially if what you're doing is working."

"It is."

"How can you tell?"

I gulp before I answer. Here it goes: "He kissed me."

Which *technically* isn't a lie. But saying *he* kissed *me* makes it seem as if I was a passive participant. No, I was definitely all in. Pebbled nipples and everything. The truth is, *we* kissed. And it was devastatingly good.

Lisa's eyes go as wide as saucers, then she places her bowl of ice cream aside and leans forward, her elbows showing in the video frame. "A kiss on the cheek?"

"No."

She breaks eye contact for a moment, then lets out a soft sigh. "This is why you wanted me to be sure about doing this, right?"

"Right. But don't read too much into it. We were on a date, and that's the conventional way to end one. Keep in mind this needs to happen for us to get to the finish line. Plus, I already told him we need to slow down. That'll buy us some time."

"I get it, I do. And I'm fine."

"You sure?"

"Yeah. Is . . . is he a good kisser?"

"Doesn't matter what I think."

"Yeah, you're right."

"I'd tell you if he had halitosis, though," I say, injecting lightness into my tone. "Because that would be a deal-breaker. But you have nothing to worry about there."

She grins, relief flooding her features. "So what's next?"

"He invited me to Cami and Bryan's couples shower next week. Remember the roller-coaster analogy? We're about to start the loop-the-loop phase."

"What are you planning to do?"

"Haven't gotten that far yet. I need to think about his pressure points. But I'll come up with something and let you know."

"Okay, good." She drops her shoulders, then grimaces before saying, "Is this weird?"

"Weird as fuck, Lili."

She throws her head back and dissolves into laughter. "This is more than weird; it's bananas."

"It's what your ridiculous ass wanted, and it's too late to turn back now."

"Is it?" she asks, her expression instantly sobering.

"Well, the landscape's forever changed. I'm now a person he kissed, so there's that. But if you want to end it here and do this on your own, I'll support you one hundred percent."

"No, that would be even more awkward than going through with the ruse. At this point, I'd be trying to steal my sister's crush. Eww. Besides, if it works out, all of this will have been worth it. He's a great guy."

"So far, that seems to be true. And if you two end up together, I think he'll make you happy. Which makes it easier for me to do this for you."

Her expression goes soft as she meets my gaze. "I knew you'd eventually think so."

Here's what I *don't* tell Lisa: It didn't take me long to figure out that Jason's a great guy. Which also makes it *harder* for me to do this for her. I'm a big girl, and I won't kid myself: I'm suppressing my interest in Jason. For Lisa.

Which can only mean one thing: This has the potential to be a big ol' fucking disaster.

JASON

My mother's in the kitchen when I arrive for Sunday dinner.

I kiss the top of her head. "Hola, Mami."

She continues to drop plantains in the pan. "Hola, mi corazón. Had a good weekend?"

"I did. Worked on that reno in Queens yesterday."

"You make me so proud," she says, then wipes her hands on a dishcloth and pinches my cheeks. "Even on a day off, you're trying to do something for someone else."

I stand there and accept her fussing because doing so is rule number one in the Code of Latinx Sons: Your mother gets to mother you as much as she wants.

When she's done, I peek inside the fridge.

"There's no beer," she says. "Nelson went to get some."

"It's all right," I say, leaning against the counter and eyeing the stove warily. "But the fire's on too high. The plátanos are going to burn if you don't turn down the heat."

She shakes her head, pretending to be disappointed. "I created a monster when I taught you how to cook."

"No, you created a guy who doesn't expect anyone to make me a meal."

"Women like that, you know. You can invite someone over and cook for them." She shrugs her shoulders. "Just a suggestion."

I didn't even know the word *suggestion* was in her vocabulary. Still, I'm on enough of a high after my date with Vanessa that I'm willing to throw my mother a crumb just this once. "Speaking of . . . I took someone with me to the reno in Queens. Sort of like a date."

She sets down the strainer and smiles. "You did? Ay, that's wonderful, mijo. Who is she?"

"Lisa's sister. Her name's Vanessa."

My mother's smile slips into a frown. "The one who didn't come inside Xiomara's dressing suite to meet us?"

"She couldn't. She was dealing with a wardrobe malfunction."

"A what?"

"Never mind. Just . . . give her a chance. She's sweet. And funny."

"If you want me to give her a chance, then I will, but if this doesn't work out, another person will come along. Maybe Vanessa's just someone for now, not forever."

"Doesn't matter, Ma. I'm not trying to get into anything serious anyway. I just wanted you to know that you can ease up on your plans to find the love of my life. One, I'm not looking for that now. And two, Vanessa's coming to the couples shower, so introducing me to a bunch of women won't be a good idea. Please don't do anything to make it awkward."

"Me?" she says, placing a hand on her chest as if she's offended. "Since when do I make things awkward?"

"Since all the time, Mami. Since all the time."

She gently shoves me out of the way, grabs a spatula, and turns back to the stove. "What does Vanessa do for a living?"

"See?" I say, rolling my eyes. "Awkward."

"I can't ask a simple question?"

"Nothing's ever simple with you. But if you must know—"

"I do."

"She's a financial planner. Just moved back home and is helping start a new office here. Before that, she was in Chicago."

"Sounds like she has a good head on her shoulders. That's something, at least."

"I'm glad you approve."

"I don't approve. I'm just not objecting. *Yet*."

"I'm starting to wonder if you'll ever think any woman is good enough for me."

"Lisa is," she says, raising a brow. "The younger one."

"Too bad I'm not interested."

"Why not? They almost look the same."

I burst out laughing. "Because I happen to care about more than just a person's appearance. I like Vanessa's personality. So that's that." I kiss my mother on the temple. "Just remember not to scare her off at the couples shower."

"If it's easy to scare her off, then she's not the woman for you."

"If you scare her off, I'll never get the chance to know one way or the other."

Just then Nelson walks into the kitchen, two six-packs in his hands. He kisses my mother's forehead before placing the beers in the fridge. "She's giving you a hard time again?"

"As usual," I say.

We exchange a knowing glance.

Nelson understands our mother-son dynamic and doesn't meddle unless he absolutely has to. He's always present in our lives, though. Watching. Listening. As if he's waiting for the moment he'll be asked to step in and give his own advice. "Let me know if you need me to distract her."

He says this with a wink and loud enough for my mother to hear.

"Go watch the game," she tells Nelson, playfully pushing him out of the room. And then she pulls me into her arms and hugs me tightly. "I only want what's best for you. You know that, right?"

"I know," I say, my chin resting on the top of her head. "But it's up to me to decide what's best for me, okay?"

"With a little help from me?"

"No."

"We'll see."

"No, *you'll* see."

This is the limit of the warning I can give my mother. I just pray she doesn't do anything to make Vanessa wary of exploring our connection. Because for the first time in a long while, I'm interested in someone. That's a huge step for me; I can only hope I don't get screwed taking it.

chapter 10

VANESSA

When I arrive at Cami and Bryan's couples shower, half of the guests are making their way through an impressive buffet line while the other half are out on the parquet dance floor.

I spot Jason immediately and take a moment to observe him in his element. Sporting black slacks and a light blue button-down with the sleeves rolled up, he looks put together and comfortable. The group of men surrounding him appear to be enthralled by whatever he's saying. Judging by their expectant faces, he's telling a story, and they're waiting to hear the climactic ending. Sure enough, I watch him gesture with a flourish, and then the group erupts in laughter, everyone dispersing like a bunch of pool balls after a break shot.

Seconds later he sees me and smiles, throwing up a hand in greeting as he makes his way over. When he reaches me, he shoves his hands into his pockets, as if he doesn't know what else to do with them, and says, "I'm glad you came."

"Thanks for inviting me. You sure it's okay that I'm here?"

"More than okay. There's no such thing as too many people at one of our parties."

"All right, I just wanted to be certain. Where should I put this?" I ask, raising a small box in the air.

"There's a gift table in the back corner. I'll show you, and then we can grab you a drink."

Before I take a step, Lisa materializes by my side. "Vanny, I need to speak with you."

"Is everything okay?" I ask, taking in her harried expression and jittery movements.

"Everything's fine," she says, swinging her arms in an arc and looking at me pointedly. "I just need to ask you something in private." She glances at Jason. "Sorry to interrupt. We won't be long." Then she lunges for my free hand and drags me through the crowd. With her head down, she marches us out of the banquet hall, not stopping until we reach the restroom way the hell on the other side of the building.

Once there, I double-check my lipstick as I wait for Lisa to explain what put a fire under her ass. She doesn't. Instead, she leans over and inspects the floor of each stall. With her facial expression set in concentration, she pulls on the door of the only stall that's locked, then does a second visual sweep of the floor. "Must be out of order," she grumbles to herself.

"Why are you doing that?" I ask, still facing the mirror. "Is this a drug buy?"

She ignores my joke. "I'm just making sure we're alone."

"They're all shaking their asses to Bad Bunny. Besides, why would anyone come all the way over here? We're in the clear. What's up?"

"I've been so busy at work I didn't realize until now that we didn't talk about the plan for today. I'm nervous as hell. Do you need me to do anything?"

"Chill, you're fine. Today is Operation Piss Off the Mom."

Lisa cringes. "Nothing too outrageous, I hope. I mean, I want this woman to be my mother-in-law someday."

"Lili, don't stress. I got this. I'm just going to make it clear that I am absolutely not the right person for her son. The key here is to guarantee that a serious commitment with me isn't within the realm of possibility. Given how close they are, pissing off his mom will do the trick. And I've got some great ideas about how to do that, but I need to be flexible. Whatever happens out there, just be ready to help."

Lisa stares at herself in the mirror and taps on her cheeks. "Okay, I can do this."

I step behind her and give her shoulders a light squeeze. "You'll have Jason eating out of your hands in no time. Remember, all you have to do is be the superior alternative to me. I *know* you can do that."

"I can do this. I can do this. I can do this." She flicks her bangs a bit, then nods. "Okay, I'll see you in there."

"Of course. And I'll call you tonight to debrief," I say, lifting the shower gift from the vanity.

She kisses my temple. "Good luck."

"Luck isn't going to get you a boyfriend, but my excellent acting skills certainly will."

She rolls her eyes before she dashes out of the restroom.

I lick my lips, then pop them for good measure. *It's showtime.*

JASON

I'm at the punch bowl getting drinks for Vanessa and me when someone tugs on the back of my shirt. I turn around and see Denise, whose usually emotive face is frighteningly blank.

"Come with me."

"Now?" I say, lifting the cups in my hands to indicate I'm busy.

Her expression hardens. "Right now."

Denise is the life of the party. The one who never takes anything seriously unless she absolutely has to. Whatever's going on can't be good. I set the drinks down. "Lead the way."

She strides out of the banquet hall and enters the empty coat check room next door.

"What's going on?" I ask. "You're worrying me."

She faces me and blows out her cheeks before she begins. "I was in the bathroom a few minutes ago. Honestly, I was planning to smoke a joint because"—she gestures to the door—"this lovey-dovey shit is making my skin crawl, and I just needed to relax a little."

"Denise, you don't have to explain all that. It's your personal business."

She draws back. "I *know* that. I'm just setting the stage for you."

"O-kay," I say, stretching out the word.

"So I went to the bathroom on the other side of the building, figuring everyone would go to the one closest to the party, and I was getting ready to light up, but then someone came in. Two people, actually." She closes her eyes. "And I just didn't want to deal. Or talk to anyone. So I jumped up on the toilet seat."

I step away, wanting to put some distance between us. "That's gross."

"I *know*," she continues, opening her eyes. "I'm not proud. Anyway, that's not the point."

"Well, what *is* the point?"

"The point is that Lisa and your *date* walked in."

My chest tightens as my brain processes that whatever she overheard has her riled up. "You eavesdropped on them?"

"I did. And I feel zero percent guilty about it. Because they're playing you, bro. And dammit, I'm *so* sorry to be the one to tell you this."

My brain doesn't have enough information to make sense of what she's saying. Lisa and Vanessa are playing me? How? Why? "Tell me exactly what they said."

"I won't be able to remember everything word for word, but the shit that stuck out to me is messed up."

I scrub a hand over my face. "Specifics, please."

"Lisa asked about"—she makes air quotes—"'the plan,' then Vanessa said today was Operation Piss Off the Mom. That she was going to do something to guarantee that Mami won't like her—not that she has much work to do there. And then Lisa said something about not wanting it to be too bad. Said she wanted Mami to be *her* mother-in-law someday."

"What the hell?"

"I know. I had the same reaction. Then Vanessa told Lisa all she had to do was continue to be the better alternative to her and eventually she would get herself a boyfriend."

"So Vanessa isn't really interested in me? She's just dating me as a warm-up for her sister?" I raise my hands in the air. "But I'm not attracted to Lisa. Never will be. What kind of ridiculous plan is that?"

"I don't know what to tell you. I just know what I heard. They're knuckleheads, the both of them. And I think we should call them out on their bullshit. Want me to get them in here?"

I put up a hand to stop her from leaving the room. "Hang on. I need to think this through." Pacing the space, I consider what my next move should be. Damn, I sensed that Vanessa was crafty, but I wouldn't have expected her to be *this* deceitful. Not in a million years. Lisa either. She's always struck me as an upfront person, but obviously she isn't. I can't wrap my head around any of it. But as I slowly come to terms with the news, I realize none of it should be surprising. It certainly tracks with everything I've experienced, doesn't it? The lies, the bullshit, the games. I *know* this is what people do, yet I let my guard down long enough to be duped by the Cordero sisters.

Denise, who's pacing beside me, shakes her head, obviously still stunned by their audacity. "Well, look at it this way: The one good thing is, Mami will be relieved. She wasn't impressed with Vanessa at Xiomara's, and as long as Vanessa's sniffing around, she's interfering with Mami's plan to find you the perfect wife. Just in time for the wedding too. Even Mami will twerk to Bad Bunny when she finds out Vanessa isn't a threat anymore. And a less-stressed Mami is a gift to *everyone*."

Denise is right. My mother isn't sold on Vanessa. When we talked about her the other day, I could tell my mother was only placating me. Maybe she was relying on that mother's intuition she's always talking about. Or maybe she learned her lesson with Elyse. Because the more she complained about my ex in the early stages of our relationship, the more adamant I became that I'd make it work. Whatever the reason, when she hears Vanessa's no longer in the picture, she'll be thrilled. And she'll immediately get back on the find-Jason-a-wife train. Final stop: marriage within a year. Which is the *last* thing I need to be dealing with on the heels of this latest blow.

The perfect solution comes to me: Let their scheme play out for as long as it serves *my* purposes. And right now, it does. For a bunch of reasons.

One, it keeps Lisa at bay until I no longer need to be around her. As long as I'm "dating" her sister, she won't be able to pursue me. And after Cami's married and off to Chile, Lisa and I won't have any reason to be around each other.

Two, I won't be forced to wreck their plan before the wedding ceremony. This is supposed to be Cami's special moment. If I say something now, though, it'll put a damper on the days leading up to her wedding. And how uncomfortable would it be for her to interact with Lisa as her bridesmaid? Worse, what if she decided to drop Lisa as a bridesmaid altogether because of this? No, this is Cami's time, not mine.

Three, it keeps my mother off my back. For a while, at least. As I discovered during the fitting, my mother's attempts at matchmaking will drive me bananas. And if she thinks I'm dating Vanessa, a woman she's only tolerating for my sake, she'll actively discourage any talk of marriage. Plus, when Vanessa and I eventually "break up," I'll be given a grace period to mend my poor battered and broken heart.

Four (and this one gives me the most pleasure, to be honest), I get to upend Vanessa's machinations and give her a taste of her own medicine. If she thinks she's going to turn me off, let's see how she responds when everything she does just makes me want her even *more*.

After going through it in my head a few times, I tell Denise my plan: "I'm not going to say anything just yet."

Denise freezes, her eyebrows snapping together in surprise. "Why the hell not?"

"Because I can use what they're doing to my advantage, that's why."

"How? And this better be good, or else I'll snitch on them all by myself."

So I explain my thinking, and as I do, her mouth drops open. When I'm done, I wait for her reaction. "Say something."

She nods repeatedly, her head tilted to one side and her mouth curved into a devious smile. "You're fucking brilliant."

"But for this to work, you *can't* let on that you know. I'm serious, Denise. Your hotheaded ass would ruin everything."

She purses her lips in frustration. "Fine. But the minute this is over, I'm going to make Lisa regret she ever messed with us." Noticing the wariness in my eyes, she adds, "Figuratively speaking, of course."

"Why only Lisa?"

"Because she's the one we're really connected to. I mean, she spent so much time with us when we were teenagers, she practically lived in our home. We've treated her like family, and this is how she repays us? Absolutely not."

I can't help chuckling.

"What's funny?"

"I'm just picturing you re-creating that Michael and Fredo scene in the second *Godfather* movie." Doing my best impression of Al Pacino's voice, I pull Denise into my arms and whisper against her ear, "I know it was you, Lisa. You broke my heart."

Denise pushes me away and laughs, her eyes flickering with amusement. "It's not *that* deep. But yeah, her fakeness is really pissing me off."

"Try to hold yourself together around her, though, all right? They can't know that we know. Otherwise, the whole counteroffensive falls apart."

"Fine. Whatever you need."

Before we leave the room, she tugs on the sleeve of my shirt. "Hey, I just want you to know that I'm sorry about this. I saw your face when she walked in. I haven't seen you interested in someone in a long time, and I realize that doesn't come easy for you."

I shrug as if it's no big deal, although she's absolutely right on both counts. Until this moment, I was optimistic about building something special with Vanessa. Slowly. Surely. But that isn't happening. Ever. Because nothing about her supposed interest in me rings true anymore. I'm over it. Over *her*. Simple as that. "It's okay. The good thing is, I learned about her motives early on. Now that I know what she's up to, there's no way we'll ever be in a real relationship."

When we reenter the banquet hall, I plaster on a smile and pretend to be unaffected by the secret I just discovered. It may take some effort, but I'm committed to making my date just as miserable as she intended to make me.

Okay, Vanessa, show me what you got. And let the petty games begin...

chapter 11

VANESSA

"Nena, ¿dónde está tu capia?"

I look up from riffling through my purse to find Jason's mother staring at me. Standing next to her, a middle-aged woman holds a wicker flower basket filled with the party favors that were a staple of my childhood.

"Oh, hello, Señora Elba. Good to see you again," I tell Jason's mother.

"Have we met before?" she says, angling her head.

I'm almost certain she remembers me, but I play along. "Yes, I'm Vanessa, Lisa's sister. We met the day of the dress fitting when I picked her up."

"Yes, yes, yes. But we didn't *really* meet because you stayed by the curtains."

"True, true. Well, it's good to meet you now."

She doesn't answer. Instead, she plucks a capia from the basket and leans in to pin it on me.

Knowing I'm committing a faux pas of astronomical proportions, I take a step back and raise my arm to block her. "Oh, that's okay. I'll just hold it. I don't want to get a hole in my blouse."

She scowls, drops the capia into my waiting hand, and mutters "Suit yourself" as she walks away.

I hold back a grin. The universe is *definitely* my accomplice today.

Suddenly Jason appears behind me. "Having fun?" he asks against my ear.

A shiver runs through my body when I register his minty breath fanning across my cheek. "Uh, yeah. The music's great." I shift to my left to put some space between us. "I was just talking to your mother."

His eyebrows shoot up. "How'd that go?"

"Fine. I think she's warming up to me."

"I don't get the sense that she was cold to begin with."

"No, but Puerto Rican men and their mothers share a special bond. I think any person in their son's life automatically starts at neutral."

He narrows his eyes. "Is that what you're trying to do? Be in my life?"

"I, um, didn't mean to say that's what's going on here. I was speaking in generalities, of course."

"Got it."

I draw back and survey his face, immediately noticing his detached demeanor. "You okay? You seem out of it or something."

He shakes his head and gives me a smile that takes longer than usual to reach his eyes. "I'm fine. Just a little tired."

"Let's sit down, then. Looks like your sister and her fiancé are going to give a speech soon."

"Sure, we're at the table up front."

He puts out his hand and I take it, trying but failing to ignore the way his long fingers interlace with mine. We weave our way through the hall and sit down as the couple begins to address their guests, Camila saying "Hola" to everyone while Bryan says "Hello." They laugh and beam at each other, after which Camila takes the lead: "We just wanted to thank everyone for wishing us well on the start of our momentous journey as a couple. Many of you have been in our lives for all the ups and downs and in-betweens, and we're so glad you're here today to celebrate with us. Gifts truly aren't the point of all this—"

"But in this recession, we'll gladly take them," Bryan adds, eliciting laughs from the crowd.

"The point is," Camila says, shaking her head at Bryan's interjection, "we feel your love and support, and that means the world to us."

Everyone claps as Camila and Bryan seat themselves in extravagantly decorated chairs facing their friends and family, the table of gifts that had been in the back of the room now next to them. *Perfect.*

Jason's mother, Elba, rises from her seat and shuffles to the gift table. "Now we get to the good part!"

"She's shameless," Jason says with a chuckle.

"She's the mother of the bride. It's her duty to be shameless."

Camila and Bryan open each gift, which Elba then presents to the guests so they can let out obligatory oohs and aahs as Lisa records the details in a logbook. It's a whole lot of nothing, honestly, and at one point I nod off, until Elba's voice pierces the air. *Why is she speaking so loudly?*

"It's very small," she tells everyone as she hands the next gift to Camila. "But maybe it'll be something useful."

My gift. She's talking about my gift. And considering the smirk she throws my way, she damn well knows it. This woman.

Camila peeks inside the box, and her lips curve into a smile. "Very nice. Thanks, Vanessa. We'll be sure to put this to good use."

"Well, don't keep it a secret," Elba says. "Show everyone what it is."

Camila's face pales. "No, we're taking a little long. Let's move on to the next one."

"That wouldn't be right," Elba says, taking the box from Camila and removing the item inside. She lifts it in the air. "It's in the shape of a flower, but what *is* it?"

Camila swallows. "It's . . . uh . . . it's a—"

"A massager," I yell from my seat. "It has warming capabilities too."

"Ooh, I need something like that," Elba says. "For all the tension in my shoulders."

"It's safe for everywhere," I add. "And super powerful."

"Looks kind of weak to me," Elba says, a challenge in her eyes. "It's so small."

I can't help countering her wiseass remark. "Believe me, it gets the job done."

"We'll see," she says. Then, to Camila's horror, her mother holds down the power button, bringing the device to life, and swipes it across her neck and over her cheeks.

"Mami, you shouldn't put that on your face," Denise warns from the back of the room.

But it's too late. Because Elba yelps, and then the suction

feature causes the vibrator to seal onto her face, stunning her into immobility.

"¡Ay, Dios mío! I can't get it off. It must be broken." Then she scurries back and forth, one hand holding the device and the other flailing wildly.

If she would just lift the device away from her cheek, she'd probably be fine, but she's being dramatic for no reason—or possibly to make me look bad.

Cami whips out her phone. "Lord, forgive me, but I need photographic evidence of what's happening right now."

Groaning, Jason jumps up to help his mother, but Denise gets to her first.

"Stay still," she tells Elba, holding in a laugh. "I can't get to the power button if you keep moving."

When the vibrator stops buzzing, Elba strokes her cheek. "What kind of massager does that?"

"The good kind," Denise says, her face deadpan.

There's snickering among the tables. When I chance a glance at Lisa, I spy her surreptitiously wiping tears from her eyes.

Jason looks over at me, his expression a mixture of awe and confusion. "A vibrator? Seriously?"

"Technically, it's a stimulator. And yes, seriously. When I asked for suggestions, you told me to get something they'd *both* enjoy." I point at the device, now safely tucked away in the gift box. "There you go."

He shakes his head and slow claps. "Bravo. You just went up several notches in Camila's eyes."

I frown. "Really? Why?"

"Because she hates all this wedding hoopla, but she will *never* forget that her mother got a vibrator stuck to her face at her couples shower." He lets out a deep belly laugh. "And when my mother figures out that she was the center of the most hilarious moment at this party, she'll eat it up like the attention-seeker she is. Priceless. I was already happy that you came today, but now I'm extra glad you did."

I give him a tight smile. Huh. That's *not* what I was going for. Maybe I'm getting rusty at this? No matter. The night's still young. There's still plenty of time to annoy Mama Torres.

JASON

Okay, I'll concede this: The vibrator was a stroke of genius.

She couldn't have known that my mother would take it upon herself to sample the "massager," but Vanessa's gift set off a sequence of events that will be imprinted in my brain forever.

I glance over at Vanessa and pretend not to notice her dejected expression. Part of me wants to laugh with her about the fiasco. Another part of me wants to wring her neck for being so underhanded. What the hell were she and Lisa thinking? It's something I'll be puzzling over for days.

"Want to dance?" Vanessa asks.

"Um, sure, let's do it."

Unlike my mother, I'm not a fan of being on display, but if Vanessa's occupied with me, she can't engage in whatever tactics she thinks will piss off my mother. What a joke. Elba Graciela Guzmán Colón is not to be messed with. If Vanessa wants to poke that hornet's nest, she better prepare to get stung in the end.

When I get to the dance floor, I finally focus on the song on rotation: Daddy Yankee's "Dura." My mother's probably going to have a fit if she pays attention to some of the lyrics. Luckily, a quick glance at her table confirms she's deep in conversation with her friends.

"I love this song," Vanessa yells as she leans in. "It's perfect for twerking."

Oh God, no. Not here. Not with my family a few feet away.

"Be kind to me," I tell her. "I'm not a big dancer."

She swings her arms to the beat, and I force myself to keep my gaze trained on her face. I will not be taken in by the way her body sways to the reggaeton rhythms pumping through the speakers. She looks phenomenal, too, with the ruffled skirt that ends above her knees fluttering against her smooth skin. Damn her, those hips definitely *do* lie.

"I'm not a big dancer, either, but I saw this video teaching people with flat butts how to twerk, and I realized I'm not half bad."

She then turns around, drops down low, arches her back, and thrusts her ass in the air.

¡Por Dios!

My cousin Héctor sidles over and begins to clap, egging Vanessa on. "Damn, primo, who's this?"

Vanessa straightens, flips her curls away from her dewy face, and puts out her hand. "I'm Vanessa. Nice to meet you."

"I'm Héctor. This dude's cousin. In case you're wondering, he's not good enough for you. Might want to expand your horizons."

She laughs. "I think I'll stick with him for tonight, but thanks."

Héctor shuffles away and joins a group of women dancing together while Vanessa spins around and starts twerking again.

If you can even call it that. Mostly she's just arching her back to the beat, her hands gripping the tops of her thighs.

"See?" she says with a broad smile. "Anyone can twerk!"

That's debatable. In fact, what I'm witnessing is a prime example of that saying, *Just because you can, doesn't mean you should*.

"You know what else I learned to do?" she says over her shoulder.

"What?" I say, flicking open the top button of my shirt. Fuck, it's hot in here.

"A split!"

And she proceeds to show me. By doing just that. In the middle of the dance floor. In a goddamn skirt. Thankfully, she's wearing biker shorts underneath so she's not flashing her underwear. Well, I'm never living this down. Never. Years from now, my family's going to remind me that I once brought a woman to Cami and Bryan's couples shower, and not only was she responsible for getting a vibrator stuck to my mother's cheek, but she also twerked herself into a split as she danced to Daddy Yankee.

My mother suddenly appears at my side and pinches my arm. "Jason, what's going on?" she asks through gritted teeth.

I need to play it cool here. Vanessa can't know she's succeeding at making me uncomfortable. "What does it look like, Ma? I'm dancing with Vanessa."

"Well, stop it. Right now."

"Want a lesson?" Vanessa asks my mother. "Anyone can do it. And you look like you could really show out on the dance floor, Señora Torres."

Heat stains my mother's cheeks, and she wrinkles her nose. "It's Señora Guzmán Colón to you, young lady. Torres is their father's name. And stop that right now!"

Vanessa freezes and rises to her full height. "Oops, sorry. I went a little too far, didn't I?"

"You certainly did," my mother says, and then she stomps away. Before she does, though, she gives me the evil eye and mimics violence by slicing a finger across her throat.

Oh shit. I'm getting an earful later, but it'll be worth it. For all the same reasons that I'm not revealing what I know about the Cordero sisters' little scheme. Still, I need to get this woman out of here before she can make any more trouble for me.

"The party's winding down," I tell her, slowing to a stop. "I'd be happy to take you home if you want."

"Oh, that won't be necessary," she says as she dabs her face with a napkin she grabbed from a passing server. "I'll just take a Lyft."

"You sure?"

"Definitely."

"I don't mind walking you out."

"Really, no need," she says, panting. "You should stay with your family. I'm sure you're itching to do something else."

She's right about that. "All right, then," I say, shoving my hands into my pockets because I don't know what else to do with them. "I'm on cleanup duty, so I should go help. Well, uh, thanks for coming."

"Thanks for letting me crash the party," she says, smiling brightly. "It was fun."

"Enlightening too," I say under my breath.

"And I'll see you Thursday for the Mets game, right?"

"I wouldn't miss it for the world."

I shake my head as I follow her off the dance floor. This has been a ridiculous day, and that was quite the performance. There's no question in my mind it requires retribution. Definitely not now. Maybe not even next week. But vengeance will be mine. Eventually. Bonus? As long as Vanessa's around, the last thing my mother will be thinking about is her usually unrelenting preoccupation with getting me settled and married.

Who's the genius now?

chapter 12

VANESSA

"Vanessa, wait up!"

I spin around and watch Lisa trot through the lobby of the banquet hall.

"You're leaving?" she asks when she reaches me.

"Yeah, my work here is done. For now."

She steps closer, her voice barely above a whisper. "That was perfect. Really, truly perfect. I almost peed my pants watching that train wreck."

"Honestly, I can't take much credit for the vibrator malfunction. It was just good luck."

"Um, I was talking about your twerking. Really fucking sad, babe. I didn't realize until today that you have no rhythm. How is that possible?"

She says all of this with a wide smile, so I snort and throw up my middle finger. "Vete pa'l carajo, Lili."

"Ooh, them's fighting words, pendeja."

We grin at each other, and my mood lifts. I may not be happy about lying to Jason, but seeing my sister relaxed and playful—around me, specifically—is enough to end my funk. I'm doing the right thing. For her. For us. And considering how amazing Lisa is, for Jason too. He might not see her as a prospect yet, but I'm confident he'll eventually figure out she's perfect for him. Which reminds me: "Listen, this is an excellent opportunity for you to charm Jason, so don't waste it. Go back in there and chat him up."

"But I never know what to say," she whines. "I never feel quite like myself when he's around, and I don't know why."

"Well, you need to figure it out sooner rather than later. If you want to date this man, you're going to have to converse with him from time to time."

"Really? I was hoping we could just communicate in bed. Like, *all* the time."

"Ew, Lili. Stop being weird."

She throws her head back in frustration. "Okay, okay, I'm kidding. It's just that I'm always so nervous around him."

I set my hands on her shoulders. "Take a deep breath. He's a regular guy. And a nice one. You can talk to him about anything. He's too much of a gentleman to make it awkward."

"Okay," she grumbles.

"Bring it in, mama," I say, stepping back and holding out my arms.

She slides into my embrace and rests her head in the crook of my neck. "Thank you. What you're doing . . . it means a lot to me."

"You're welcome. And I know. But let's not forget your piece of the equation, too, okay? For this to work, he has to be drawn to you eventually."

"Got it."

"Well, well, well. What a touching display of sisterly love," a voice behind us says. "You two must be *thick as thieves*."

Lisa stiffens in my arms, and we spring apart as if we've been caught red-handed. Which is silly. We're related, and we can damn well hug if we want to.

Lisa turns around and groans. "Ugh, what do *you* want?"

The person ignores her question, then meets my gaze. "I'm Denise, by the way. Jason's sister. We didn't really meet the other day."

I accept the offered handshake, immediately noticing that her grip borders on being *too* firm—purposefully so, I bet. "I know who you are. Your reputation precedes you."

"If Lollipop over here is the source of that reputation, don't believe it. She's a poor judge of character."

My sister purses her lips, her eyes narrowing into slits.

"Well, she called you 'scarily brilliant,'" I say with a smile.

Denise's eyes widen, then she glances at Lisa before she dons an impassive expression. "Did she?"

"She did."

"And *she* is right here," Lisa says through gritted teeth. "Again, Denise, *what* do you want?"

"Nothing from you, believe me." She eyes us both, then lifts her arm, showing us the cigarette she's holding. "Just needed some fresh air and a smoke. Was going to light up a blunt earlier in the bathroom, but I got distracted by . . . something. This will have to do for now."

Oh damn. Was Denise in the bathroom when Lisa was losing her shit? No, that can't be. We went to the far side of the building, and my sister checked all the stalls. So I should take Denise's words at face value. I mean, if she overheard our conversation, she would have flipped out on us, right? That seems to be her style: She strikes me as the kind of person who'd easily get into a brawl at a Waffle House on a Sunday and represent you in court on a Monday. This woman is definitely going to wreak havoc on the world when she gets her law degree.

Lisa stares at the cigarette dangling from Denise's lips. "What a disgusting habit."

"Settle down, Lollipop. I only smoke when I'm stressed. Doesn't happen that often."

"Because you're always too busy stressing everyone else," Lisa says. "Which reminds me, when are you going to get back to me about the plans for Cami's bachelorette party?"

Denise crinkles her nose as if there's a foul odor in the air. "I'll get back to you when I get back to you. It's bad enough that Cami's forcing me to wear a dress for her wedding, but for her to make me work with you on a ball-and-chain party? Unforgivable."

"You'll get over it—like a big girl should."

The bite to my sister's words matches her sarcasm. Yikes, these two don't know how to play nice at all.

"And if I don't?" Denise says, stepping in front of Lisa, trying to intimidate her.

My sister remains unfazed. "Then you'll only remind everyone that you're selfish and you make everything about you. Honestly, it wouldn't surprise me in the least."

"Do you really think so little of me?"

"Nope. The problem is, you think so little of yourself. The tough act only gets you so far. I can see right through it."

Denise grimaces. "Whatever. You're such a damn know-it-all."

"And you know absolutely nothing."

They're staring at each other with daggers in their eyes, the tension around them so thick that a fight just might be imminent. As entertaining as this is, I need to intercede here. "Okay, okay, children. Why don't we play the quiet game?"

"She started it," Lisa says, pouting.

"And I'll happily finish it," Denise replies.

I step between them. "I'm putting you both in time-out." Placing my hands on Lisa's shoulders, I look at her meaningfully and add, "You. Isn't there something you should be doing right now?"

Lisa's frown relaxes. "Right. I'm on it." And then she pivots away from Denise and me, not even sparing Jason's sister a second glance.

I give Denise a once-over, and she peers right back at me through narrowed eyes. "I get the sense you're not my biggest fan."

"What gave you that idea?" she asks.

"Well, it looks like you're seconds away from body-slamming me."

She shakes her head as if to clear it. "Sorry. It's your sister. She riles me up. You're just collateral damage."

"Are you *sure* that's all?"

"I'm sure," she says, nodding.

"Well, that's something, at least. But let's be honest, I think it's safe to say you two rile each other up."

"Fair," she says, nodding gravely.

My Lyft driver's arrival saves us from engaging in idle small talk, although Denise doesn't seem like the type to suffer through mindless chatter anyway. "There's my ride. Take care, Denise."

"Take care, Vanessa."

I can sense her watching me as I go, but I don't dare look back. Before I shut the passenger door, though, she calls out to me.

"Yeah?" I ask.

"My brother likes you," she says, her eyes flickering with an emotion I can't quite place. Sadness, maybe? "Don't break his heart, okay?"

"Okay," I say confidently, throwing up a sarcastic thumbs-up.

Besides, Jason's heart isn't mine to break, and if all goes as planned, Lisa will capture it in due time.

JASON

"Can I help with the chairs?" a voice over my shoulder asks.

I turn and find Lisa staring up at me.

Guests are still mingling at the front of the room, so I'm starting at the back and hoping they'll take the hint that the party's over.

"Sure, that would be great," I tell her.

"Do we need to break down the tables too?"

"No, those came with the facility. The chairs are rented, though, so Manny and I are responsible for returning them on Monday."

"Got it," she says, folding a seat in seconds and placing it on the flatbed cart I borrowed from a job site.

We work together quietly, each of us apparently lost in our own thoughts. I'm not saying shit to her unless she initiates a conversation. Who the hell knows what these two are planning?

The best approach is to take my cues from her and try to dodge and weave as best as I can.

After a while, Lisa clears her throat. "So did you enjoy yourself today?"

"I did. You?"

"It was great. I'm so happy for Bryan and Cami. They're truly perfect for each other."

"How so?"

Her brow furrows. "What?"

"You said they're perfect for each other. I'm wondering why you think so."

"Uh, you don't?"

"I didn't say that. I'm just . . . never mind."

"No, no. I get it now. Um, well, let's see. Cami and I have been best friends forever. And I always knew when she was into someone. I also knew when she lost interest. Honestly, I had whiplash keeping track of her crushes. That didn't happen with Bryan, though. In fact, she didn't say much about him at all. I think she was scared because her feelings for him didn't follow the same pattern. Anyway, they seem so comfortable together. Not forced or anything. And it's just as clear they adore each other. You know that old crap some people say: 'I love you, but I'm not *in love* with you'?"

I nod.

"The thing is, Bryan and Cami manage both." She shrugs. "I don't know, I guess it's hard to explain."

"Actually, I think that's really insightful. And I agree with you: They *are* a good match."

She beams at me as I struggle to think of something else to

say. Cami's the extent of our connection, and the only person we've ever talked about, so I latch on to my sister's upcoming move as a topic. "She'll be heading off to Chile soon. How are you holding up?"

Her shoulders drop. "I'm going to miss her, of course, but I'm doing okay. She's just a FaceTime call away, and I'm planning to visit as soon as they're settled. It's going to be weird not hanging out at your mom's house, though."

"I'm sure my mother won't mind a visit every now and then."

"Yeah," she says quietly. "But it won't be the same. I guess I just got used to it being my second home."

"Well, now that your sister's back in town, you can use that time to reconnect with her, right?"

She nods enthusiastically, her eyes brightening. "Right. We have a lot of catching up to do."

"Good, good." I place the last set of chairs on the cart and lean on the handle. What else is there to say? I got nothing. "So, um, I'm going to start loading my truck. Thanks for your help."

She straightens. "No problem at all. I'll see you around."

"Take care, Lisa."

"Take care, Jason. Oh! And have fun at the Yankees game!"

"The Mets, you mean."

"Of course, of course. How silly of me. Big difference, right?"

"Definitely," I say with a curt nod.

She angles her head at me, perhaps sensing my annoyance with the whole charade she and her sister have concocted. So I school my features. Because my plan won't work if either sister suspects that I know what they're up to.

And honestly, I'm not all that mad at Lisa. She isn't a bad

person. She's just misguided as hell. We're not a match and never will be. As long as I don't forget that the same holds true for her sister, I should be fine.

So why did it bother me so much to discover Vanessa's part in the scheme? And why am I still looking forward to spending time with her?

There's only one answer that makes sense: *Damn. I'm a masochist.*

chapter 13

VANESSA

Confession: I *like* baseball. The prospect of seeing the Mets play in Citi Field actually thrills me. Today, however, I'm going to *hate* America's favorite pastime. There will be yawning. *So* much yawning. And complaining. *So* much complaining. Sure, this is going to take some effort, but you better believe I'm up for the challenge.

As I wait for Jason outside the Jackie Robinson Rotunda—he's taking the subway from Brooklyn—I watch the spectators shuffle past, laughing, bumping shoulders, and joking with one another. Their excitement is palpable, and my only regret is that I can't join in their enthusiasm. Not outwardly, at least.

A few minutes after arriving, I spot Jason separating from a crowd heading my way. He's wearing a striped Mets jersey, a pair of loose faded jeans, and a brandless royal-blue baseball hat.

I chuckle as he approaches.

"What?" he asks, his eyes twinkling.

"I was just thinking that if we lose each other in there, it won't be my fault."

He looks down at his clothes. "Something wrong with what I'm wearing?"

"Uh, you look like every other male here over the age of five."

He shrugs, his grin widening. "This is the dress code. Period. Not my fault you didn't get the memo." Appraising my outfit, he grimaces. "Speaking of which..."

Now it's my turn to look down at my clothes; they're my accomplices, after all. "I wanted to dress the part, but they didn't have any Mets gear at the sporting-goods store by my apartment."

"So you wore a Phillies jersey? That team is their biggest rival."

"Is it?" I ask innocently, knowing full well this getup could lead to a scuffle with a drunk fan.

"It is. Which means that if we end up in jail, it'll be *your* fault."

"You'd fight for me?" I say, batting my eyelashes.

"I'd fight *with* you. Prepare to throw down too."

"Ah, chivalry isn't dead; it's just egalitarian."

"Exactly. Besides, I have a funny feeling you'd hold your own in a fight. Ready to head in?"

"If we must."

"C'mon, where's your joy for experiencing new things? This'll be fun."

"I doubt it, but I promise to keep an open mind."

"*That*," he says, pointing at me and grinning. "*That* is definitely not keeping an open mind."

He takes my hand, his fingers warm and strong, and we're

swallowed by the crowd of people entering the stadium. After making our way inside, he turns to me, "You hungry?"

"I can eat."

"Good. There's a burger at the Shake Shack with my name on it. How does that sound?"

"Oh, um, I'm not really in the mood for red meat. Hurts my tummy."

He gives me a thoughtful nod. "I had a feeling you'd say something along those lines. They serve a 'Shroom Burger, though. It's excellent. Fried portobello with gooey cheddar and Muenster on a potato bun."

"Yikes. All that cheese. I'd definitely get the runs."

He barks out a laugh. "Damn, just let it all hang out, why don't you?"

"Well, you asked. Figured I could be real with you."

"You're right. I did ask. And I appreciate that you're being *real* with me."

Something about his tone makes me peer at his face, but he's reading the menu for one of the concession stands in the concourse. I'm being paranoid. There's no way he's playing mind games. "You know what I'd love? A—"

"Salad."

"How'd you know?"

"Lucky guess."

"Huh. I'm sure there's a—" I freeze.

"What's wrong?" he asks in an alarmed tone.

"They serve Nathan's in here."

"And?"

"And it's only the best hot dog known to man."

"I thought you said you didn't want beef."

Shit, he's right. But these hot dogs are on another level, and I didn't factor the possibility of having one when I made my plan to be annoyingly picky. I'm physically incapable of passing by this stand. To him, I say, "I can make an exception for Nathan's. For some reason they don't hurt my stomach the way burgers do."

"How convenient," he mutters.

"Oh, and the crinkle-cut fries that you have to stab with the red fork thingy. I'll be in heaven. And truth be told, that Shake Shack line is out of control. We'd spend the whole game waiting to order."

"Fine, let's grab you and your fussy tummy a Nathan's hot dog."

"You're getting one, too, right?"

"Absolutely. If I can't get a burger from Shake Shack, a Nathan's dog is the next best thing."

Well, now I feel bad for depriving him of something he was looking forward to. But wait. That's what I'm *supposed* to be doing. *Get it together, Vanessa. Take no prisoners.*

With our ballpark snacks in hand, Jason and I meander to our seats at the end of a row behind first base. It's warm but not oppressively so, and the sun is hiding behind a swath of fluffy white clouds. Because it's a day game, kids seem to be carpeting the place wall to wall. Mr. Met, the mascot with a ridiculously humongous baseball head, is high-fiving kids and dancing to the preopening music being blasted through the stadium's speakers.

"These are great seats," Jason says, his eyes on the Mets dugout as he opens a mustard packet and preps his hot dog. "Not too far. Not too close."

"Too many rug rats, though," I note.

"You don't like children?" he asks, frowning before he takes a bite of his dog.

"As a concept, sure. In reality, eh, I could do without them. How about you?"

"I'm part of the Big Brothers program, and I can't wait to be an uncle someday."

"So kids are cool as long as you can return them to their rightful owners at the end of the day?"

"Exactly."

"I like the way you think," I say with a wink.

"We're growing by leaps and bounds. I never would have imagined you saying that a week ago."

"Honestly, same." After taking a few bites of my hot dog, I ask, "Anyone you're looking forward to seeing?"

He turns so I can see the back of his jersey.

"Lin-dor," I read. "Is he good?"

Of course I know Francisco Lindor is good. He's an Afro Latine shortstop from Puerto Rico. My father, who derisively calls him by his nickname, "Paquito," was pissed when the Mets picked up Lindor because he knew his least-favorite team had scored big. Fans booed Lindor during his first few appearances, and then he went on to hit three home runs in a single game during the 2021 Subway Series and just decimated the Yankees that night. I watched that game at a sports bar in Chicago and became an instant fan, not that I'd *ever* mention any of this to Papi.

"He didn't look great in the beginning, and the fans were rough on him, but he's finally found his footing. Just watch him play. He brings the excitement this franchise needs."

"Cool. Okay, so wake me when something interesting happens."

"I'm starting to think this was a bad idea."

"What?"

"Bringing you to the game. You're not into it."

"I wanted to see the stadium anyway. It's on my bucket list of things I should do as a New Yorker. Don't feel bad that I'm not super into it."

"I don't feel bad. I just think someone who's a true fan could have used your ticket instead."

With my jaw dropped, I whip my head to meet his gaze and find him staring at me, a smile dancing on his lips.

I stick out my tongue at him. "Fine. Point taken. I'll be a better date from now on."

"Is that what this is? Another date?"

"Definitely not a date if you're asking."

He leans in and lowers his voice. "Would you like it to be?"

I straighten in my seat, mentally brushing off the tremor that went through me when his breath feathered over my neck. "Is this a trick question?"

"No tricks," he says, putting up his hands, the container of fries we decided to share resting precariously on his lap. "I'm just trying to get a sense of where your head is."

"Okay, well, if that's the case, this is probably the right time to tell you that I was in a relationship before I left Chicago and I'm not ready to jump into another one. And you should also know that I tend to take things slow. *Really slow*. If none of this has you running for the hills yet, then I'd like to hang out with you and see where it goes. How does that sound?"

He leans to the side and nudges me with his shoulder. "Sounds like we're hanging out and seeing where it goes."

Okay, if I'm being honest, the vibe between us is way too positive for my liking, but he gave me an opening and I took it. Now I just need to focus on making a bad impression on him. Somehow, I need to give him an inkling that everything isn't what it seems. So I'll bide my time and wait for the perfect opportunity to be messy. Which is always the fun part.

As luck would have it, that chance doesn't take long to materialize. In the fourth inning, third baseman Mark Vientos hits a foul ball into the stands. By some miracle that calls back to my brief stint playing softball in college, I manage to dive past Jason and catch the ball with my bare hands. *Motherfucker*, that hurts.

"Holy shit!" Jason exclaims. "That. Just. Happened."

"I can't believe it!"

A few feet away, a young boy, probably seven or eight, looks at me with pleading eyes. Oh, there it is. Maybe I can slip the ball to the kid later, but for now, I know exactly what I need to do.

Bless me, Father, for I am about to sin.

JASON

"Sorry, kid," Vanessa tells the little boy next to us. "I'm keeping this one for myself."

"C'mon, you're not even a fan of the game," I tell her.

"But catching the ball awakened something in me."

"Seriously?"

"Seriously."

Shaking my head, I drop into my seat. Stunned by Vanessa's rudeness—he's a kid, for God's sake—I dart a glance at her face and catch her devilish smile before it slips away. Malcriada. How could I forget that her little assignment is supposed to make her look bad so her sister will come out on top? That's the only explanation for her behavior that makes sense. And if by some small chance she's actually as heartless as she seems right now, well, then she deserves what's coming to her.

I jump up and egg on the kid's parents. "How rude is that? What's this world coming to, am I right?"

"Yeah," the mother says, puffing out her chest. "How could she do that to a *child*?"

Vanessa gulps, her face flushing. "I caught the ball. I'm allowed to keep it."

"Boo," I chant. "Boo."

Waving my arms around, I motion for everyone to join me. Soon after, our entire section is booing Vanessa.

"I can't believe you're selling me out like this," she cries, looking mortified and sinking in her seat.

"I'm not the one who didn't give the ball to a"—I look over at the kid's parents—"How old is he?"

"Seven!"

"A seven-year-old!" I say, and the crowd goes bananas. It doesn't help that Vanessa's wearing a Phillies jersey, which all but signals she's the enemy.

Even Mr. Met gets in on the action, shaking his stubby index finger at her. Then he points at the Jumbotron, which is displaying Vanessa's image with the word *Spoilsport* above her head.

"Hey, check it out!" I shout. "You're up there!"

Vanessa looks at the Jumbotron and scrunches up her face. "Oh Jesus."

With her head bowed, she hands the ball over to the kid, and the people in the stands throw up a wild cheer.

Laughing, I collapse into my seat. "That was the right thing to do. Don't you feel better?"

"No," she grumbles, crossing her arms.

Well, I feel better. But I hate—and I mean *hate*—that her antics somehow make her even more adorable to me. *No, Jason. Do not let her dazzle you.* She's a schemer. And schemers can't be trusted. I need to dish out as much bullshit as she does. Sooner or later, Vanessa's going to figure out she's messing with the wrong man.

chapter 14

JASON

"Oh, c'mon. You're still upset about what happened back there?"

Vanessa and I are sitting in a neighborhood bar near Citi Field. I'm still hyped after watching the Mets decimate the Reds 7 to 2, but Vanessa's pouting as she swirls a cocktail straw in her pomegranate martini, her head hung low so all I can see are her toffee-colored curls.

"I'm not upset. I'm disillusioned."

"About?"

She whips her head up and gives me a disbelieving stare. "*You*. I thought you were one of the good ones, but then you got people to *boo* me. And my *face* was on the damn Jumbotron."

"You took that ball from a seven-year-old. Have you no shame?"

She lifts her chin defiantly. "It was *my* ball. I risked injury to my hand to catch it. That kid just stood there with his dopey eyes and chocolate-smeared cheeks."

"Oh, okay. So you *don't* have any shame."

She rolls her eyes.

I'm so damn tempted to tell her that I know what she's up to, but it's also fun as hell to mess with her. I reach over and shake her hand playfully. "It was a joke. No harm, no foul, right?"

"Right," she says, her gaze clouding. "I'm over it."

She's probably wondering how it all went wrong, but I'm not educating her about shit.

As our server clears our table, I spy Vanessa taking a deep breath and squaring her shoulders, as if she's decided to shake off the preceding train wreck and pivot to another tactic.

"How'd you end up a Mets fan?" she asks. "I thought all Nuyoricans rooted for the Yankees."

"When it came to deciding, it was easy. My dad—my real dad, I mean—was a Yankees fan. So I chose the Mets."

"But why?" she asks with a laugh.

"Because he's a piece of shit, and I didn't want us to have a baseball team in common." The words just fly out of my mouth as if they couldn't wait to escape. Fuck. I was so proud of myself for one-upping Vanessa, I forgot that I need to be on high alert around her at all times.

Before I can tell her to disregard my outburst, she says, "That's an excellent reason."

And just like that, my little tantrum isn't as uncomfortable as I thought it would be. Because this is what Vanessa does: She lulls you into being open with her, and then she passes no judgment when you say too much. At first, this aspect of her personality charmed me, but now I know it's a part of her power. She gets people to reveal themselves while she remains hidden behind an infuriatingly attractive mask.

"So Nelson's your stepdad?" she prods.

"He's my mother's second husband." I shrug. "My sisters call him Papi, but that sounds weird to me. I mean, he's been a constant in our lives for a long time, yet I have a hard time thinking of him that way. Doesn't really matter."

"I wonder if it matters to him," she says softly.

"He doesn't seem to care."

As far as I'm concerned, Nelson's fine. My mother's happy now, and that's all that matters. Although he's been around awhile, the moment the situation changes, he'll be gone too. I'll make sure of it.

"Or maybe he cares, but he doesn't want to ruffle any feathers by pushing you one way or the other."

"You mean he's hiding his true feelings." I draw back and pretend to be shocked. "People do that?"

She shakes her head, her lips twisted, then she says, "C'mon, you know they do."

"You're right. I definitely do." I inwardly wonder if she's thinking about the double meaning behind my words. I hope it's making her squirm on the inside. To her, I say, "In the end, though, Nelson and I are on good terms. We like each other. Respect each other too. Our dynamic works for us."

"Fair enough, then."

"So now that we've dissected my relationship with my mother's husband, tell me about being a financial planner. Was that what you always wanted to be?"

"Definitely not. But I'm good with numbers. And I'm super organized. Managing other people's money takes advantage of my skill set. I needed a well-paying job with long-term stability, mostly because I wanted to be able to support myself and send any extra money to my parents."

"So no burning desire to be a James Beard Award–winning chef? A prima ballerina? A world-class athlete?"

"Too risky," she says, shaking her head. "Even if I'd had the talent, which I didn't, I couldn't let my future be dictated by chance. I wasn't choosing a career for me; I was choosing a career for my family."

I stare at her for a moment before I speak. Why are this woman's layers so damn interesting to me? I really wish they weren't. "That's a lot of pressure to put on yourself."

She shrugs. "It's what poor, first-gen college students do. The ones who realize not everyone gets the opportunity to improve their family's situation, at least. Chasing some unrealistic dream would have squandered the chances I'd been given. Thanks to me, my parents have a retirement fund. It isn't much, but it's something. And once they sell the store, I'll help them find a home of their own. A place like Sueños. Knowing they'll be okay helps me sleep at night."

"Those are some serious oldest-daughter vibes."

"Tell me about it."

"What about Lisa? Does she help?"

"She does. Lisa's the one who's been keeping an eye on them while I got to leave home and make a new life in Chicago. She works her ass off at her own job and does shifts at the store on the weekends. But financially? I don't really expect her to. She's not swimming in money, and she deserves to save for her own future."

"What about what *you* deserve?"

She lets out a bitter laugh. "Believe me, I've gotten more than I deserve."

And see, this is the shit that kills me. I want to be able to feel nothing in this moment. To take her word for it. But the sum of Vanessa's parts have me in a damn choke hold. What *is* it about this woman?

Maybe it's her contradictions. She's a person who'll pretend to like me as part of a silly scheme meant to hook me up with her sister. She's also a person who will think of her family first when choosing a career. Yeah, people are complex and complicated and all that, but something tells me I haven't even gotten to all the layers that make Vanessa who she is. And damn, that intrigues me. So I dig a little deeper—because I can't seem to help myself. "Why don't you feel entitled to more?"

"I didn't say that."

"You implied it, though. By saying you've gotten more than you deserve."

"I meant that I've had my fair number of breaks. Private school. College on a mostly full ride. An excellent job right after graduation. That's enough for me. Other people deserve good breaks too."

"Like your parents. And Lisa."

"Exactly."

"I understand now."

Her eyebrows quirk up. "You do?"

"Yeah, you feel guilty."

Her eyes go impossibly wide, and then she stands abruptly. "I need to use the restroom."

I stand with her. "Listen, I didn't mean to upset you—"

"You didn't," she says, waving me off as she looks around. "I'll be back in a minute."

I watch her leave, not wanting to care about her as much as

I'm starting to. Even though I should know better. Even though I *do* know better.

Vanessa returns a few minutes later, the skin at her temples damp, as if she sprinkled water on her face to cool off.

She slowly lowers herself onto the chair, her lips pressed tight.

"Everything okay?" I ask.

"Yeah. I just..."

"Whatever you're going to say, it's fine. Tell me."

She opens and closes her mouth, then opens it again. "Remember when I said I wanted to take things slow?"

"Of course."

"I meant that about *everything*. The conversation we had a couple of minutes ago? That was more than I wanted to get into today. Too much. Too soon. Can we just enjoy each other's company without trying to uncover every facet of our personalities?"

Ah, I see what's going on here. She's saying what a person would say when they have no intention of building a future with someone. She doesn't need to get to know me—not the *real* me—because that isn't what we're about. More importantly, she's warning me not to delve too deeply because she's terrified to let anyone get to know her—the *real* her. "We can go as slow as you need to. And we'll stick to the basics. Like, when's your birthday?"

"February twenty-third," she says, her body noticeably less tense now that I've let her off the hook.

"You're a Pisces. Explains a lot."

"I'm not even going to ask. People who pay attention to astrology scare me. When's your birthday?"

"June twentieth."

Her eyes narrow as she does the calculations in her head. "Ooh, that's next Thursday."

"Yup."

"Any plans?"

"Nope. I'm not big on celebrations."

"Noted. Favorite snack growing up?"

"Easy. Now and Laters."

"Nice. What flavor?"

"Grape, of course. You?"

"Green apple Jolly Ranchers," she says. "Used to swipe them from the ten-cent bin in my parents' store."

"Sticky fingers too. I'm not surprised. Well, my favorite color's blue. What's yours?"

"Red."

We stare at each other, then I burst out laughing. "See how boring this is?"

She smiles. "We don't have to go to extremes, you know. We can find a middle ground. Something that works for both of us. Something that satisfies your need to be nosy and satisfies my need to be—"

"Guarded? Cagey? Evasive?"

She draws back and narrows her eyes. "Chill out, Mr. Thesaurus. I was going to say *mysterious*."

"You say mysterious, I say evasive."

"You say evasive, I say careful."

"You say careful, I say circumspect. I can do this all day."

She smiles. It's a genuine one this time. Big and assured. And I love that something that I said transformed her face that way. "I like you, Mr. Torres."

"I like you, too, Ms. Cordero."

And that's a problem. Because as much as it's true, I can't be with someone who's as deceitful as she is. It figures that the one person to spark my interest in years is the one person I could never trust.

Fuck, this sucks.

chapter 15

VANESSA

Me: Hey! Heads up: Tomorrow is Jason's bday.

Lisa: I know. Are you two going on a date?

Me: No, I have something else in mind.

Lisa: Something messy?

Me: Of course.

Lisa: And?

Me: And what?

Lisa: Aren't you going to tell me what it is?

Me: I'd rather you have plausible deniability.

Lisa: Should I get him something?

Me: Have you gotten him a gift before?

Lisa: No.

Me: Might be weird to start now.

Lisa: Maybe I'll send him a text.

Me: Sounds good. I'll let you know how it goes.

Lisa: OK. 😊

✖ ✖ ✖

As I wait at the Midtown rendezvous point near Jason's worksite, I remind myself that my plan is solid by cataloging a few facts about him:

One, he's not a big fan of public displays of affection.

Two, he's a bit of a grump at work, in part because he's younger than many of his employees and thinks he needs to be Mr. Serious to get their respect.

Three, he's not an attention-seeker. It's not that he wants to fade into the background; he's simply not interested in being at the forefront of anything.

What I'm planning will make him want to murder me. It's so delicious, I can hardly wait to see how it comes together. And if this prank doesn't send him scurrying into Lisa's arms, I'll give up my vibrator for a year. No, a week. A week makes the same point, right?

"Ms. Cordero," a voice behind me says.

I spin around and survey the white man I suspect I've been speaking with on the phone the past few days. "Henry?"

"In the flesh."

He reminds me of our IT guy in the Chicago office, right down to the chinos and blue V-neck sweater-vest over a slouchy T-shirt. I suppose that's part of his deal; he's meant to blend in with his surroundings.

"Great to meet you, Henry. Thanks for arranging this on such short notice."

"Our pleasure. Coordinating special moments with tight turnarounds is what we do best."

I point across the street. "There's his makeshift office."

Jason's current worksite is a boutique on Fifth Avenue that's expanding to incorporate the retail space next door. It's the namesake of a designer I've never heard of because super-high-end clothes aren't ever a part of my discretionary budget. I should ask Jason if he gets a discount. *Or maybe you should focus on the task at hand, Vanessa.*

Turning to Henry, I ask, "Are you ready for him?"

"Sure. We're all in position."

"It might take me a bit to get him to the right spot, but I'll manage it somehow."

"No rush on our part. We're getting paid by the hour, after all."

"Shit, I appreciate the reminder. Time for me to hustle."

I readjust my tote bag, then station myself along the western side of the park so I can corner Jason when he gets here.

The store's windows are covered in brown builder's paper, making it impossible to see inside, but I know from Jason's partner, Eric, that the birthday boy is here for a site inspection and they're taking a lunch break at noon. After I explained to Eric that I wanted to celebrate Jason's big day, he agreed to help me with my (undisclosed) surprise.

The goal is to get Jason to Bryant Park across the street. You can't get more public than that.

The doors of the store open right on time, and a steady stream of workers carrying bagged lunches shuffles outside and heads for the park. Jason eventually appears with Eric by his side. They're talking animatedly, and I spend a moment surveying Eric, who I'm seeing in person for the first time. He's tall, dark, and bald, and if someone told me he was related to Morris Chestnut, I'd believe them. Next to Eric, Jason looks just as impressive. Jesus, it shouldn't even be legal for these two to be friends, and judging by the stares they're getting from passersby, the general public agrees with me.

Eric points in the vicinity of where I'm standing, and then they jog across the street together. Seemingly in slow motion. Seriously, they're like an old *Baywatch* commercial—minus the red rescue cans, of course.

As soon as they make it across, I step out in front of Jason, causing him to almost stumble into me.

"Vanessa," he says, his eyes wide. "What are you doing here?"

"It's your birthday, so I thought I'd surprise you with lunch." I pat my tote. "Are you free?"

"Well, uh, Eric and I were going to grab—"

"No, we weren't," Eric says. "I'm just delivering the package. Happy birthday, man."

Jason and Eric give each other dap, then Eric grins at me.

"Nice to meet you," he says.

"Likewise. And thanks for everything."

"My pleasure. And I'm guessing his too."

Jason rolls his eyes. "Bye, Eric."

"I'm out," Eric says, waving as he saunters down the walkway adjacent to the park's lawn.

We watch him get swallowed by the crowd, and then Jason and I face each other.

"Are you cool with this?" I ask sheepishly.

"Definitely. This is sweet of you." He looks around. "Want to grab a table?"

"Yeah, that'd be great."

Seating at the park is at a premium, but the person who conveniently rises from the black wrought-iron table a few feet away is part of the surprise.

"We're in luck today," I say.

"He must know it's my birthday."

He does, I think to myself. *He absolutely does.*

"I brought some sushi from Hatsuhana. Eric said you're a fan. Hope that's okay."

"That's *more* than okay. It's perfect."

As I unpack my tote, Jason peeks inside the to-go containers, then looks up at me, his eyes narrowing. "You're eating with me, right?"

"Of course." Then I tilt my head. "Why? You think I'd poison your sushi?"

He chuckles nervously. "No, no. I just wanted to be sure."

"I went with the salmon lovers."

"Ah, that's my favorite," he says, unwrapping both sets of plastic chopsticks and handing one over to me.

Pulling out our beverages, I say, "And I'm told green tea pairs perfectly with sushi. I figured you wouldn't want to drink on the job."

"I'm floored by all of this, Vanessa. Truly. I didn't want to make a big deal about my birthday, so this is just how I'd do it. Lunch with a friend and a beautiful day in the park."

"I'm glad you're enjoying it."

He bites into a salmon avocado roll and squeezes his eyes shut. "So good."

I stare at his lips as he chews, then mentally smack myself

upside the head. Nope, indecent thoughts are not allowed. *I'm doing this for Lisa. I'm doing this for Lisa.*

We chat about the expansion project he's working on as we eat, and when we finish a few minutes later, I give the preestablished signal to begin the surprise.

It starts with a woman twirling by our table and handing Jason a rose.

"Just because," she says.

With his mouth slack, he takes it, then mutters, "Thank you." To me, he adds, "That was odd, wasn't it?"

"So weird," I say as I happily sip my tea.

Then the sounds of Kool & The Gang's "Celebration" float over the lawn. Another woman leaps into the air and ends her startling move by kneeling in front of Jason with two roses.

"What the hell is going on?" he says to himself.

"It's New York. Weird shit like this happens all the time."

"Not to me, it doesn't."

"Well, I guess today's your lucky day. Maybe even your *birthday*."

His gaze snaps to mine. "You didn't."

"And what if I did?"

"I'd hate you for the rest of my days."

"Wow, then I guess I didn't."

Next, a guy does the robot and drops four roses on Jason's lap. The women join him in a synchronized dance, and each time the song hits the chorus, a new group of dancers merges with the current crew, some of them tossing roses at Jason as they leap through the air.

Jason's eyes pop open with each new wave of people, and it's glorious. By now his employees in the park have caught on to the hijinks, and even Eric, who's leaning against a tree trunk nearby, is watching in amusement. The spectacle is drawing a crowd, and Jason definitely notices.

"This is wild," he says, heat staining his cheeks.

"Happy birthday."

"I'm never recovering from this. With the people I work with, I mean."

"I hear you need to be more approachable. This will help."

"You've *got* to be kidding me."

"I kid you not. You'll seem relatable this way."

"Because I can be embarrassed like the best of them?"

"No, silly. Because you know how to have fun."

When the song ends and Jason's hands are filled with two dozen roses, the crowd of onlookers claps for the performers. A few of his coworkers come over and slap him on his back, and a litany of congratulatory shout-outs ensues:

"We didn't know it was your birthday, boss!"

"Happy birthday, man!"

"¡Feliz cumple, bro!"

Jason flops back in his chair and mumbles something that sounds like "Thanks."

And now for the grand finale. I reach into my tote. "Oh, I almost forgot to give you your present!" With a flourish and a huge smile, I set it on the table. "Go ahead, open it."

"Should I?" he says, looking at it warily and then glancing at his employees.

"Of course you should."

Jason carefully opens the package, and his body goes rigid as he registers what's inside.

"Let everyone see!" I say, clapping my hands like a seal.

"I really shouldn't."

"Aw, c'mon, boss," an employee says. "Let us see it. She's proud of it, man."

So he pulls the book out of the exquisite gift wrapping I did all by myself.

One of the workers reads the title: "*How to Live with a Huge...*"

"*Penis*," another one finishes.

Their laughter trails off as the book's implications settle in, and then they exchange furtive glances with one another and with Jason. Seconds later, they quickly say their goodbyes, scrambling across the street like they're running from the bogeyman.

Eric, who's joined the fray, doubles over, and as he's walking away, he shouts over his shoulder. "Oh yeah, she's a keeper."

But judging by the murderous expression on Jason's face, if he had his choice, I'd be a goner. Now I have him exactly where I want him: a few dates away from ditching me. Perfection.

chapter 16

JASON

Vanessa thinks I'm going to lose it, but I'd never give her the satisfaction. Somehow, by the grace of the man upstairs, I pull all that emotion into the center of my body and release it on a shaky exhale. I must admit, if I didn't know what she was up to, this latest stunt would have me seriously questioning her grasp of basic dating norms. Touché, Vanessa. Tou-fuckin-ché.

"How'd you know?" I whisper.

"How'd I know what?"

"How'd you know I needed this?" I stare off into the distance and sniff. "All these years, I thought I was alone." With a deep sigh, I sift through the book. There's a page with an actual paper ruler so you can measure yourself. Jesus Christ. "Now I know there are people out there just like me. Trying to navigate life with this . . . thing that's more than anyone should have to handle." I glance at Vanessa's face—her eyes are bulging and her lips are parted. "It's so heavy, sometimes my back starts aching." I flip through the table of contents. "Huh, I wonder if there's a section about that? So yeah, thank you. Seriously. I'm going to start reading it tonight."

She swallows. Hard. "Oh, I'm glad you, uh, think it'll be useful." She tries to sneak a peek at my crotch. "It was a guess."

"It was a good guess, then. For obvious reasons, it's a touchy subject, but since you raised it, now I don't have to be nervous about your reaction if we ever get to that point. *Not* that I'm assuming we will."

Now she's blushing furiously, and oh man, I'm enjoying the hell out of her discomfort.

"Well, I'm, uh . . . I'm glad," she croaks out.

"Somehow, you've pushed me out of my comfort zone and made my birthday special. So thank you." I take her hand, trying very hard not to laugh. "Listen, duty calls for now, but when can I see you again?"

She tilts her head and considers me for a moment. "You still want to?"

"Of course. Why wouldn't I?"

"Huh. Okay. Well, I'm going to a cookout this Saturday. For my new office. One of my coworkers is hosting it. I'll hardly know anyone, and the food will probably suck because it's a potluck, but you're welcome to come with me. We can be awkward and uncomfortable together. How does that sound?"

"Sounds perfect."

She jerks her head back. "It does?"

"Haven't you figured it out by now? Anyplace with you is where I want to be."

"Oh, that's sweet," she says, looking dazed. "I just thought social stuff isn't your jam."

"It isn't, but I'll suffer through it. For you. And I'll even bring a dish so you don't have to."

"That's . . . very kind of you, Jason."

I point over my shoulder. "So, uh, I need to get back there, but you'll send me the details about this weekend?"

"I will."

"Great. Take care," I say, then press a kiss against her forehead. "And thanks again. For everything."

I chuckle to myself as I wait for the traffic light to turn red. When I look back at Vanessa, she's still standing by the table in the park, her eyebrows squished together as though she's working something out in her head.

I fucking love this. And I'm not even done.

× × ×

Eric's mouth twitches the moment I enter the store. "So that's Vanessa."

"That's Vanessa."

"She's Black."

"And a woman, Captain Obvious."

He has the grace to look embarrassed. "Sorry. I was just picturing someone else when you said she was Puerto Rican."

"We come in all sizes and colors, man. You're from NYC, you should know that better than most."

"I'm ashamed to say I went with the default."

"Let me guess: Jennifer Lopez."

"Exactly. I'll have to think about why that is. But anyway, I can see why you're into her."

"Don't even, man. You helped her with all that shit."

He throws up his hands and makes a shrugging gesture. "I didn't know. All she said was that she wanted to make your birthday special."

"No, she wanted to annoy the hell out of me."

Eric's eyebrows shoot up. "Why would she want that?"

I sigh. "Because it turns out that she's not really interested in me. Her sister is."

"I'm not following."

"The sister has a crush on me, and they've come up with this stupid-ass scheme they think is going to send me running to her. Vanessa's supposed to be the poisonous asshole. The sister's the antidote."

"Fuuuck," he says, holding his chin as he steps back. "How'd you even find out?"

"Denise overheard them talking about their plan at the couples shower."

"Yo, that's wild."

"Yeah, it is. So now I'm messing with Vanessa, too, and she has no clue."

"Why not call her out?"

"Because if I do, it'll blow up Cami's wedding plans. Denise is about to kill Vanessa's sister as it is. Plus, my mother's harassing me about finding someone to settle down with. She's not impressed with Vanessa, so as long as she's around, my mother's going to leave me alone."

"Why wouldn't your mom throw some women your way, then? To get between the two of you."

"Because the last time she tried to dissuade me from dating someone, it backfired."

His chin lifts in understanding. "Elyse."

"Yeah, Elyse."

"So you're just messing with them now?"

"Exactly."

"Look at you, being all devious and shit."

"Yeah, I'm even surprising myself."

"Well, on a serious note, I'm sorry. I had high hopes for you two. I thought she was a person you could move on with."

"She isn't."

"Then be careful," he says, squeezing my shoulder. "If you take this too far, you might catch feelings anyway."

"Not gonna happen. Trust me."

"If you say so."

"I do."

Yeah, I'm not catching feelings for anyone. Vanessa may be interesting, despite the bananas scheme she's committed herself to, but that doesn't mean I'll ever *fall* for her. I have way more sense than Eric gives me credit for. And *I'm* the one who's in control of this situation. Full stop.

chapter 17

VANESSA

"Thanks again for joining me," I say to Jason as we climb the staggered walkway leading to my coworker's home. "I'm meeting some of these people for the first time, and it'll be nice to know a friendly face is near."

"Not a problem. I'm always game for hanging out with you."

Why, Jason? Why? I've been nothing but annoying as fuck around you.

"Another thing," I say, "if I don't immediately introduce you to someone, it might be because I forgot their name or never knew it in the first place. If you could—"

"Vanessa, relax. You're here to get to know your colleagues. And have a little fun. I'll introduce myself if I need to."

"Right. Okay. I can do this." I raise the bottles of rosé in my hands. "And when all else fails, liquor is an excellent icebreaker."

Jason playfully jostles the bowl of potato salad he made. "And if that doesn't work, my world-famous potato salad will do the trick."

"I can't believe you went to all that trouble. When I hear *potluck*, I think wine. Or chips and dip."

"It's a cookout, Vanessa. Potato salad is *always* the way to go."

"Well, Lisa tells me you're a fantastic cook, so I know it's going to be a winner."

"Trust me, you're gonna love it."

"So what's in the bag?"

"The extras. The mayo always gets absorbed in the potatoes during transit, so I bring extra dressing to add when we're ready to eat. Along with some delicious mix-ins."

"Sounds tasty. You're going to make me look good just by association."

"I sure hope so," he says cheerfully.

When we reach the top of the steps, we take the path to a side gate and follow signs to the backyard. It's huge, an expanse of meticulously manicured grass enclosed by a black wrought-iron fence, with a playset in the corner and a dozen Adirondack chairs sprinkled around two large picnic tables.

After a dizzying round of introductions among the twenty or so guests, Jason and I help ourselves to Arnold Palmers made with fresh lemonade and cold-brewed iced tea. Not long after, Julie Cho, our host, waves her hands in the air in a bid to get everyone's attention.

Charles, the manager of our new office, who I'm delighted to learn is Black because it means I won't be the "only," uses his booming voice to help her out. "All right, people. Julie's on the mic."

"I appreciate that, Charles." She positions herself between the picnic tables. "Hey, all. I'm not going to take up a lot of time with speeches. I just wanted to take a moment to acknowledge how thrilling it is to be opening this new office with you. Meridian Financial is going to make its mark in the New York market, and I hope you're all as proud as I am to be a part of this exciting new venture. Yes, there will be ups and downs ahead, but we've got a good group here, and I know we're ready to handle whatever challenges come our way. For the moment, though, enjoy the amazing food you all brought, take advantage of the games set up in the far corner of the yard, and definitely get yourselves some wine because I purchased enough to fully stock a cocktail lounge. The buffet is open. Now, let's grub and get to know one another."

A few people raise their cups and say "Hear, hear," while others head straight for the buffet line.

Jason uses this as his cue to prep his potato salad, which has been on ice since we arrived.

"He's a fantastic cook," I say to the white woman next to me. She's an HR manager, if memory serves. Barb's her name, I think. "People are going to be asking for the recipe as soon as they get a taste."

"I'm glad he made it, then," Charles says, watching the preparations. "Potato salad is no joking matter. Can't just let anyone bring it."

"So true," Jason says, grinning. "Let me just add a little bit more of this mayo dressing, and we'll be all set." He folds in the dressing with a spoon, and then he snaps his fingers. "Almost forgot the mix-ins."

"Mix-ins?" Charles asks skeptically. "That doesn't sound right."

"Don't worry, I got this. Been making this family recipe for years, and it's always a hit."

With a flourish, Jason whips out Ziploc bags of different foods—peaches, raisins, sunflower seeds—and adds them to the salad. Oh no, are those bacon bits?

"Oh *hell* no," Charles mutters. "You need spices, mayo, mustard, paprika. Maybe onions. *Maybe.*"

"Give it a shot, man," Jason says. "You might surprise yourself."

My eyes go wide when my gaze lands on the last plastic bag. Are those Skittles? M&M's? Oh my God, this is a nightmare.

"Peanut M&M's," Jason says. "For extra crunch."

"What the hell are you making?" Charles asks. "A fucked-up ice cream sundae?"

"I'm telling you, it's good. Yeah, it's a bit unconventional, but the flavor profile works. You just need to be adventurous. Right, Vanessa?"

"Uh, yeah, sure. It all sounds so yummy. Can't wait to try it."

"No waiting necessary," he says with way more cheer than is warranted. "Since you're lucky enough to know the cook, you get to try it first."

"Oh, that's okay. Potato salad is so, uh, filling. I was going to grab some my second time through the buffet."

"What? No way. And miss the chance to try some? We can't have that. Because I'm telling you, it's not going to last very long." He takes a plastic spoon and scoops a heaping portion of potato salad. "Say ahh."

I want to duck and run away, but what would my colleagues think? I've already talked up Jason's cooking to everyone. Shit. How was I supposed to know making potato salad is his apparent kryptonite? All the ingredients are familiar to me, so it can't be that bad, right?

"C'mon, Vanessa," Jason prompts. "You're holding up the line, sweetie."

I close my eyes and open my mouth. Jason makes the sound of an airplane and spoon-feeds me his potato salad surprise. Oh God, what is this? The flavor that hits my tongue reminds me of that period during my childhood when I inhaled whatever was in front of me. When foods melded together because I ate them so quickly. There's so much going on in my mouth right now, and it's zero percent pleasant. It's like I have flavored nuts and rusty bolts and screws being tossed around in there.

"How does it taste?" Jason asks.

I open my glistening eyes to see him looking at me hopefully. "So good," I say, still chewing. "Is there water, though? I'm a little parched."

"Here," Jason says, handing me a cup. "Take mine."

You're brave, Charles mouths behind Jason's back.

"Want more?" Jason asks.

"No! Um, what I mean is, I'd rather everyone else get a chance to taste it. I'm just going to run to the bathroom real quick. I'll be sure to get some more salad the next go-round."

Now I'm the one scrambling as if the bogeyman's chasing me.

When I return from the bathroom a few minutes later, I spy Jason chatting with Charles and make my way over to them. I glance at Jason's plate, which is piled high with a serving from every dish at the cookout. Except his world-famous potato salad. *That bastard. I should have known he was up to something.*

"Hey, Charles, I need to steal Jason for a minute."

"No problem," Charles says, bowing as he steps back.

"What's up?" Jason says. "Everything okay?"

"I refuse to believe that's your usual potato salad recipe."

He looks at me innocently, but I'm not convinced.

"Why? You didn't like it?"

"It had peanut M&M's in it. What the hell, Jason?"

His dark brown eyes crinkle at the corners. "I *might* have tweaked it a bit."

"Why?" I stare at him a moment, and then it hits me: "Oh, you're devious. To pay me back for the flash mob, am I right?"

"Exactly."

"What's the big deal, though? I thought it was a sweet gesture."

"Did you now? Is that why you were laughing your ass off? Nu-uh, you were getting me back for the Jumbotron incident."

"Was not. It was your birthday, and I wanted to do something special. That's all."

He steps in front of me, overwhelming my senses with his presence. "Look me in the eyes, Vanessa."

Oh God, this is hard. The angles of his face, the cleft in his chin, those pouty lips. How can I pretend to not be affected by this man? I sway on my feet as I battle my desire to lean into him. Somehow I manage to remain aloof. "Okay, I'm looking."

"Can you honestly say that you arranged that flash mob because you thought I'd enjoy it?"

"I—"

"Wait. Before you answer . . ." He takes three giant steps back. "Just want to be sure I'm not collateral damage when you get struck by lightning."

I fall over with mock laughter, then quickly straighten, my face deadpan. "Har har, you're so funny . . . and heartless."

"No, I'm practical. Now, what's your answer?"

"Yes, okay, I did it to annoy you," I say, unable to hold back my smile. "And because I thought maybe you'd get a kick out of it too."

His eyes go soft, and I'm momentarily dazzled by this version of him.

He takes three giant steps forward, landing directly in front of me, then he flicks one of my curls. "Thanks for being honest."

"You're welcome."

"But I'm not sure the potato salad is enough payback for the flash mob."

"Bring it."

"I don't do dance battles," he says.

I tilt my head. "What?"

"You said 'bring it.' Sounds like you're challenging me to a dance battle. Am I wrong?"

"Oh God, what am I going to do with you?" I ask, throwing up my hands in fake frustration.

He gives me a silly grin. "I'm sure you'll figure it out. And in the meantime, let me make amends."

"Amends for what?"

"The Great Potato Salad Incident."

"Is that what we're calling it?"

"We are."

"Okay, so how do you propose to make it up to me?"

"I'm cooking dinner for the family Thursday night. At Cami's place. A sort of send-off for her before all the wedding chaos begins. Your sister will be there too. Join us."

"Are you sure you want me there?"

"I'm sure. But there's a catch."

"Okay..."

"I need you to be my sous chef."

"That's not a good idea. Trust me, I'm a terrible cook."

"Do you know how to use a knife? A can opener?"

I narrow my eyes at him and purse my lips for a moment before answering. "Of course."

"Then you're hired."

"Okay, I'll come, but on one condition."

"What's that?"

"You don't put potato salad on the menu. Deal?"

"Deal."

Gah. Why isn't he following the program? He should have had enough of my shenanigans by now. Instead, he's giving as good as he's receiving, and I'm barely focusing on my mission. I'm supposed to be making him miserable, but he seems to be enjoying my company and wanting more of it. And honestly, this unfortunate development thrills me. What the hell is happening, and how do I make it stop?

JASON

"Ready to get your second round of potato salad?" I ask Vanessa.

She's cheesing so hard, and I'm captivated by her unguarded demeanor. "Absolutely not. I wouldn't—"

Whatever she was going to say gets swallowed by a gasp.

"What is it?" I ask, noticing her expression hardening.

She shakes her head as if to clear it. "Nothing, really. Saw someone I didn't think would show up today."

I twist around to see the "someone" who just arrived: a white man who looks to be in his early thirties. Tall, wiry, and a dead ringer for that actor from the *Deadpool* movies. His gaze sweeps over Vanessa with familiarity. I hate him on sight. "Bad blood between you two?"

"That's the head of the Chicago office. He made it possible for me to be here."

There's so much she isn't saying, which, given that this is Vanessa, shouldn't come as a surprise. "Wait a minute. Did you *want* to be transferred?"

"I didn't have a choice. I pissed off the wrong person."

The picture I'm getting isn't flattering. Of him. And all it does is confirm my initial reaction to his possessive gaze. I grit my teeth, then will myself to calm down. "What do you mean?"

My steely tone gets her attention. "Forget I said anything, Jason. It's not a big deal, I promise."

"Do you want to head out? I'm here to do whatever you want. Whatever you need."

Clearly fighting back tears, she looks up at me. "I'm not upset about him. I'm upset about the situation I put myself in. And I just need to not lose my shit in front of my new colleagues. Can you help me with that?"

I pull her close and press a soft kiss against the corner of her mouth. "Consider it done."

"Thank you," she says, burrowing into my embrace.

The jerk circles the perimeter of the gathering, but his gaze keeps returning to Vanessa. Yeah, this man is whipped, and she's obviously not interested. I maneuver us away from the crowd, just in case there's a confrontation. As expected, he slowly makes his way over to us. Throwing on my game face, I straighten to my full height and slide my hand around Vanessa's waist.

"Good to see you again," he says to her.

"I'm surprised you're here."

"The execs wanted my expertise, so I was visiting on business. Figured I'd say hello to the new group." He extends his hand to me. "David Warner. You are?"

"Jason Torres."

He looks between us. "A friend?"

"Whatever she wants me to be."

"Huh," he says. "Interesting. Are you a financial planner, Jason?"

"No, I own a construction firm."

"Ah," he says. "A potential client, then."

"I'm not looking for financial planning advice at this time, but I will say Chicago's loss is New York's gain."

David clucks his tongue. "Fair point. But you know what they say: New York is for your twenties, everywhere else is for a lifetime."

Vanessa groans. "No one says that."

"Give me a minute of your time," the jerk says, invading her personal space.

She sidesteps his advance and shifts close enough that our bodies are touching. The satisfaction I'm experiencing from that simple move is well out of proportion for what it probably means, and that's definitely on me.

"Is what you want to talk about related to work?" Vanessa asks him.

"You know it isn't," he says, imploring her with his eyes to give him a chance.

"Then no, you won't be getting any more minutes from me." She places her hand on my chest. "I'm thirsty. Let's grab something to drink." Over her shoulder, she adds, "Have a safe trip back to Chicago, David."

"Can I call you before I leave?" he asks her.

"You're welcome to, but I blocked your personal number, so good luck with that." Then she pulls me along to the beverage table.

After grabbing two glasses of wine, I hand one to her. "Do you want to talk about it?"

"Not at all."

"I'm a good listener."

"I know you are, but this isn't a story fit to be told. Nor is this the place."

"Let's get out of here, then. You've done the rounds. You've met your coworkers. Let's get some real food somewhere and talk."

She studies my face and smiles. "You're a sweet guy."

"But?"

"But I think I just want to go home and clear my head. Alone. Maybe I'll see you when you're working at the store tomorrow?"

I step back and take a final sip of wine. "Of course. We're moving at your pace, remember?"

"Thanks for being so understanding."

"You'd be surprised by how much I understand, Vanessa."

She tilts her head and peers at me, but she doesn't say anything in response. That's Vanessa for you: She only shares what she absolutely has to. I shouldn't be disappointed, but I am. And even though letting me into her life isn't part of her agenda, I want it to be. That's a big problem—one I have no clue how to solve.

chapter 18

VANESSA

"You're supposed to be on vacation until your new office opens. Why are you here?"

My mother's staring at me as she rings up a customer. The register is like a typewriter to her; if she had to, she probably could charge three dozen customers per minute. And she doesn't even need to look at the number pad.

"Hello to you, too, Mami," I say as I lean over and stash my purse behind the counter. "I'm fine this morning. Thanks for asking."

She flicks my forehead. "Cuidao. No seas atrevida."

"I'm not being fresh," I say with a laugh. "You basically told me to leave."

"No, I didn't. I'm basically telling you to get a life."

"Ouch," I say, holding both hands over my heart. "You don't want me around?"

"Of course I want you around. I *always* want you around." She looks at me meaningfully. "But only if you want to be here."

And there it is. A subtle reference to that *one time* when the store was the last place I wanted to be. It's doubly disconcerting to have it thrown back at me by my mother, who's essentially my twin; seeing her disappointment is like staring at a reflection of my own self-loathing. I pretend not to understand what she's alluding to—it's easier that way—and busy myself by straightening the magazine rack near the deli. "Where's Papi?"

"He's out back getting some supplies."

She watches me as I wander around the store, then lifts her chin as if she's worked out a puzzle in her head. "Aha, I think I know what's going on."

"What, Ma?" I ask, wearing a blank expression. "What's going on?"

"You're sniffing around because Camila's brother will be coming later."

"Jason? Hardly. One, I'm not sniffing around. Two, he's already invited me over, so there's no need for me to sniff around anyway." I catch her eyes going round, so I quickly add, "For *dinner. At his sister's house.* He invited me for dinner with his mother and sisters and Lisa on Thursday."

My mother's strained expression softens. "So you're just hanging out with us today?"

"Yeah, if that's okay with you. And if Lisa wants to head out early, I could cover for her. Or if you need to run errands, go ahead."

"You don't mind?" she asks, raising a brow.

"Not at all."

"Great," she says, whipping off the apron she's always wearing even though she never steps foot in the deli section. "Then I can do my compras now. Fine Fare is having a sale on bistec."

Do my parents own a grocery store? Yes. Do they buy groceries somewhere else? Also yes. La Flor is for quick pickups: bread, milk, the occasional vegetable when you've forgotten a key ingredient. But Fine Fare is for stocking the fridge.

We quickly switch places, and then she opens the door. "Oh, Clara's son is always trying to be cute. If he comes by, tell him we don't sell individual cigarettes anymore. His mother can buy a whole pack if she wants, and she needs to come get them herself."

"Got it," I say, nodding.

"Thank you, mija! Tell your father I'll only be a minute."

As soon as she's gone, my father returns with a stack of boxes in his hands. "Your mother left?"

"Yeah, she's going to the supermarket. Said she'll be back soon."

He shrugs. "Your mother is always moving. Can't keep still to save her life."

"And you wouldn't have it any other way."

"That's true." He studies my face as I wipe off the counter. "It's nice to have you here."

"It's nice to be here."

"We missed you," he says with a wide smile that emphasizes the fine lines around his eyes.

"I'm not going anywhere."

"Good, I like the sound of that," he says, nodding, then he lifts the boxes in his hands. "I'm going to get ready for the morning rush."

"Need help?"

"As long as you handle the register, I'll be fine."

"Okay, Papi."

I continue to straighten up the counter area, content in the knowledge that my parents still want me here. This feels right: being home again, that is. And although I was thriving in Chicago from a professional standpoint, I wasn't nearly as successful in my personal life there. My relocation wasn't entirely voluntary, yet I can't say that I'm hating my new normal. It's comforting to be around my family again. It's heartening to be rooted somewhere, to be anchored to the people I love.

My father and I work well as a team for about an hour, and then Lisa relieves me, explaining that she needs to start now so she can leave early to get her nails done.

"This is perfect, then," I tell her. "Use this time to chat up Jason. I won't be here, so you'll have a captive audience."

"Okay, but what do I say?"

"Just talk to him, Lili."

"Okay, okay," she says. Then she licks her lips. "I'm just nervous."

"You'll be fine. Show him who you are. Talk about your interests. Ask about his. Be drama free, and give him a glimpse of how easy you two would be together."

She nods, biting her lip. "I can do that."

"I *know* you can."

Minutes later, I'm counting the money in the drawer before handing it off to Lisa when the digital doorbell chimes and a voice I never expected to hear in this place greets me.

"Hello, Vanessa."

I whip my head up, my mouth parted in shock. "What are you doing here?"

Standing in front of the counter, looking as if he's headed to play a round of golf at Van Cortlandt, is my former lover, David Warner.

What the fuck?

He smiles at me, pretending that all is well between us. I glare at him as heat courses through my body.

The nerve of this man.

Lisa senses my distress and places a hand on my arm. "Is everything okay? Need me to get Papi?"

"It's okay, Lili. I can handle this."

Narrowing my eyes at David, I motion for him to follow me outside. I'm not putting up with his games anymore. This bullshit ends now.

× × ×

"You left me no choice," David tells me. "This is the only way I could see you."

I'm pacing the area in front of the store, trying but nearly failing not to lose my shit.

"How'd you find me?" I ask, scowling at him.

"Easy. I listened when we were together. And I remember you saying your parents owned a bodega on 106th Street."

He pronounces *bodega* like Bogotá, Colombia, and I want to smash his face in.

"This is harassment, David. I don't want you here."

"I just wanted an opportunity to explain," he says, reaching for my hand.

"Explain what?" I say, dodging his touch.

"I think I made a mistake recommending you for the New York office. It didn't turn out the way I planned. And I miss you."

"No," I say, shaking my head vehemently. "We are not doing this. There are absolutely no circumstances under which we are anything but professional colleagues."

"You don't mean that," he says, moving closer.

I put up a hand to stop him. "David, listen to me. We are *never* going to happen. I'm a novelty for you. I wasn't interested in a relationship, so you're inevitably desperate for one. Because that's how these things work, right? But if you thought about it—*really* thought about it—you'd recognize that you screwed me over, and that *kind of* puts a damper on whatever love story we could have had."

David runs his fingers through his hair and lets out a frustrated sigh. "People make mistakes. If you would—"

"Is there a problem here?" a voice behind me asks.

I squeeze my eyes shut.

Oh my God, no. Not Jason. Not now. Beam me the fuck up, Scotty.

I spin around and face Jason. "It's nothing. I can take care of this."

A muscle ticks in Jason's jaw. "Are you sure? I'm happy to stay here until he leaves. Or make him leave if he gives me a reason to."

"I'm sure," I say, placing a hand on his chest. "There's no need for you to be involved."

His eyes flash with hurt, and then his expression goes blank. "Fine. I'll be inside if you change your mind."

Jason stomps off, but not before glowering at David as if he's seconds from slamming my boss's face against the concrete. It would serve the man right if Jason did just that.

"So he really is your boyfriend?"

"I've moved on, David. You should too."

David can make of that response what he will. I don't owe him an explanation.

"Listen, I just want to do my job," I continue. "It didn't work out between us, but it's over now. And in a way, this move will be good for us. It's a clean break."

"So that's it?" he says, sadness clouding his features as he stares at me. "You felt nothing for me?"

"I did feel something for you. Not love, but affection and respect. All of that was extinguished the moment you retaliated against me."

The word *retaliated* seems to set off a warning bell in his mind, as if he suddenly realizes the implication of his actions. He steps back, and his face turns crimson. "I'll leave you alone. Sorry if I went too far."

"You did. Let's just push ahead from here."

"Okay," he says, his shoulders sagging in defeat.

Before he walks away, I stop him. "And David?"

He turns around. "Yeah?"

"I saved every voicemail, every text, every card attached to the lilies you used to send."

He doesn't answer, but judging by how his skin pales, I think he understands my point. And then he scurries away, throwing up his hand to hail a cab when he's put some distance between us. Yeah, good luck with that.

"You okay?" Jason says behind me.

I jump at the sound of his voice. "God, you scared me. I thought you were inside."

"I was standing by the door," he says, his face unreadable. "Just in case."

"Thanks, but it's handled. I have a funny feeling I'll be dealing with David exclusively by email from now on."

"Good," he says, his expression grim. "Your dad and Lisa wanted to know who he was."

"Did you tell them?" I ask, pinching the skin at my throat.

"I claimed not to know."

"Thanks again."

He opens his mouth, then snaps it shut.

I can only imagine what he's thinking. Yes, I'm a mess. And yeah, I don't always make the best decisions, but this move to New York is my chance to start fresh. It figures that David would try to drag me back to hell and that Jason would be around to witness it. "Go ahead. Say what you want to say. I'm sure I've heard worse."

"You told me there was no need for me to be involved," he says, walking toward me, then stopping when we're inches apart. "Before. When your boss was here. But I'm already involved. And I only backed off because you asked me to. I just wanted you to know the state of play. Ball's in your court now."

Unable to formulate a pithy response, I simply nod.

Honestly, a part of me wanted him to be involved too. I can easily imagine a scenario in which Jason is my partner and has my back. I can just as easily picture a future in which we ride-or-die for each other. Which can only mean one thing: I'm officially in over my head.

chapter 19

VANESSA

The Thursday after the Great Potato Salad Incident, Jason and I are chatting as we cook Cami's bon-voyage meal. Correction: He's cooking; I'm prepping the ingredients for sofrito. He hasn't brought up the incident with David, and I'm more than appreciative of the reprieve. Especially because we're not alone. The rest of the guests are in Cami's living room, going over the wedding details and occasionally poking their heads in the kitchen to see how much longer they have to wait before dinner's ready.

Soon, people, soon.

Well, that is if Jason stops being a tyrant in his sister's kitchen. Even the relatively simple process of mashing more garlic in the pilón requires his supervision.

"Hazlo con más fuerza," he says behind me.

"I don't need your instruction, Chef Ramsay. I'm putting enough effort into this as it is."

"Hmm. I thought you said you don't speak Spanish."

"I can understand most of it just fine, and you're being overbearing in both languages."

He raises his hands in the air and backs off. "Okay, okay. The sofrito is yours."

"Thank you."

"I'm going to need it in a minute, though."

"Oh my God, remind me to never be your sous chef again."

He gives me his side smile—the one where only one corner of his mouth lifts—and I can almost envision us being this easy with each other for real. Well, we *are* this easy with each other for real, but Jason has no clue I'm hoping he'll end up with my sister. Speaking of... let's get back on track, shall we?

"You know who should be doing this with you?" I ask.

"Who?"

"Lisa. She's a great cook. She'd probably be able to show you a thing or two."

"Think so?"

"Oh yeah. She'd be all over this if you called her in here. Even as a teenager, she knew what she was doing. It's like she popped out of the womb with a talent for cooking."

"We'd probably clash in the kitchen, then. I mean, you *did* just compare me to Gordon Ramsay."

Shit. The point is to bring them together, not give him reasons to think they're incompatible. "Nah, I think you'd find a rhythm with each other."

"Maybe. Still, I like cooking for people, so it doesn't bother me one bit that you're not handy in the kitchen."

"It doesn't?"

"Not at all."

Dammit. As usual, Jason's brain isn't cooperating. It's frustrating as hell, but I need to roll with it, don't I? "Hmm, that's been one of those things I've always wondered about. Whether someone I dated would expect me to make amazing Puerto Rican dishes and be disappointed when they learned I'm only good at making coquito."

"Well, you don't need to worry about that with me. Feeding people brings me pleasure."

I watch him as he pulls the roasted pork from the oven. After setting the pan on the stove, he breaks off a juicy chunk of meat and pops it into his mouth. "Mmm," he says, closing his eyes. Then he breaks off another piece and offers it to me. "Say ahh."

I open my mouth for a taste, his gaze settling on my lips as I chew. "Oh my God, I think I just had my first food orgasm."

"Glad I was here to witness it," he says as he continues to stare at my lips.

Holy. Shit. The devil must be chuckling right now.

I step back and gesture with my hands at the minced garlic in the pilón. "Ta-da. All done."

"It's about time."

"Easy now. Let's not be ungrateful."

"Me? Ungrateful? Never. Impatient in the kitchen? Always."

"I *knew* there was a flaw somewhere."

"Oh, believe me, there are many."

"Name another."

He thinks about it for a moment, then says, "I tend to tiptoe around my problems because I hate conflict."

"C'mon, don't keep me hanging. Examples, please."

"My longest relationship in college lasted a year too long because I didn't know how to break up with her."

"Jason."

"You asked," he says, wincing. "Now it's your turn."

"To what?"

He tilts his head and gives me a blank stare. "To tell me one of your flaws."

"I would if I could, but I don't have any."

"Vanessa."

"Jason."

"Vanessa."

"Okay, okay. I'm terrible at remembering important dates—birthdays, anniversaries, and so on. You lucked out only because you told me your birthday the week before."

"*That's* your flaw?"

"I'm sure there are others, but that's the one I'm sharing with you."

"Right. Of course."

"What do you mean, *of course*?"

"You don't share much about yourself, Vanessa. And yeah, we agreed to take this slow, but I want to get to know you, too, and I get the sense that you're stalling for some reason."

Shit. This is the problem with being a starter ex to someone who's emotionally intelligent: They can spot your bullshit a mile away. In college, the guys I dated didn't care if I opened up to them, but Jason's not a teenager, and he's noticing that I'm not fully invested in our budding relationship.

Honestly, I don't know *how* to be open. Anyone with a sense of self-preservation knows you need to tread lightly when sharing your secrets. Because anything you share can and will be used against you. Still, if I don't say *something*, Jason might get suspicious. So I'll tell him an unflattering fact about me. Lord knows there are tons to choose from. "The guy you met at the cookout, David. He isn't just one of my bosses. We also dated for a while."

"I figured as much."

"And he pushed for my transfer because I broke things off. He's punishing me. Essentially, I fucked my boss, and now I'm being screwed for it."

"That was *not* what I thought you were going to say."

"What? You thought I was the one pushing for a serious relationship?"

"Exactly."

"Right. Because it's *always* the woman who wants more."

"I realize that is a stereotypical assumption."

"It is. But that speaks to one of my flaws too. I couldn't give him more because I *hate* sharing things about myself."

"Why?"

"People never like what I tell them. Case in point, I dated my boss, a supremely foolish thing to do. And now I bet you're thinking it doesn't speak well of my judgment."

"I don't think any less of you now than I did a minute ago. I'm more concerned that he got away with sexual harassment."

"I was going to leave Chicago no matter what."

"But you should have been able to do that on your own terms. You could—"

"Jason, leave it alone. I don't *want* to do anything about it. Yeah, it was a costly lesson, but I won't be putting myself in that position again. I've made peace with what happened."

"Simple as that?"

I nod. "Simple as that."

"You're way more complicated than you let on, though. But I

get it: You've been burned in the past, and this is your way of protecting yourself."

"Easy, Dr. Phil. I don't have enough money to pay you for therapy."

"Can I give you a hug instead?"

"Why?" I say with a laugh.

"I think you know why."

We stare at each other for a long moment, then I set down my knife and open my arms. He pulls me close and wraps me in a tight embrace. Against my hair, he says, "Thank you."

"For what?"

"For sharing a piece of you. I know that wasn't easy."

"I'm trying."

What I don't say is that I'm trying *for him*. And the realization knocks me upside the head. There's no reason for me to be doing anything *for him*. Hell, I'm sending mixed signals even to myself, and that's a recipe for disaster.

I step out of his arms and rub my hands together. "We better get back to cooking. Your family's going to kill us if the food isn't done soon."

"Right," he says, snapping his fingers. "I need to make the rice real quick."

"Is there anything else I can do?"

"Yeah, actually. Would you mind setting the table?"

"Okay, *that* I can handle." I spin around and peruse Cami's cabinets.

"She said we could take whatever we need."

"Got it."

As I'm reaching for the plates, he clears his throat. "So, uh, I've been meaning to ask you something."

"Sounds ominous," I say, turning to face him.

He smiles. "Could be."

"I'm all ears."

"So, uh, Cami and Bryan. Let's just say they pride themselves on going against the grain. There won't be a bachelor or bachelorette party. Instead, they're calling it a 'going out with a bang' celebration, and they want to do it together."

"Sounds cool so far."

"You'd think so, but I'm not sure. Because they asked Lisa and Denise to plan the event. It's going to be the people in the wedding party and any significant others: Cami and Bryan, me, Denise, Lisa, and Bryan's brother, who's the best man, and his girlfriend. It's just a day at a spa in Hudson Valley, and we'd be staying only one night. Anyway, I was wondering if you would like to come along? Not as my girlfriend or anything, but as my friend who will make it less painful for me to be there."

"When is it?"

"This Saturday."

"I suppose that could be fun."

"But don't blame me if it isn't."

"Wow, you're really selling the experience."

"Sorry. I just worry about Denise. She's got a sick sense of humor, and I wouldn't put it past her to arrange for strippers and shit."

"Oh, I'm definitely coming, then."

"And if it isn't clear by now, I'd love for you to be my date for the ceremony."

"Mr. Torres, are you using me for cover at your sister's wedding? Want me to fend off all the women trying to catch your eye?"

His shoulders tense, and his gaze bounces all over the room. "What? No! I'd never do something like that."

I laugh. "Relax, I was just kidding. And sure, I'd love to be your date. Luckily for you, my dance card is empty."

"Great. Okay. That's good. Great."

"Are you all right?"

"I'm fine. Just happy that we'll be spending more time together."

So am I. Because I'm losing control of this situation, and I need to redouble my efforts. Yeah, it's time to take my irritation tactics to the next level.

× × ×

"And what did *you* do?" Elba asks me, passing the platter of pernil to Cami.

"I made the sofrito. Jason walked me through it." Elba looks at me as if she's expecting me to say more, so I add, "And, uh, I'll be helping with the cleanup."

"Do you like to cook?" she asks.

"I hate it." Which is true. "Lisa's the one who can cook her butt off. And she bakes too. I tend to just order from DoorDash or Grubhub." That's also true. "I'm a lover, not a fighter. I'm an eater, not a cooker. Which means Jason and I are *perfect* for each other."

Lisa giggles, Denise clenches her jaw, and Elba flares her nostrils. This is working out just as I hoped it would.

I stare at my sister meaningfully, trying to remind her with my eyes that she has her own role to play this evening. Thankfully, she catches on quickly.

"Oh, I almost forgot," she says, jumping up from her chair and crossing to the hall closet. She reaches inside and pulls out a black garment bag. With a broad smile, she hands it to Jason's sister.

"What's this?" Denise asks tersely, her head cocked to the side as she stands.

"Cami and I thought you'd like this."

Denise unzips the bag, revealing a two-piece suit that's cinched at the waist and in the same shade of pale blue as Lisa's bridesmaid dress.

With her brow furrowed, Denise swings her gaze between Lisa and Cami. "You bought me a suit?"

"No, I *made* you a suit. Cami and I know you don't want to wear a gown, so we thought it would be nice to come up with something else. My seamstress skills are a little rough, but I think it'll work once I take it in at the waist."

"But I didn't ask for you to make me a suit," Denise says, her voice rising. "And you," she says, addressing Cami. "Why didn't you talk to me about this first? Why go behind my back?"

Cami looks at her sister and blows out an exasperated breath. "Because it was a surprise, Denise. Goodness, we were trying to make you happy. I can see now we've only managed to piss you off. How surprising."

Denise throws up her hands, the garment bag swinging wildly. "And now you're making me out to be the bad guy. I'm just shocked *she* would even do this."

"You're welcome, by the way," Lisa says, her jaw tight.

"See?" Denise says, pointing at Lisa across the table. "*This* is why I don't want you to do anything for me. Don't think I'm beholden to you or some shit. This changes nothing."

Lisa tilts her head back in frustration. "Jesus, I didn't expect it to."

"Mija," Elba interjects gently, addressing Denise. "Wear whatever you want, but I think it's nice that you have a choice."

Her mother's voice seems to calm her. "Yeah, I guess," she says as she sits and drapes the bag over the back of her chair.

Lisa and I exchange a furtive glance. This was supposed to be her moment. An opportunity to show Jason how caring she can be. And I, for one, know she spent countless hours of her meager spare time this past week obsessing about every aspect of the suit before I even mentioned the idea of using it to gain Jason's favor. Per usual, however, Denise is here to muck up our plans. How could such a sweet gesture cause so much strife?

Camila, bless her heart, monopolizes the conversation from there, obviously wanting to ease the tension generated by Lisa's gift. As we devour the meal, she shares her and Bryan's plans for decorating their new place in Santiago. Lisa doesn't engage much; nor does Denise. The tension's too fresh.

If there's a bright spot in the evening, it's Jason's food. His pernil and arroz con gandules could go up against my mother's any day, and that's truly saying a lot. Is there anything this man *can't* do?

When we're all done, I jump up and gather everyone's plates.

"I'll help you," Jason says as he rises to his feet.

"No, no," I say, putting an arm out to stop him. "You did all the cooking. Enjoy this time with Camila. She's leaving soon, and you won't get to spend time with her like this for a while."

His eyes soften. "Thank you."

I turn away quickly, shutting down the flutter that zips through my chest. Sure, this evening hasn't gone as planned, but

I still have a job to do. Scanning the kitchen, I contemplate how to annoy everyone without totally ruining their special family time. When my gaze lands on the caldero on the stove, I know exactly what I need to do: throw the pegao in the garbage.

Humming to myself, I spoon the remainder of the rice into a large Tupperware container, then I scrape up the crusty rice bits stuck to the bottom of the pot. In my family, pegao is its own food group. When Lisa and I were younger, we competed for the right to clean the caldero because that person would have dibs on the pegao. And something Gordon Ramsay didn't understand when he tried his own recipe: Pegao isn't *made*; it just happens.

My breath quickens as I lean over to shovel it into the trash bin. This is Latine heresy. I shake my head. No, I can't do it. Not if this is the last authentic Puerto Rican meal Camila will eat before she moves to Chile. So I spoon it into a small to-go container and hide it in her pantry. Then I tackle the rest of the dirty dishes. I'm washing the dinner plates when I hear a gasp beside me. *Jackpot.*

"Where's the pegao?" Denise asks, her eyes bulging.

"The what?"

"Pegao, Vanessa. It's the rice at the bottom of the pot. Thin, crispy, delicious."

"Oh, I tossed it," I say nonchalantly.

"What? Why? What is wrong with you?"

Jason comes over and puts his hands out as if he's refereeing a boxing match. "Hey, hey. What's going on?"

"She threw out the pegao."

"I'm sorry. I didn't realize anyone would want burnt rice."

"¡Madre de Dios!" Jason's mother mutters, her head bent and her hands folded on the table.

Good thing she's not looking at me, because if she did, I'd cackle. Out of all the shenanigans I've engaged in to annoy them, this might be the one that causes this family to banish me forever.

"It's not a big deal," Jason says. "She didn't know."

"How is that possible?" Denise counters. "Everyone knows you don't throw away pegao. I'm starting to wonder if she's even Puerto Rican."

"Wow, that's a low blow," I say more forcefully than I intended. "And *she* is standing right here."

"Must you always be so nasty?" Lisa asks, staring at Denise with daggers in her eyes.

Denise sucks her teeth and storms off down the hallway. Seconds later, the bathroom door slams shut.

I look down at my shaking hands. Well, that went sideways in the worst way. Denise's reaction, as innocuous as it probably seemed to her, touched a nerve I try really hard to ignore.

Jason leans over me and turns off the faucet. With gentle hands, he steers me away from the others. "She didn't really mean that."

"Oh, yes she did."

"You're right. She did. And shame on her for questioning your identity. I'll speak to her about it later."

"It's fine. I don't want to hijack this evening any further. This is about honoring Camila, not babying me."

His lips thin, then he says, "I'm not babying you. I'm caring about you. There's a difference."

I whip up my head to meet his gaze, and for a split second, I'm completely lost. What the hell am I doing? And *why* am I doing it? I told myself this man needed to be humbled. I pretended I needed to vet him for my sister. But all I want to do right now is tuck myself into his side and hug him fiercely. So the solution, of course, is to get away from him as quickly as I can. "I'm going to head out and give all of you some time with Camila."

He holds on to my hand, as if he doesn't want to let me go just yet. "I don't want you to leave like this."

I ease my hand from his grasp and wave away his concern. "I'm completely fine. Please don't worry about me."

"That's just it. I don't think I have a choice."

Our eyes meet, and my mouth goes dry. There's such yearning in his expression. It's as strong as the yearning in my heart. *No, no, no, no, no.* I need to shut this shit down. Whatever he's feeling. Whatever I'm feeling. It's not right. It never will be. "I *really* need to get home."

"Okay," he says, threading his fingers through his hair. "I'll walk you out."

"I'm good. Please. Go check on Denise."

"All right."

When I look up, Lisa's staring in our direction, her head tilted as if she's seeing us in a new light. If she needs assurances that we're still on track, I'll give them to her later. I can't do it now.

Before I go, I tip my chin up at Camila. "There's a small to-go container of pegao in the pantry. I saved it for you and *only* you."

She blows me a kiss, and I return her much-needed affection with the same gesture. Seconds later, I'm out the door.

I don't exactly know what happened back there, but I won't beat myself up about it. Even in college, I had off days as a starter ex, so I'm not concerned. That's what this is: an off day. I'll be in top form again in no time. All I need to do is remember my assignment: Be the catalyst for a relationship between Lisa and Jason.

Unfortunately, to do that, I also need to erase any inkling of my attraction to my sister's crush, and with each day that passes, that task seems more and more undoable.

chapter 20

JASON

"So what's on the menu at this hoity-toity spa?" I ask.

Eight of us are squeezed into a rental van heading to the Mother Earth Wellness Spa in New Paltz, New York. Google Maps tells me it'll take us a little over an hour to get there.

My question is met with silence. The organizers, Lisa and Denise, are glaring at each other. "Oh, damn. What happened?"

Cami, who's sitting in the front row with Bryan, turns around. "They couldn't play nice long enough to arrange anything, so I took matters into my own hands."

Everyone groans.

"It's going to be great. This spa isn't into doing the same ol' thing, so I'm really excited about the day they've planned."

"Care to clue us in?" Bryan's brother, Sam, asks.

He seems fine. His girlfriend, Willow, however, can't be bothered to show even a little bit of interest in getting to know us.

"Nope," Cami says. "I'd like to keep it a surprise."

Because I don't like surprises, I pull up the spa's website and click through its pages. The philosophy is simple: Back to basics. Using the earth's resources to create a holistic spiritual and physical life. Yawn. I click on a few photos. One catches my interest immediately: a couple receiving massages as they enjoy an incredible mountain view. Now *this* I can get with.

Next to me, Vanessa looks as if she's fighting the urge to fall asleep, her head tilted at an angle and her eyes blinking nonstop.

"Rough night?" I ask her.

"Yeah. Did a favor for someone that kept me up later than usual."

"This is perfect, then. There *must* be massages in our future."

"I'll probably fall asleep on the table."

Yeah, my brain goes there, picturing Vanessa on a table, her body naked underneath a bright white sheet. *No, Jason. A naked Vanessa is not in your future.*

A young white woman wearing a gray spa uniform greets us as soon as we get out of the van. "Welcome to Mother Earth everyone. This is the Torres and Atkins party, correct?"

"Correct," Cami says excitedly.

"Wonderful. I'm Summer."

"Of course she is," Denise mutters beside me.

I bump my sister on the shoulder. "Shh. Remember what I said: You better act right this weekend."

"Yeah, yeah, I know," she grumbles. "I'm on your shit list. Got it."

Exactly. After the stuff she pulled at Cami's going-away dinner the other day, she should be happy we're on speaking terms. Sure, Denise was frustrated because she knows what Lisa and Vanessa are up to and Lisa's gesture set her off, but that doesn't excuse her tirade. Honestly, though, she's my sister, and I can't stay mad at her for long. Doesn't mean I won't use her guilt to my advantage, especially because I need her to remain calm this weekend.

"I'll be your concierge during your stay," Summer continues. "We've arranged your accommodations according to Ms. Torres's requests. If you'll follow me, I'll escort you to your rooms."

We take our overnight bags from the van and follow Summer down a long outdoor path. The grounds aren't immaculately groomed. Instead, a variety of bushes and plants grow wildly, some even obstructing parts of the walking trail.

"Watch your step," Summer warns. "A few of these plants think they rule the place." The path eventually leads to a suite of bungalow-style cottages. At the first one, which appears larger than the rest, she pulls out a card and reads it. "Your group is scheduled for activities at our Oasis spa behind the main building at ten-thirty a.m. You'll find maps and your attire inside your rooms. Please meet out there at your appointed time, dressed and ready to begin your experience. If you need anything, the phone inside your rooms will connect directly to me. Now, for the room assignments. Cottage 1 is for Camila and Bryan."

"Yay," Camila says, taking two key cards from Summer. "Bye, guys. See you soon!"

She trots off to her cottage, Bryan carrying their bags behind her.

"Cottage 2 is for Sam and Willow."

"Cool," Sam says.

Willow finally looks up from her phone. "Is there a bathroom in there? Because I don't camp. I just glamp."

Beside me, Vanessa snorts.

"No need to worry," Summer says. "All the cottages are

equipped with first-class amenities, including fully functioning bathrooms."

Sam and Willow break off from the rest of the group, and Summer grimaces as she watches them go.

"Moving on," she says. "Cottage 3 is for Lisa and Vanessa."

"That works," Vanessa says, eyeing me with a grin. "I thought they were going to pair me with you. Was wondering if this was the start of an oh-no-there's-only-one-bed situation."

I have no idea what that means, but whatever. It's cool if she doesn't want to share a room with me. Not like we're dating or anything.

"Which leaves Jason and Denise in Cottage 4."

"Nice," I say. "Ours has a porch swing."

Denise disagrees. "Lovely. Sharing a room with my older brother. Ah, I'm living the dream." She shakes her head. "Tell me there are two beds."

"Two queens, yes," Summer says, nodding patiently.

"Fine," Denise says. Turning to me, she adds, "But the minute you start crop dusting, I'm kicking you out."

Summer clucks her tongue. "Oh, just to be clear, we only allow the legally prescribed amount of marijuana in the designated outdoor areas of the spa."

"What?" Denise says. "Crop dusting isn't . . . never mind."

Lisa clears her throat, and we all turn in her direction. "Um, listen, uh, Jason and Vanessa, I know you guys are kind of . . . talking or dating or whatever. So I'm happy to room with Denise if you two would prefer to be in the same room."

Vanessa's eyes go wide, and she tilts her head at Lisa as if she's truly confused by her suggestion. Ah, this must not be a part of the plan. The younger sister's going rogue.

"Absolutely not," Denise says. "I will not stay in the same room with her."

"What the hell is your problem?" Lisa asks.

"You. *You* are my problem. You're the fakest person I know, and I do not want to be around you any more than I have to."

"Jesus, fine," Lisa says, walking away from our group. "I was just trying to give Jason and Vanessa some alone time."

"I'm sure," Denise mutters under her breath.

Lisa freezes, her head snapping up, then she spins around, pointing an accusatory finger at Denise. "You know what I think is the problem? You're *jealous*. You haven't liked me since day one. You can't stand that Cami confides in me. You can't stand that Cami prefers to hang out with me. Maybe if you got your own damn friends, you wouldn't be so concerned about hers."

"This has nothing to do with Cami. I don't give two shits about your relationship with her. This is about—"

"Denise, stop," I say, interrupting before it's too late. "This isn't the time or the place. It's Cami and Bryan's time, not yours, not mine, not anyone else's. Let's just chill this weekend and remember why we're here. Got it?"

Her expression dulls as she digs her sneaker into the dirt to stomp out her frustration. "Got it."

"Okay," Summer says, her expression blank. "The room assignments are staying as is, yes?"

"Yes" we all say in unison.

She hands us our key cards. "Then enjoy, everyone." Summer practically flees after that, likely wondering what the hell is wrong with our group.

With her arms folded across her middle, Vanessa glances at me and mouths *Sorry*.

Not your fault, I mouth back.

Whatever's going on between our sisters has been brewing for years, and the little scheme Vanessa and Lisa cooked up is only worsening the situation. Let's hope a decent massage will mellow everyone out.

chapter 21

VANESSA

"What the hell was that?" I ask Lisa as soon as she closes the door to our cottage.

"What was what?"

"All of it," I say, waving my hands in frustration. "The suggestion that I room with Jason. That argument with Denise. From top to bottom, that was awkward."

"I don't know," she says, looking at me with her doe eyes. "I was trying to help. Figured it couldn't hurt if you two stayed together and you did something ridiculous."

"Staying in the same room together would complicate things, though. And I don't want either of us to be uncomfortable."

She tilts her head and seems to ponder this for a moment. "Sorry, I wasn't thinking."

"It's fine. More importantly, are you okay?"

"Why wouldn't I be?" she asks, drawing back.

"That whole exchange with Denise was intense. And I know

you don't like confrontation, so to see you go at her like that caught me off guard."

"It's just Denise," she says as she inspects the room. "That woman is all bluster. A shit talker on steroids. I just didn't want her to think she could run all over me."

"Clearly, she can't. She brings out the fierceness in you like no one else. But Jason's right: This is Cami and Bryan's weekend. Try not to provoke her, and try to ignore her if she provokes you."

"From now on, I'll be an angel. Promise."

"I'll believe that when I see it." After taking a deep, cleansing breath, I circle the room as I survey it. "Not bad. This must be costing them a fortune."

"It isn't. Bryan's parents wanted to pay for something, and Cami's parents finally relented and said they could pay for this."

"Goodness. Must be nice to have disposable income like that." I walk over to the bed closer to the window and claim it. "Dibs."

"Fine with me. The serial killer will get you first."

"Says the person closer to the door."

Ignoring that remark, she hauls her travel bag onto a luggage rack, then sits in an oversized wingback chair in the corner of the room. I can feel her watching me as I inspect the linens for bedbugs.

"Something on your mind?" I ask, lifting the mattress.

"Always."

"Care to share, then?"

"Funny you should say that. I was going to ask you the same thing."

"Out with it, Lili. I don't have enough coffee in my system to deal with your mind games this morning."

She draws in a long breath, then exhales slowly. "Okay, I was hoping you'd just tell me, but I should know by now that's not how you operate. What's the deal with the guy who came by the store the other day? Is he an ex-boyfriend or something?"

"Something like that."

Lisa jumps up and scowls at me. "Right. Nice talking to you, sis."

She's poised to close herself off in the bathroom, and I'm tempted to let her go, but I can't very well expect Lisa to let me back into her life if I don't let her back into mine—embarrassing mistakes and all. "Wait."

She pauses, looking at me over her shoulder.

"His name's David Warner, and he's technically my boss. That may change once the new office is up and running, but for now he's my superior."

"And you dated him?" she asks, turning to face me.

"We slept together."

"Is he the reason you're back in New York?"

"Yeah, he arranged my relocation."

She narrows her eyes. "Against your will."

"I didn't ask to be relocated, if that's what you're trying to get at."

"And you didn't object? Through official channels, I mean."

I drop my chin and shake my head. "It's better this way, Lili. Staying in Chicago under the circumstances would have been a nightmare. Now I get to be back home with all of you, and I won't lose my seniority."

She steps forward and takes my hand. "I'm not judging your choices. I'm just trying to understand what's going on."

"I appreciate that. I really, really do," I say, my voice unsteady.

"So why'd he come by? Is he badgering you?"

"He wanted us to rekindle our relationship. I told him in no uncertain terms that was never going to happen."

"Good," she says. "And if he gives you any more trouble, please tell me. We can figure out what to do together, okay?"

"Okay."

"Vanny..."

She tugs at her earlobe, which makes me nervous about whatever topic she's about to broach.

"What, Lili? Don't hold back on me now."

"Are you sure this is what you want? To be in New York, I mean. With us?"

My heart constricts when I realize why she's asking me these questions. My God, I really hurt them all those years ago. So much so that my own sister isn't sure I want to be here. I shouldn't be surprised: I did a terrible thing, and then I abandoned them, sending money every month to assuage my guilt. If I could erase the memory of that day in their minds and mine, I would in a heartbeat. But I know I can't. All I can do now is show them that I'm ready to call this place home and that they mean everything to me. "I'm sure, Lili. I wouldn't want to be anywhere else."

She pulls me into a tight embrace, enveloping me in her warmth, her soft curls tickling my cheek. After a long moment, we slowly separate, plopping down onto our respective beds at the same time. We each scoot forward enough so that our knees touch.

Desperately needing to change the heaviness of our conversation, my gaze settles on the spa-issued clothes resting on the dresser. "What kind of outfits are those?" I ask, eyeing the plain white tank and white sweatpants neatly folded and tied together with a ribbon. "Oh no. You know what this means: We're going to do yoga."

"What's wrong with that? It's exactly the kind of thing I'd expect at a place like this."

"You don't mind getting into all those poses? I can't imagine I'll look cute twisting myself into a pretzel."

She reaches over and taps my nose. "Good thing you're not worrying about looking cute, right?"

"Right, of course," I reply, not meeting her gaze. "In fact, the weirder I can make this, the better for our cause."

"My thoughts exactly. So let's change before Cami shows up and drags us out of here."

"Ooh, maybe I'll pretend to be gassy and rip a bunch of fake farts while I'm doing poses."

"Please don't. You might not be trying to impress him, but that might take me out of the running just by association."

"Ugh, you're no fun."

"Whatever. I have a rep to protect."

"Fine. I'll come up with something."

She gives me a sidelong glance. "You always do, sis. You always do."

× × ×

As far as I can tell, the Oasis is a clearing in the woods. Which is fine. At its center is a huge square pit that appears to be filled with dirt. Which is *not* fine. The staff at Mother Earth can try to sell this as a luxurious, all-natural cleansing bath, but it's nothing more than a mud pit, and I have no intention of wading in it. "I'm going back to the room for a nap."

Lisa spins me around and drags me behind her. "Oh no, you're doing this with me. Remember what Mami used to say: 'You girls need to stick together.'"

"She didn't mean this."

"It's a catchall phrase. She meant everything."

"Fine, but if I get a yeast infection, I'm sending you my doctor's bill."

"How about I give you a couple of my five-dollar Ulta gift cards instead?"

I'm ridiculously easy to please, and Lisa knows it. "Ooh, deal."

We make our way to the front of the pit and join the others, all of whom are wearing the exact same outfits as we are.

I sneak a peek at Jason, and everyone else fades into the background. Good Lord, the tank top he's wearing accentuates his broad shoulders and tapered waist, and the standard-issue sweatpants, which are sitting obscenely low on his hips, highlight his strong thighs. I shouldn't be ogling him, but I'm stunned by the way his appearance is affecting me, so I'm staring even harder to try to make sense of my reaction.

He saunters over to me and waves a hand in front of my face. "You okay?"

"Um, yeah, sure. Fantastic. Fabulous. Never better."

Shut up, Vanessa.

"Good morning, everyone. My name is Mindy, and I'll be your guide for this morning's activities. First, I'd like to congratulate Camila and Bryan on starting a new journey of spiritual love and commitment. Second, I'd like to congratulate you, their friends and family, on supporting them on this journey. Now, you may be wondering what we're doing back here, so I'm going to explain it all. You see, Cami wanted to do something that would nourish your body, detoxify your mind, and reduce stress. Mud wrestling is designed to do all three."

I lean over and whisper in Jason's ear. "Did she just say *mud wrestling*?"

"She did."

"I'm going home."

He gives me a half grin and continues to listen to Mindy.

"The clay in this oasis is a deep-cleansing formula that will moisturize and brighten your skin while drawing out impurities from your pores. But you won't just be diving into it. You'll also be engaging in friendly combat designed to de-stress your mind. This is the perfect time to let your inhibitions go, channel negative energy out of your life, and vent in a healthy and safe environment."

"I'm *so* ready, Lollipop," Denise says, staring down Lisa.

Cami waggles her eyebrows at Bryan. "So am I."

Mindy smiles. "That's the spirit! Okay, the reason you're wearing all white is because that is a crucial part of the challenge. The aim of the game is simple: The first team to be completely covered in mud from head to toe loses. I'll be watching and refereeing as necessary. Whenever someone is what we call 'mud soaked,' I'll ask them to climb out of the pit so the remaining people can continue. Any questions?"

"What if I don't want to mess up my hair?" Willow asks.

Mindy nods. "That's simple. We have plastic bonnets for anyone who wants them."

"Is this full contact?" Denise asks. "Like, can I throw an elbow to bring down my opponent?"

Mindy frowns. "The goal should be to get your opponent dirty, not hurt them. And I didn't think this needed to be said before, but I'll say it now: You cannot hold your opponent's head under the mud. Doing so will disqualify you and might even get you kicked out of the spa."

Sam raises a hand. "Is there a prize?"

"Glad you asked, and yes, there sure is. Each member of the winning team gets an extra thirty minutes added to their massage session."

There's a bunch of oohs among us when she makes that announcement.

Jason turns to Cami. "*This* is what you planned for us?"

"Isn't it great?" she says, with absolutely no sarcasm detected.

The group is silent, and Cami's smile slips.

Who the hell cares if it's messy and uncomfortable and will render my underwear useless. The bride is stressed and wanted to plan something fun for her friends and family. The least we can do is not make her feel bad about it.

I walk over to her and put my arm around her waist. "It's a fabulous idea. I mean, how many people get to say they've mud wrestled before? Now I get to check this off my bucket list!"

"Mud wrestling was on your bucket list?" Cami asks, her eyes bright again.

"No, but only because I didn't have the imagination to think of it. But I'm putting it on there and checking it off in one day, so I'm excited to do this."

The others reluctantly murmur their approval.

"All right, everyone," Mindy says. "We put your names in a hat to select the teams, and it just so happens that Cami and

Bryan are opposing captains. The people joining Cami are Sam, Denise, and Vanessa. The people joining Bryan are Lisa, Jason, and Willow."

"Perfect," a narrow-eyed Denise says as she rubs her hands together.

Lisa points two fingers at her eyes, then points them back to Denise. *Bring it*, she mouths.

I will, Denise mouths back.

"Go ahead and climb in," Mindy tells us. "I'll blow the whistle once every person puts a thumb up in the air to let me know they're ready."

As we file into a line to enter at the shallowest part of the pit, Jason tugs on the back of my tank top.

I look at him over my shoulder. "What's up?"

"Thanks for what you did back there."

"What did I do?"

"You took Cami's feelings into account. You made this about her, not us. I just wanted you to know I noticed. And I appreciate it."

"It was nothing."

He gazes at me affectionately. "Well, it was something to me."

Oh God. My heart is racing, and I'm not even sure why. Maybe it's because I'm never the nice guy in any scenario. If there's mischief to be had, I'm your girl, but bone-deep goodness? That's never been me. Still, Jason thinks I'm a decent woman, and I almost wish I could live up to the person he's built in his head. If he knew what Lisa and I were up to, though, he'd realize how wrong he is.

"Okay, bring it in for a team huddle," Cami says, pumping

her hands to get us hyped. "We don't want to overthink this. The point is to have fun. But we should make sure to have each of them covered. I'll take Bryan."

"I just bet you will," Denise says, winking at her sister. "And I've got Lisa."

"I just bet you do," Cami says, giving Denise a wink in return.

"Okay," I say, stepping in. "I know there's no love lost between you and my sister, but take it easy on her. She's not as tough as you, Scrappy-Doo."

"I'm sure she can take care of herself."

"Fine, be that way. Just remember I'm not as nice as she is. And don't complain when you find yourself tag-teamed."

"Threatening me with a good time, are we?"

"Ladies," Cami interrupts. "I need the extra massage time, so set aside your differences and focus on your job: getting the other team mud soaked. Got it?"

"Got it," we all say.

"Sam, I assume you want to cover Willow?"

"Absolutely," he says.

"Okay, that means Vanessa's on Jason."

Something about her phrasing sends a flutter through my belly, then my mind goes to places it really shouldn't, imagining me literally on top of Jason in various positions. I fan myself as I pace, willing my unruly thoughts to get the hell out of my head.

"Vanessa?" Cami says. "Thumbs-up?"

"Oh, right." I quickly place my raised thumb in the air.

"All right," Mindy says. "I'm seeing everyone's thumbs, so here's the whistle in three, two, one!"

Before Mindy's mouth is even on the whistle, Denise charges for my sister, who slides to the side and hooks her leg around Denise's ankle, bringing her down in seconds. It's a thing of beauty, this takedown, and I'm so shocked that I take too long to register that Jason's eyeing me like prey.

"Watch out, Vanessa!" Cami yells. She's pretending to wrestle Bryan, but all they're doing is rolling around in the mud like hogs in heat. "You're our best chance."

I circle the perimeter, using my peripheral vision to keep an eye on Bryan's team, Jason especially.

"Denise is out," Mindy shouts.

"Damn it," Denise grunts, wiping mud off her face as she wades to the ladder.

Willow, who opted for a plastic cap, is slathering mud on her body in an apparent attempt to disqualify herself.

"You're not even trying," Bryan says to her.

"I'm running a marathon in two weeks. I can't afford to get hurt."

"Willow's out!"

Realizing his girlfriend's no longer in play, Sam pivots and chases after Lisa. Letting out a loud battle cry, he lunges for her, tackling her so hard she lands face-first in the mud.

Mindy blows the whistle. "Time-out!"

Denise, whose face is beet red, sneers at Sam. "What the hell? That was uncalled for."

Sam laughs. "Chill. We're on the same team, remember?"

"Wish I could forget, you asshole."

I trudge through the dirt to check on Lisa. "Hey, you okay?"

Blinking rapidly, she shakes her head as if to gather herself. "I'm fine. He just caught me off guard."

I put out my hand to help her up, but Denise materializes by my side and offers Lisa her hand instead. She doesn't say anything, so she and Lisa simply lock themselves in a staring standoff. Eventually, Lisa relents and takes Denise's hand.

Jason appears by my side and whispers in my ear. "I think we're witnessing a breakthrough."

"Miracles do happen."

"Checking in," Mindy says. "Thumbs-up if everyone's okay."

Everyone gives her the signal.

"Okay, Camila and Bryan, you're out. Lisa too. Which leaves Sam and Vanessa from Cami's team and Jason from Bryan's team. Whistle on three."

As soon as Mindy blows the whistle, Jason and Sam both get into a sumo squat. I edge away from them, fully intending to win this game by being the last person standing. Jason and Sam charge each other, arms and legs flailing as they try to bring each other down. Jason's face is scrunched in concentration, and I'm mesmerized by the way his muscles flex as he and Sam roughhouse.

Denise raises her hands to her mouth. "Finish him, Jason!"

"You're on my team," Sam says through gritted teeth.

"You're a jerk," Denise yells back.

Jason uses the distraction to his advantage and wraps his arms around Sam's torso. In an impressive show of strength, Jason lifts Sam in the air and drops him into the mud, then rolls him like he's making a burrito.

The whistle blows. "Sam's out."

Jason's eyes gleam as he peers at me, his broad chest heaving. Oh shit, I'm the only target left. Maybe winning by process of elimination isn't one of my better ideas.

chapter 22

JASON

If I were an evil man, I'd make it my mission to get mud in every available crevice of Vanessa's body. But I'm not an evil man, so I settle for pelting her with mud balls instead.

The first lands in the center of her chest, and as she's looking down at the spot where she was hit, her mouth parted wide, I land another on top of her head.

"Oof," she puffs out. "Is that how you want to play it? It's on, Torres."

"Let me see what you got, Cordero."

"Stop talking smack and get on with it, you two," Lisa yells.

Vanessa heeds her sister's call and gathers mud in her hands, then starts flinging it with the precision of a Major League Baseball player. As I dodge the mud bullets and gather my own clumps, she whales on me, delivering stinger after stinger as everyone, including my own teammates, cheers her on. The front side of my shirt is plastered with wet clay, so I turn away, hoping to protect my sweatpants.

I land a few bombs on Vanessa's tank and can't help noticing how delicious she looks in a top that's clinging to her body in all the right places. I ping her in the forehead just for being gorgeous.

"Ow," she says. "That one stung."

"Sorry."

"No, you're not."

I shrug. "All's fair in mud and war."

She narrows her eyes and looks down at her shirt, then, with a wink in my direction, she tugs the front of it up and over her head as I stand there motionless.

Fuck.

She's wearing a gray sports bra that emphasizes her phenomenal tits. As I watch her bend over and gather mud in a makeshift shirt-bowl, my teammates yell at me to move my ass. But it's too late, because the next thing I know, I'm staring at a slingshot full of mud being launched across the pit. The entire glob rains on me like a volcanic eruption, landing on the bottom half of my body as intended. How the hell is she so precise?

Mindy blows that damn whistle again. "Jason's out."

"Yes!" Cami shouts, pumping her fists. Then like a victorious gladiator, she declares, "The extra massage time is mine."

"You could have just paid for it," Denise observes.

Cami shoves her away. "Don't spoil the drama."

Vanessa and I stare at each other, my goofy grin matching hers.

I approach her carefully, my hands raised in surrender, then I drop them for a sportsmanlike handshake. "You bodied me out there."

"I know."

"How'd you land so many bombs?"

She looks up in the air, pretending to think hard. "Wait. I didn't tell you I played softball in college?"

"You *definitely* did not."

"Huh, it must have slipped my mind."

"I'm sure." And since I'm a good guy, I wipe some of the mud off her face as she stares up at me. She shudders when I touch her. It's a brief reaction, but I notice it because I notice *everything* about her. "You look great this way. Mud is your color."

"Funny, I was thinking the same thing about you."

I wonder if that's true or if it's all part of her act. Damn, this woman is messing with my head—and she sure as hell knows it. It would be foolish of me to forget those important facts. "I need to grab a shower. Enjoy the extra-long massage."

I stomp off, knowing she's probably confused by the sudden change in my attitude. I'm confused by it too. Because if I haven't caught feelings, why am I so upset, and why is keeping my distance from her so damn hard?

✖ ✖ ✖

Now this is the life. Worries? What worries?

I'm sprawled out on the oversized porch swing in front of my cottage, punching a few of the dozens of pillows tossed onto the daybed to get them just right, when I hear the crunch of footsteps on gravel nearby. I look up and see Vanessa slowly making her way up the path. She's humming, her face all glowy and tipped to the sky, as if she's hoping to draw the sun's warmth onto her skin.

I should ignore her. Save myself the grief. "How was your massage?" I call out.

Yeah, I'm a pendejo.

Vanessa startles, then smiles when she sees it's me. "The massage was a dream. I think I'm still in it. And if I am, don't wake me."

"I'm flattered that I'm in your dream." I pat the daybed. "Join me?"

She takes a step forward, then hesitates. "I should check on Lisa."

"I'm sure she's fine."

"Okay."

Well, that was easy. I'm trying not to read too much into how quickly she gave up her protest. Again, this could be a part of her scheme, so concocting a fairy tale from nuggets like this one would be foolish.

She settles onto the daybed, shifting a couple of pillows to make a plush headboard, then lying back against them. "Oh yeah, I'm definitely still dreaming."

We're content to just sit in silence, the sounds of tweeting birds and leaves rustling above us serving as our soundtrack. Until loud laughter causes us both to sit up. After tracking the people responsible for our disturbance, I whistle with my fingers to get Cami's and Bryan's attention. "Yo, take that noise inside."

Cami's head snaps up, and she sticks out her tongue at me. "We're going, we're going." Vanessa and I watch them saunter through the door of their cottage, and seconds later, we see Bryan's hand placing the DO NOT DISTURB sign on the knob.

"You hate to see it," I say.

"Having trouble accepting that your sister has sex?"

"No, I'm fully expecting to be an uncle someday, so I've gotten over that hump. But I can't wrap my head around either of my sisters having sex for fun."

Vanessa laughs. "Maybe because you shouldn't be wrapping your head around your sisters having sex at all."

"True, true. Consider the thought pulled out of my head. Happy?"

"Very." She chuckles.

"What?"

"I'm imagining you as an uncle someday. Those kids are going to run all over you."

"And I'm going to enjoy every second."

"You're really looking forward to it?"

"Hell yeah. However it happens. Natural childbirth or adopted, doesn't matter to me."

"You mentioned wanting to be an uncle before, and now I'm curious: Why don't you want to be a father yourself?"

This is the kind of question that usually unnerves me. It's the start of a conversation that tells a woman I'm not a forever type of guy. But Vanessa isn't asking because the answer matters to her own life plans; she's just being inquisitive—or maybe she's scouting for Lisa. Either way, the stakes are low, so I tell her the truth. "It's not that I don't have it in me. It's just . . . I don't want to wreck some kid's life." When I see her eyes go wide, I add, "Don't get me wrong, I like children. I could even see myself taking care of my kid and being ridiculously happy doing it. But that requires a healthy and loving relationship between the parents, and in my mind, the likelihood of that happening for me is zero."

"Why is a bad relationship inevitable?"

"Because someone always fucks up. It'll be me. Or it'll be them. But one of us will do the wrong thing, say the wrong thing, and then we'll grow apart. And the one who gets hurt in all that mess is the kid. It's not fair."

"Is that what happened with your dad?"

My chest tightens at the mention of him, and I grimace. "You don't want to know what happened with my father."

She inches closer and taps my hand. "I wouldn't have asked if I didn't want to know. It's part of who you are. That matters."

Being around Vanessa confuses me. On the one hand, I shouldn't believe anything that comes out of her mouth. On the other, I absolutely do. Maybe I'm so desperate to find any true feelings between us that I'm seeing them where none exist. "I don't really like to talk about it. With anyone. Cami has no clue what went down."

"What about Denise?"

"She's the one exception. Because Denise is nosy and stubborn and bossy as hell."

"I won't judge. I promise. I'd be the last person to judge anyone about anything."

Again, I believe her. About this at least. Settling my head against a pillow, I close my eyes. It'll be easier to share this if I can't see Vanessa's reaction. "When I was a kid, I thought my dad could do no wrong. And I felt special. Being the only boy meant we had a bond that was different from the relationship he had with my sisters. Or so he told me. And I ate all that shit up. He took me fishing. He took me to Yankees games at the old stadium. He took me to his work. I was in awe of him. He had his own office in an apartment building he supervised. Took me around when he went to tenants' homes to check on things. Or

I'd stay in his office while he did his job. Watched TV there. Or did homework after he picked me up from school, and then we'd go home together."

"Sounds like things were good for a while."

"They were," I say, nodding, my eyes still closed.

"But then he started bringing people along on our outings. Women, specifically. Women he'd met in the building where he worked. Told me they were friends. I was so young and gullible, I believed him. And then I got older. Wiser. And I finally figured out what he was doing. What he was doing to my mom. He was basically using me for cover. By that time I was older, and I had my own interests anyway. So I stopped hanging with him. Made up excuses not to be around when he wanted us to go out."

"How old were you?"

"When I finally figured it out? Thirteen, fourteen maybe."

"That's a lot for anyone to deal with, let alone a teenager."

"Yeah, I was moody and angry, and no one except my father knew why. I didn't tell a soul. There were so many times I tried to say something to my mother, but I punked out. I didn't want the girls to experience the pain I had. I didn't want to be the reason my family fell apart. How messed up is that?"

She caresses my arm, letting me know she's still here, still listening. "Your family was already broken, though, and your father was the reason, not you."

"On a certain level, yes. I can see where you're coming from. Mom eventually found out on her own and threw him out. But I could have said something before then. Saved her those years she wasted on him. Whenever he acted like everything was good, like he adored my mother, I wanted to blurt it all out. He was so fucking fake. I even threatened to tell her once, but he said it would crush my mother. That I'd understand one day, when I had my own wife. As if my cheating on this person who didn't even exist yet was a foregone conclusion."

"But you don't believe that. I can tell."

"No, but I'm starting to think I'll never get close enough to anyone to prove him wrong. And it's never them, it's me. Because I'm always waiting for the other shoe to drop. For someone to reveal their true selves and ruin everything. That's what my father did to my mother. That's what my ex did to me. I've seen it over and over, so I have a hard time expecting anything else." I sit up and sigh. "I don't know. This subject's too heavy for a porch swing in front of a cottage in the Hudson Valley."

She sits up, too, her mouth curving into a smile that seems forced. "Actually, I think all of these conversations happen in this type of setting. At least they do in the movies. Except we should have waited until early evening. And started a fire. Oh, and how could we forget the wine?" She leans over, takes my hand, and gives it a tight squeeze.

I turn my head and stare at her. This is Vanessa's superpower. Listening without judgment. She doesn't pretend to have the answers, but I can feel, to the very center of my being, that she cares. That she's heard every word, turned each one over in her brain. In this moment, I *know* she has feelings for me. Never mind that she's holding back a secret that makes me question her integrity and my own sanity.

Could I ever move past the scheme if she confessed to it?

Maybe.

Probably.

Because it's the deceit that doesn't sit right with me. And now she knows why. If she voluntarily told me about her and Lisa's plan, I might be able to laugh it off as the ridiculous start to our relationship. A glitch in the operating software that we could fix in the update and shake our heads about months from now. God, I hope that's where we're headed.

Vanessa breaks our gaze, then she stands and stretches, a sliver of skin peeking out from below her pink top. I'd love to kiss a path along her stomach, brush my cheek against it. Or just lie here with her a little longer and listen to her voice as she tells me something real. That would be every bit as nice.

After looking out at the lake across from the cottages for a long moment, she says, "It's okay not to trust people. They should give you a reason to. And if they don't, they're not worth your time. You'll find the right person, Jason. Someone who deserves your love. Maybe not tomorrow. Maybe not next week or next month. But someday. You're too good of a man not to."

How can she say that so easily, knowing what she and Lisa are attempting to do behind my back? And then it dawns on me, as clear as the cloudless sky above: In her mind, the right person could never be her.

× × ×

A bloodcurdling scream wakes me from my sleep, and I fight the sheets trying to get up. "What the hell?"

"You heard that too?" Denise says from her bed.

"Yeah," I say, pulling on a fresh pair of sweats.

"It came from Vanessa and Lisa's cottage."

"I'm going to run over there and make sure they're okay."

"Or you could let the axe murderer kill them both."

"You're not so heartless as to want them dead, are you?"

She shrugs. "I'd settle for a mild injury. A sprained ankle or something as they run through the woods."

I shake my head as I pull open the door. "Back in a minute. Hopefully."

As soon as I step onto our porch, I see light coming from their cottage, then I hear another scream. Louder this time. So I sprint across the grass, leap over their steps, and bang on the door. "Vanessa! Lisa! It's me."

Lisa opens the door, her face scrunched in amusement.

"What's going on? Is Vanessa okay?"

"There's a spider in our room. The big baby can't deal."

"May I?"

"Sure," she says, stepping back from the door. "Maybe you can help me find it, so the rest of us who aren't scared of spiders can get some sleep."

When I enter the room, my gaze immediately lands on Vanessa, who's standing on top of her bed and doing an excellent impression of a person stomping grapes. She's wearing sweats from top to bottom, she has some kind of neon-green cap on her head, and her face is covered in pink goo.

"I hear there's a spider in here," I say, holding in a laugh.

"Yes, please, please, *please* find it. I won't be able to sleep unless I know it's gone."

"Don't worry, V, Jason and I will get it." Lisa may as well puff out her chest and tell us she's here to slay dragons.

"O-okay," Vanessa stutters.

I survey the room. "Where'd you last see it?"

"Under my bed."

Lisa glides in front of me, a tissue in her hand, and bends over as she lifts the edge of Vanessa's comforter. This sister's wearing a cutoff top and tiny shorts. Emphasis on *tiny*. As I look between them, I can't help wondering if this is a part of their ruse. A scheme to get me to their room so I can see Lisa in revealing clothing, while the sister I'm supposedly trying to date is dressed to lug moving boxes to a rented U-Haul.

Lisa sticks her head under the bed. "I see it!"

"What the hell is going on in here?" a sleepy-eyed Denise asks from the door that Lisa apparently left cracked open.

Meanwhile, Lisa's having a conversation with the likely nonexistent spider underneath her sister's bed. "Come here, you brat. I'm not afraid of you."

"Is it big?" Vanessa asks, the back of her hand pressed against her forehead. "It's huge, isn't it? Oh my God, oh my God, get it out, get it out."

This might be the worst acting performance in the history of acting performances.

Lisa jumps up triumphantly, raising the now-crumpled tissue in her hand. "Got it."

"Don't kill it," Denise says. "Toss it outside."

"Great idea," Lisa says, walking to the door.

I try to stop her. "Wait. Let me see what kind it is. So I know what to look for in case there's more."

"More?" the sisters ask, their eyes going round.

"Yeah, spiders tend to make nests under beds, especially in the evenings when it's cooler."

I have no idea if that's true. I'm talking out of my ass because I'm committed to messing with them.

Lisa scurries to the door and rushes through it. "Absolutely not. I'm just going to toss it outside like Denise suggested."

Before I can catch a glimpse of the definitely empty tissue, she waves it out the door. "There. Spider all gone."

I chuckle at the ridiculous lengths these women are willing to go to for the sake of Lisa's unrequited crush. "That was badass, Lisa. I'm impressed."

She does a curtsy, then takes a bow, grinning from ear to ear. "Thank you."

"Oh my God, y'all are being silly," Denise mutters. "It was a spider, not a bear."

"I still think I should check under there. Just in case."

"Please do," Vanessa says, her voice thin. "I didn't think about nests."

Making a big show of getting on all fours, I whistle as I shine a light on the floor underneath Vanessa's box spring.

"See anything?"

"Oh shit," I say.

"What?" all the women ask.

"It's a nest, all right. I think you got the mama, and now the babies are scrambling everywhere."

Vanessa lets out a high-pitched scream, jumps off the bed, and tugs the comforter loose. Lisa scrambles over to her bed and does the same. Then they're both scurrying to the door and flying past Denise, who's focused on Lisa's tiny shorts.

"Where are you going?" I ask, laughing.

"We're sleeping in your room," they call back.

"On the floor," Denise yells over her shoulder as she stares after them. When we hear a door slam shut, she turns to me, a wicked grin wiping away the tired expression she had a minute ago. "Let me guess, there are no spider babies under the bed."

"Maybe there are," I say with a chuckle. "But I didn't see any."

"I like this version of you," she says, bumping my shoulder with hers before she walks through the door. "Haven't seen you let go like this in years."

Here's the thing: She's absolutely right. And I hate that Vanessa and her antics, as wacky as they've been, are the cause.

I take a deep breath and let it out slowly, mentally giving myself a pep talk. The wedding's next week. After that, Vanessa and I don't have to cross paths ever again if we don't want to.

Am I holding out hope that Vanessa will reveal the truth about her and Lisa's scheme before the reception ends? *Yes.*

And if she doesn't, will I blow the lid off the ruse as soon as Cami and Bryan say goodbye to their guests? *Damn right I will.*

chapter 23

VANESSA

"You look beautiful, Lisa."

I'm staring at my sister's reflection in the full-length mirror in my apartment as she puts the finishing touches on her makeup for Cami and Bryan's wedding. Both the ceremony and reception will be held at the 3 West Club, a boutique hotel in Midtown Manhattan. Since the venue's a quick drive from my apartment, Lisa's getting ready here.

"Thank you. I was worried, but Cami came through for me and actually chose a dress I could use again."

"Is Denise wearing the dress or the suit?"

"Who knows. She's butch, so I thought she'd want to wear the suit, but she'll probably choose the dress to spite me."

"No matter what she decides, I'm sure she'll look great."

"Definitely. She'll still be annoying, though."

"Speaking of, she seemed halfway decent to you on the ride home from the spa last week. Did you two hash out your differences?"

"I wouldn't go that far, but she admitted that she's been a bit harsh to me in the past, and I conceded that I've always thrown my and Cami's closeness in her face." She shrugs. "It's a start, I guess."

"Good. I'm glad I won't have to worry about you two murdering each other at the reception."

I playfully bump Lisa out of the way so I can put on my own lipstick. She stands close, watching me with her top teeth tucked into her lower lip.

"What?"

"I want to talk to you about the starter ex stuff."

"You want to stop?" I ask, my eyes lighting up as I spin around to face her. Inwardly wincing at the traitorous eagerness in my voice, I stumble my way through a clarification. "I mean, I'd understand, is all I'm saying. I'm here to do whatever you want, and if it's too much for you, we can figure something out."

What I don't tell her is that the scheme is too much for *me*. Because my feelings for Jason aren't platonic, and I'm bound to mess up everything if we continue this ruse.

"What? No, nothing like that. It's just ... today's my best friend's wedding, and I don't want anything to sabotage it. So maybe lay off the antics for today."

Oh, that's not where I thought this conversation was headed. She's *not* rethinking the arrangement. My heart sinks, but I don't give myself the space to contemplate how I would have responded if she wanted to call it off. My feelings don't matter. *Lisa* matters. *Her happiness* matters. I'm doing this for her. With that reminder firmly in place, I ask, "Just be Jason's date, you mean?"

"Exactly," she says, nodding. "Don't start a conga line. Don't twerk. Don't serenade the bride and groom. Or tell embarrassing stories at your table."

"But what am I supposed to *do*?"

She takes my hands in hers. "Just be yourself. Can you do that?"

I don't even know what being myself looks like. I'm *always* someone else. Always playing a role. Someone more worldly. Someone not a few monthly paychecks away from being poor. Someone not stressed. Someone happy. Someone who has no fucks to give. Although most of the time I'm none of those things. "In other words, be me without the shenanigans."

"Just for today."

"Okay."

I don't tell Lisa this, but I have my doubts that I can meet the challenge. I'll try, though. And I'll enjoy my time with Jason. Maybe even pretend we're a real couple doing real couple shit. And then I'll get back to being what Lisa needs: the person who'll help her secure the man of her dreams.

Never mind that he may very well be the man of my dreams too.

× × ×

"You both look stunning," Jason says, greeting us in my building's vestibule.

"Thank you," Lisa says, twirling so he can get the full effect of her gown.

He pulls me to him and kisses my cheek. "Now your turn."

"Hell no. You're supposed to sneak glances at my ass when I'm distracted. I'm not just going to *give* the view away."

"Of course," he says, chuckling. "How silly of me. But in case my awestruck expression isn't clear enough, you're stunning, and I'm looking forward to spending time with you."

I slide my hands down the lapel of his black suit jacket. "And you clean up real nice, I must say." That's an understatement, really. He's heart-stoppingly gorgeous, and I'm sure he'll be turning several heads throughout the day and evening.

Lisa clears her throat, her forehead creased as she swings her gaze between us. "We should get going."

"Right," Jason says, a flush creeping up his cheeks. "Cami arranged for a Lincoln and a driver. We're over here."

We all climb into the back of the car, Jason taking the middle. It's a fitting place for him to be—even if he doesn't appreciate the irony.

"Excited?" Lisa asks him. "Your little sister's getting married today."

"I don't know that it's sunk in yet. She's heading to Chile soon after this, so my head's all messed up. My baby sister's grown, and it feels like it happened overnight."

"Stop that," I say, giving him a teasing grin. "You skipped favorite-uncle status and just went directly into dad mode."

"Get used to it. It's kind of how I feel. And don't be surprised if I cry. It's bound to happen, for sure."

"Aww, poor baby," Lisa says. "Don't worry, we'll be around to cheer you up."

Jason turns slightly in my direction. "Just wanted to give you the heads-up that I might be leaving you alone from time to time. Wedding party duties and all that."

"Of course. I expected to be on my own a bit, so do what you need to do. I'll be charming and engaging and find people to help pass the time."

"But don't have *too* much fun without me. And save me several dances, okay?"

"My dance card tonight has only one name on it, and it's yours."

He takes my hand and squeezes it. "I like the sound of that."

My and Lisa's eyes meet, then she raises a brow. Yeah, I'd be wondering what's going on too. But if she doesn't want me to engage in any shenanigans today, I can't very well be an asshole to him. There's not much I can do to assuage her concerns for the moment—with Jason between us, no less—so I let that look go for now.

Minutes later, we arrive at 3 West Club and find Denise pacing the lobby. Dressed in the tailored pantsuit Lisa created, her short hair buzzed on the sides and layered in waves on top, she's as gorgeous as her brother. The genes are *ridiculously* strong in the Torres family.

She gives Lisa a small smile. "The suit is amazing. I should have told you that from the jump. Thanks for designing it."

"You're very welcome," Lisa says softly. "It's perfect on you."

Straightening abruptly, Denise mumbles something about us looking nice, then tugs on Jason's wrist. "It's chaotic up there, and I can't do it alone. Mami and Nelson are crying. Cami's crying. Shit, the friggin' makeup artist is crying, and I have no idea why. Been waiting for you for what feels like forever."

"And so it begins," Jason mutters as Denise pulls him away.

Lisa stares after them, then turns to me, her expression pensive. "You two are getting close."

I laugh. "That *was* the plan."

"Was it?" she asks, a smile dancing on her lips. "I thought you were supposed to be a terrible date so I could come in and sweep him off his feet."

"You still can."

"Can I, though? Is that what you want?"

"Yes, of course, Lili. That's what I've *always* wanted."

"Why? Because you think you don't deserve him?"

"I was never meant to," I whisper.

"And yet you're falling in love with him anyway."

There's no anger in her voice, just resignation. It guts me. She didn't ask for much, and I couldn't even give her that. I let her down. Again. "I'm *not* falling in love with him, Lili." Pleading with her to listen, I add, "He's yours, I promise."

She pats my hand as if I need to be mollified. "Babe, only one of two things can be happening here: Either you're lying to me, or you're lying to yourself. I think we both know which it is. Besides, there's something else I never really considered when we went down this road: Jason can't be mine if he doesn't *want* to be mine. And it's pretty obvious he wants *you* to be his person."

"I . . . I don't know what to say. We can still fix this, Lili. We can."

"Is that *truly* what you want?"

I stare at her, unblinking.

She nods. "That's what I thought. On that note, I need to join the rest of the wedding party." She leans over and pulls me into her arms, then kisses my cheek. "Everything's going to be all right, Vanny. A crack in the foundation isn't going to tear down the whole house. We'll talk later."

What the hell does *that* even mean? I'm poised to ask her, but she's already slipping away. Fine. Until we can talk, I'll just do my best to hold it together. No drama, no theatrics, no nada. I'll pretend all is well. It's my MO anyway. But Lisa's wrong about one thing: Nothing's okay. Because even if she gave me her blessing to explore my feelings for Jason, I'd still be the villain in this story—and I always will be.

JASON

"¡Ay, bendito! Te ves como un ángel."

My mother's right: Cami *does* look like an angel.

"Just wait until Bryan tears into her tonight," Denise mutters beside me. "The devil will be working overtime."

"¡Cállate!" my mother warns.

"Must you poke her?" I ask Denise. "Even today?"

"I wouldn't be me if I didn't," she says, her eyes twinkling with mischief.

Cami turns so everyone can see the full effect of her dress. She doesn't appear to be nervous. Surprisingly enough, she's the picture of serenity, even as the makeup artist messes with her face.

"I gave her an edible," Denise tells me.

Of course.

My mother fans her face. "I will not cry. I will not cry. This makeup *must* stay on."

"Do you need something, Ma?" I ask. "Water? Ginger ale?"

"Ay, mijo, I'm fine," she says, basking in the attention. "Just a mother realizing her babies are growing up."

I grin, thinking about Vanessa's comment earlier. Yeah, I did sound like the doting, overdramatic dad. Unable to help myself, I look down at my phone screen and shoot off a text to her.

Me: You good?

Vanessa: Fine. I tend to attract uncles and grandpa types. Two are vying for my attention right now.

Me: Tell them you're taken.

Vanessa: But I'm not.

Me: Kind of hate that.

I wait for the three dots to appear on the screen. They don't. It guts me that she has no answer to give. Which is when I realize I'm in too deep already. Fucking Eric. He called it, didn't he?

What do I do now? How can I expect her to confide in me if we're just friends? Or a potential fling. Or whatever. Not once have I told her my feelings run deep. Not once have I given her a reason to abandon this ridiculous plot to trick me into dating her younger sister. The *why* is obvious: I'm scared as hell that I'm barreling into a disaster.

But if I want us to have a shot, I need to put myself out there and just hope she doesn't crush my heart.

"I'll be right back," I whisper to Denise.

"What the hell? The ceremony's going to start soon. Mami will freak out if you're not here."

"Cover for me, then."

I slip out of the bridal suite and rush down the stairs to the Solarium, where the ceremony will be held. The room is bright and airy, the decorations simple but tasteful. Everything fits Cami's and Bryan's personalities perfectly: classic, no fuss, comfortable.

I spot Vanessa immediately, her golden-brown curly hair a beacon among the straight- and dark-haired people around her. She's stunning in a long royal-blue dress that skims her curvy figure. From the front, the dress appears prim, but the rear view is a different story altogether. The back is largely open and held together by a few silver straps that look delicate enough to give with a single tug. Her silver stiletto sandals highlight her toned calves, which I can see through the side slit that ends just above her knee. I know she's wearing makeup, but it's so subtle I'm imagining this is how she would look the morning after a night in a bed—preferably mine—that hasn't been used for sleeping.

She sees me, too, and strides in my direction. We meet in the middle of the aisle that separates the room into two sides.

"Everything okay?" she asks. "You look anxious."

"I'm fine. Everything's good. I don't know why I needed to get this off my chest right now, but I do. I lied."

She tilts her head and frowns. "About what?"

"The other day when I invited you to be my plus-one. I said I wanted you here as my friend, but that's not true. We can take as long as you need, explore this as slowly as we feel is necessary, but I want to be more than your date. When I'm up there in the bridal suite, I want to be able to say that I need to get back to my girlfriend downstairs. I just want to be on the same page about that and know that we're working toward something. And if you're not ready for that, I'm okay with that too. It's just . . . I don't think I've ever said those words. And you obviously can't read my mind, so I wanted to put that out there." I take a deep breath and exhale with a laugh. "All right, I'm done."

"You sure?" she asks, her eyes sparkling in amusement.

"I'm sure. The floor is yours."

She steps closer and slips her hands around my waist, looking up at me with a mixture of nervousness and longing. "I thought you'd be tired of me by now."

"Hardly. We're just getting started."

"In that case, I should probably tell Tío Francisco that I have a boyfriend."

"Little known fact: He's not my real uncle. We don't even know who he's related to. Just showed up at one of our parties back in the day and has been a part of the family ever since."

She laughs.

"I want to kiss you," I tell her, bending a fraction to whisper in her ear. "Properly. Thoroughly. But not here."

"Later, then," she says softly, her eyes flickering with promise. "I'm counting on it."

"See you after the ceremony," I say, my fingers lingering on hers as we slowly drift apart.

I take only three steps, and I'm already tempted to return to her.

Yeah, I'm in so deep I'm drowning.

× × ×

"Jason, my man. It's so good to see you!"

"Hey, Torres, give me a ring next week. I might have a job for you."

I'm distracted by my errand as I make my way through the guests mingling on the Solarium terrace, occasionally shaking hands with a cousin or some other distant relative. It's tight in here. And now that the ceremony is over, people are being freer with the liquor and their voices.

I spot Vanessa and wave at her as she approaches. "Hey, have you seen your sister?"

She raises a brow. "No, I figured everyone was taking photos. I was hoping to speak with her myself."

"We thought we were done, but the photographer called us back for one last group pic. Something about wanting to take a photo with us standing on the staircase."

"I'll text her." Vanessa's fingers fly across her phone's screen, and then we wait. "Hmm. She's not answering. Bathroom, maybe?"

We leave the Solarium and take the stairs to the level immediately below us. Vanessa pushes open the bathroom door and returns seconds later. "Not there."

"Shit, my mother's going to throw a fit. Denise is missing too."

I stride through the hall, until Vanessa stops me with her hand on my arm. "Hey, it was a beautiful ceremony. Most of the photos are done. Everything's going to be fine."

"You're right," I say, letting out a breath. "I'm just used to doing the wrangling in this family."

"I get it."

"And now that I'm calm, I seem to remember we're due for a kiss."

"We are," she says, waggling her eyebrows.

I chuckle, then look around and take her hand. "This way."

We power walk to the end of the hall, and then I pull her into a lounge. I stop abruptly when I see that the room's already occupied. "Fuuuck" is all I can think to say.

What. Is. Going. On? No, it can't be. My eyes *must* be playing tricks on me.

"What's wrong?" Vanessa says, jumping in front of me. "Oh God."

Yeah, I'm glad I'm not the only one seeing this train wreck. I need another witness; otherwise, no one would believe me.

"What the hell?" Vanessa asks, her eyes blinking furiously. "Are we in the Upside Down?"

"Sure looks like it."

Why? Because we're watching my sister nuzzle Lisa's neck as they lean against a wall, the skirt of Lisa's gown bunched up and fisted in Denise's hand.

"Privacy, please?" Denise says, turning her head in our direction, her mouth curved into a wicked grin.

A flush creeps up Lisa's cheeks, and then she hides her face behind the lapels of Denise's suit jacket. They don't spring apart, though.

Well then.

"You're both needed for another photo," I say, pulling a stunned Vanessa away. "Might want to wrap this up."

Outside the room, Vanessa rubs her eyes. "Did that just . . . ?"

"It did."

I hope Vanessa's processing the implications—because I sure the hell am. There's *nothing* stopping us from being together now. Obviously, Lisa's moved on to someone else. Never mind that the someone else is my sister. So if there's any chance Vanessa's feelings for me are real, she doesn't need to hold back anymore. God, I hope that's the case. I want it more than anything.

My phone buzzes, so I pull it out and read the screen. "It's Nelson. Wondering where the hell everyone is. Let me take this photo, and then I'll come right back to you."

"Of course. I need a minute to myself anyway."

She doesn't meet my eyes, but there isn't enough time to parse out what's going on in her head. I squeeze her hand. "Don't go too far. I won't be long."

Because this? This changes *everything*.

(I hope.)

chapter 24

VANESSA

I watch Jason leave, and then I slump against the wall. My brain can't even process what I just saw or how this affects my and Jason's relationship. But I know this: There's no chance he'll ever date Lisa after what we witnessed. I mean, maybe it was always a long shot, but now it's an *impossible* shot. Worse, I hate myself for being happy about this development.

See? Terrible.

I'm tempted to speak with my sister and try to unpack what's happening, but I highly doubt she's interested in anyone other than Denise at the moment. What to do? Where to go? How to feel? So many questions and zero answers. Nothing's making sense in my head.

I rush up the stairs and sprint into the first room I find. Dark wood paneling covers the perimeter, and a built-in bookshelf spans the entire length of one long wall. Two green velvet chaises face each other in front of the floor-to-ceiling windows overlooking the Manhattan skyline. As I struggle to catch my breath, I trace a finger against the spines of the books whose titles pass in a blur. I'm too wired. Too confused. Overwhelmed by the knowledge that Lisa isn't—or shouldn't be—trying to win Jason's heart anymore.

I drift over to the mirror opposite the bookshelf. I'm the same person I was when I entered the 3 West Club a few hours ago, but so much has changed. Does Jason sense it too?

As if my thoughts have conjured him, he appears in the library and quietly closes the door behind him. The click of the lock sounds in my ears like a gong.

Within seconds, he's behind me, studying our reflections in the mirror, his eyes drowsy and just as unfocused as mine. "Are you okay?"

"Not really," I say, my voice unsteady.

Because for once, that's the truth. My body is coiled tight, a million nerve endings pinging all at once. Every moment I wanted to touch him but held back returns in a rush, as if all of my repressed feelings have finally gathered enough force to barrel through the floodgates. I'm on overload, and I'd do *anything* to feel Jason's hands on my body.

He steps closer, his chest creating a wall of heat at my back. "What's wrong?"

"Nothing's wrong, exactly. It's just... seeing Lisa and Denise together threw me for a loop. I was not expecting them to be glued to each other like that."

He peers at me, his brow furrowing. "It bothers you? Seeing your sister with Denise?"

Disappointment laces the tone of his voice. I meet his troubled gaze in the mirror and shake my head. "It doesn't bother me in the way you might be thinking. God, nothing like that. Lisa's never hid her bisexuality from me or my parents. It just surprises me. Those two specifically. First, I thought they hated each other, then I thought they were only tolerating each other. For Cami's sake."

"*Hate*'s a strong word. The way I see it, they've always provoked each other. Now we know why."

"I guess."

"There's something else messing with your head, though. Tell me."

His voice is urgent, hopeful, and I can't pinpoint why. I'm seconds away from revealing the truth about the ruse, but I realize it isn't only my truth to reveal. It's Lisa's too. "I don't think I can."

His lips thin.

"I'd rather show you."

Because *this*? This is *my* truth and my truth alone. And I want to give it to him freely.

He gives me a questioning look, his teeth pressing gently on his bottom lip. My arms fall to my sides, as if I'm offering myself to his scrutiny. Am I really doing this?

"Whatever you need," he says softly, urgently. "Anything."

That promise unleashes my restraint. So I push my ass against him and take one of his hands, drawing it across my stomach. He sucks in a breath, and the sound of his desire flips the switch in my brain that controls any rational thinking. I want this, I want him, and I don't want to consider why this is a bad idea. Our entwined hands lift the hem of my dress slowly, his long fingers traveling across my skin wherever I direct them—the top of my thigh, the curve of my hip, the swell below my belly button.

"You're so warm," he murmurs against my ear. "So soft."

I drag his hand over my panties, and he closes his eyes, breathing through the contact as if he's using all of his reserves to keep himself under control, to let me steer his hand in whatever way I choose.

"Here's where it's aching," I say. "I need you to make the ache go away."

He cups me, then freezes. "You want my fingers inside you?"

"Yes," I say with a moan. "Your fingers. Your mouth. Your dick. *Please*."

He scrunches the fabric of my underwear, as if he's making a fist with it, then he delves underneath, tracing his digits *so close* to where I want them.

"Don't tease me."

"I'm not teasing. I'm exploring every inch of you. This could take hours. Days, maybe. Might want to settle in for the ride."

"Now you're just being cruel."

He doesn't respond with words. Instead, he slips his free hand up my back and around to my shoulder, where he drags down the thin strap of my dress, baring one of my breasts. "Look at that," he says, flicking a nipple. "Qué bella." Unable to stay upright any longer, I fall back against him, and he immediately buries his face in my neck. "Here's one."

I open my mouth, ready to ask him to explain, but then I feel it: One long finger. Slipping inside me.

"How's that?"

"So good," I say, squeezing my eyes shut.

"Here's two."

"Oh God. *Yes*."

"Want three?"

"Please."

"Open your eyes first. Watch us in the mirror."

I open my eyes, but my vision is blurred; when it clears, I see the strain in his face, the sheen of sweat across his upper lip. He's taking this slow, but it's a struggle for him. Then I focus on my reflection, and I'm stunned by what's in front of me: My hair's disheveled, my lips are parted and wet, and my chest is heaving.

"What a sight we are," he says.

"Three," I eke out. "You promised me three."

He slips another finger inside me, his thumb working my clit. "There you go."

I nearly fall to the floor, but he holds me steady. "Yeah, that's it. Just like that."

"Fuck, Vanessa," he says, his eyes closing for a moment. "My fingers are soaked. Now I'm imagining this wetness all over my dick." He tilts his pelvis against my butt, as if he's envisioning what it would be like to move inside me.

"There's no need to imagine. I want that as much as you do."

"This isn't how I pictured our first time."

"You thought about it? Before today?"

"I went to bed imagining it in my head. More times than I should have."

"I don't think I can wait. Not anymore. Now that..."

"Now that what?"

"Nothing. I'm not making any sense." I shake my head. "I just need you."

Jason grimaces. "I don't have anything on me. No protection."

"Have you been with anyone lately?"

"Not for eight months. And I've tested negative since then." He hesitates, then asks, "You?"

"I got tested when I came back here. I had to."

He pins me with a piercing gaze, but he doesn't push me to tell him more. That's all I think I can bear to say about that anyway.

"I'm on the pill too," I add.

"Are you sure this is what you want?"

"*Yes.*"

My one-word answer galvanizes him. He pulls out of me and tugs my panties down my legs. "Step out."

I do, and then he slips the scrap of fabric inside his pocket.

"We won't have much time," he says against my ear. "Someone will come looking for one of us soon."

"It's okay. I just need this. Need you. Don't want to think about anything else."

With one hand, he unbuckles his belt and flicks open the top button of his slacks. With the other, he cups my pussy.

"Yes, Jason. Hurry."

The sound of his zipper ricochets all over the room, and then he's tugging down his pants and bunching up my dress at my waist. "The couch?"

"No, right here," I whisper as I place my hands on the console table.

He caresses my back and gently pushes me forward, guiding me to bend over, as he lines up the head of his dick against my entrance. "I'm so hard right now. Jesus, V, what the hell are you doing to me?"

"The same thing you're doing to me. Hurry."

He covers my body with his, places his left hand over mine, and pushes inside.

"Fuck," we say in unison.

He groans as he inches forward. "Incredible."

He's big. Thick. Filling me with no room to spare. "God, you *did* need that book."

He chuckles, his chest vibrating against my back, but when I squirm against him, he hisses, all humor forgotten.

"God, Jason, please move. I need you so much."

My words seem to be his undoing, because now he's caging me in, his fingers clutching mine, and he's moving in and out of me in earnest. I'm tingling everywhere, and my updo is a wreck, but I have no fucks to give except the one I'm giving this man. I tighten my core, and Jason shudders against me.

"Yes, that's it, baby," he groans. "Squeeze just like that. I want to feel you on every inch of me."

I'm blissed out and overwhelmed. All I can do is chant his name and moan in rhythm with each stroke. My entire body is hot, adrenaline coursing through me.

He nibbles on my ear, ratcheting up my pleasure. "Knew we'd be like this together, but didn't dare hope. Fucking fire. Electric."

"Addictive," I choke out, a tear slipping down my cheek. "Oh God, so good."

"How can I make this everything for you? What do you need?"

Somehow, his voice gets past the ringing in my ears. "I need to touch myself."

He slows, waiting for me to snake my hands between my legs and massage my clit. "Good?"

"More than good."

And then he speeds up, smoothly, like his only job is to be attuned to my body and satisfy its desires. Jason nuzzles me. Inhales my scent. Scrapes his teeth against my neck. I'm a bundle of nerves expanding, then coiling tight. The sweetest pressure fills me. I want this feeling. *Precisely* this feeling. As many times as he's willing to give it to me. No one else will do.

"Oh God, Jason. I'm going to come soon. Are you close?"

"I'm close," he grunts. "But don't wait for me. I don't want to miss seeing you fall apart."

I stare at his reflection in the mirror and watch the way he rocks into me, my fingers furiously circling my clit.

He meets my gaze, then says, "Open your mouth." When I do, he places his thumb inside. "Bite down if you need to. I want you to leave a mark I can see tomorrow."

My eyes fall closed, the pleasure so intense I'm seeing stars behind my lids. He's making me crave things I never imagined I would. Soon a tingle teases me, then flares into a warmth that spreads throughout my body. "Oh God, I'm going to come."

"Bite," he says as he slams into me.

I don't worry if I'll hurt him. I just press my teeth into his skin as the orgasm rocks me from head to toe.

"Jesus, Vanessa," he says, trembling behind me while he chases his own orgasm. "Fuck, fuck, fuuuck."

When we descend from our highs, we stare at our reflections, both of us panting. Eventually he pulls out and looks around in a daze. "Do you need me to . . ."

"I'll take care of it."

"I'm guessing you can clean up in there," he says, breathing hard and pointing to a doorway in the corner. Stunned. He looks stunned by what we just did. Me too, Jason. Me too.

I let the skirt of my dress fall and stagger to the restroom. In a stupor, I quickly use the bathroom and dab my face with a tissue. I'm a literal and metaphorical mess, but I don't regret what

Jason and I just did. No, I only regret that there are so many secrets between us.

When I return, Jason's dressed and rubbing the back of his neck.

"Everything okay?" he asks.

"I'm wondering how I'm supposed to go back out there and put together intelligible sentences."

"No idea," he says with a chuckle. "I'm only smiling and nodding for the rest of the night."

I laugh. "We're ridiculous."

"Ridiculously good together, you mean," he says, caressing my cheek.

I step forward and kiss him sweetly. "Sir, you are so much more than I bargained for."

And that much *is* true. I never imagined Jason and I would be together like this, bringing each other pleasure, reveling in the feel of our bodies igniting.

"Come home with me," he pleads. "Stay the night. Let me worship every part of you."

"Yes, I'd love to."

There's no hesitation in my voice, and perhaps there should be, but for once, I'm going to enjoy the here and now and worry about the inevitable clusterfuck later.

chapter 25

JASON

I'll be the first to admit that my sister's wedding isn't the highlight of my day. Yeah, I know you're judging me, and that's okay. Now, don't get me wrong. I won't soon forget the ceremony, which was as special and as romantic as Cami and Bryan's relationship. Plus, my stomach and feet are still recovering from the dinner and dancing during the reception. But Vanessa's coming to my *home*, and before long, we'll be in my *bed* (and other places), where she'll inevitably wreck me from head to toe. I can't wait.

I take her hand as she climbs out of the town car.

She scans the street, then my apartment building's redbrick façade, and nods. "Impressive."

"Before you get any ideas, let me be clear: I'm not independently wealthy. TAG was the contractor that renovated these apartments, so I had an in with the landlord."

"You've got friends in rent-controlled places. In New York, that's like hitting the lottery."

"Believe me, I know."

"Let's see the rest, Mr. Torres."

I unlock the front door, then gesture for her to walk ahead of me.

"Elevator?"

"I'm on the second floor. It's easier to take the stairs."

"But my feet are killing me," she whines. "The least you can do is offer to carry me."

I stare at her. "Are you being serious?"

Her lips twitch. "Of course not."

I pull her close and press my mouth against hers. "All that sass is going to get you in trouble someday."

"Is that a threat?" she asks, her eyes flickering with naughtiness.

"It's a promise."

I like this new version of us. Playful. Intimate. Unconstrained.

Minutes later, Vanessa's ambling through my apartment for the first time. She scans the kitchen, taking in the marble countertops, the white subway tiles, and my favorite feature, the midnight-blue shaker cabinets. "You did all this?"

"I did."

"With a designer's help, right?"

"That would be Eric. He has a gift for this."

"Oh, you guys are a dream team, then."

"I'd like to think so."

She circles the island, her hand gliding over its surface. "This is gorgeous."

"Thank you." I set my keys on the counter. "Want something to drink?"

"Any chance that wine fridge actually holds wine?"

"I have cab, merlot, and chardonnay."

"Look at you, being all worldly and shit."

"I'm not a wine guy, so you know. They're all gifts from clients. Figured since the apartments are outfitted with wine fridges, I may as well use mine."

"Let's crack open the chardonnay."

"Coming right up."

"While you do that, can you point me to the bathroom?"

"First door down the hall."

She gives me a once-over, then saunters away, her ass and hips swaying seductively. I take a deep breath, marveling that this same woman wanted to string my balls across a telephone line a month ago. She isn't acting outlandish. She isn't engaging in any sabotage. She isn't even trying to annoy me. She's just being herself. This is almost everything I was hoping for.

After filling two glasses, I set them on the coffee table in front of my couch, shrug out of my jacket, and wait.

And wait.

And wait some more.

A few minutes later, Vanessa calls out to me. "Jason, can you come here a sec?"

I peek into the bathroom and find it empty, so I enter my bedroom and pull up short. My vision narrows on the gorgeous *naked* woman sprawled across my bed. "Fuck. Me."

"That's the idea," she says, arching her back, her brown nipples hard and begging for attention.

I attack the buttons of my shirt as I continue to devour the visual feast before my eyes. "You cheated."

"How?"

"I wanted to undress you."

"Another time."

"I like that you're already thinking about next time. I like that a lot."

She squirms on the mattress as I remove the rest of my clothes, and when I'm done, her gaze falls to the space between my legs, her eyes blazing with lust. "God, you're so sexy."

"You wouldn't waste those words on me if you saw yourself through my eyes." I crawl over her and place a kiss on her forehead. "Being this close to you feels like a drug. My heart's racing, my body's warm all over. I'm lightheaded, V."

"Are you sure you're not having a heart attack?" she asks, grinning.

I pinch her thigh, and when she yelps, I smooth my hand over the spot. "That's for the sass. I gave you fair warning."

"I'll be good from now on, promise."

My nose skims hers, and then I lick my way inside her mouth. She immediately massages my back, sinking her fingers into the muscles there. Wanting to play with her tits, I slowly pull away, then straddle her hips as I place her arms above her head. My chest squeezes at the sight. The heady mix of confidence and vulnerability in her expression humbles me. She's trusting me to give her pleasure, and I intend to deliver.

I caress her face, then snake my hands across her neck, down to her belly, and back up to her breasts. "What do you like? Soft or rough?"

"Both," she says. "Soft in the beginning, rough when I'm coming."

Her words supply my brain with wicked images of what soft and rough look like, and my cock hardens even more. I toy with her nipples, lightly, leisurely, as if I don't have anything else in the world to do but play with these beautiful peaks.

"Oh God, yes," she says, pressing her tits together and squirming beneath me. "They're so sensitive. That's perfect."

I lift myself to a sitting position beside her and tap her arm. "Move to the left, baby, and raise your knees. I need a little more room."

She stares up at me as she complies, her expression dreamy.

Just you wait, sweetheart. In a minute, you're going to be so blissed out you're going to forget your name.

After positioning myself perpendicular to Vanessa's body, I stick my head between her thighs. Making space for me, she spreads herself wide and gently rests her left leg across my back. I place a hand against her stomach and drag my mouth along her inner thighs. I kiss her mound, breathing in her scent. This is heaven. Plain and simple.

"Sideways oral?" she says, her torso rising as she digs her fingers into my scalp. "Ten out of ten. Would recommend."

My dick is rock-hard against my belly, and I have to shift to gain relief from the friction. And then I dive in, trailing my fingers all over her cunt, gathering the wetness and spreading it along her folds.

"Jason, please," she begs. "I need your mouth."

"Can I play a little? With my fingers?"

She throws a hand over her face. "Oh God."

I lift my head. "Oh God, bad, or oh God, good?"

"Oh God, I don't think I'm going to survive this, and I really don't care."

I place my mouth on her thigh and smile against it. "Maybe I should get going so I don't create unrealistic expectations."

Her belly shakes under my hand. "Nope. Too late. Expectations have been set and must be met. I—"

A long, side-to-side lick against her inner lips silences her.

"*Shiiiiit*, that's so good."

She's so damn wet I have to pull her hood back so I can focus on her clit. Then I lick her in earnest, alternating between soft and hard flicks as I press two fingers inside her pussy. Vanessa's murmuring nonsense, gripping the sheet as she writhes against the mattress. Her clit becomes more engorged the longer I lick.

"Yes, that's it, Jason. I'm close. *So* close."

I hover against her back hole, waiting to see if she's cool with my fingers there.

"Yes," she pants. "I want that too."

I'm determined to make her see stars, so I lick everywhere—her lips, her clit, her soaked opening—and then I press my hand against the skin above her hood and suck her clit like a man possessed. Within seconds, Vanessa's torso shoots off the bed as she arches her back and comes as if she's been rocked by an explosion.

Fuck, that's sexy.

She blinks her eyes open and takes my hand. Giggling, she traces something against her mound with my finger.

"What was that?" I ask.

"Your signature. If I had spray paint, I'd let you tag your name on it."

Before today, I would have told anyone who asked that I don't have a possessive bone in my body, but the idea that Vanessa would metaphorically sign over her pussy to me awakens feelings I never imagined having this soon in our relationship. But I want *more*. I want to know that I'm giving my heart to someone who won't crush it on a whim. Telling me about her initial plans to date me for her sister would help quash my misgivings. Am I being unfair? Unrealistic? Who knows. This is all uncharted territory for me. But if I think too hard about all this, I'll spiral. Tonight is about letting go. About releasing everything that's been pent up inside us. The hard stuff can come later. Vowing to live in the moment, I bark out a laugh and pull her up. "Don't sign off so fast. We're not done yet."

She sighs happily. "I was hoping you'd say that."

✕ ✕ ✕

"Enough," Vanessa groans out as she collapses against the pillow. "I'd like to be able to walk tomorrow."

I fall back on my pillow and tug her close. "If you're able to walk tomorrow, then I'm not doing my job as well as you claim."

"I promise you, you're doing an outstanding job. Ten out of five stars. Guaranteed promotion. With benefits."

"Oh yeah? What kind of benefits?"

"Blow jobs, rimming, and pegging, oh my!"

I look down at her and she returns my stare, her expression serious. Seconds later, she lets out a high-pitched cackle. "You should see your face."

I'm grinning so hard, and I can't imagine a more perfect way to end the night. Except there's the small matter of her and Lisa's scheme that keeps coming to the forefront of my mind. "Are we going to talk about it?"

She sobers, peering at me as if she's trying to gauge my mood. "Talk about what?"

"Lisa and Denise."

"Who conveniently scrambled away every time we tried to approach them tonight."

"You noticed that too?"

"For sure. Maybe they're still trying to work it out in their own minds. I know I certainly am. Where the hell did *that* pairing come from?"

"No idea. I'll confess, I always thought Lisa had a crush on me. I guess I was wrong."

I'm serving up an opening for her to tell me the truth, just as I did in the library at the 3 West Club. I hold my breath, waiting to see how she'll respond.

"Lisa's a hard one to read when it comes to everything, including her love life."

A nonanswer if ever there was one. She certainly isn't confessing anything tonight. But I don't want to end the evening on a sour note, so I'll let it go for now.

"I just hope they don't hurt each other," I say softy. "Heartbreak isn't fun."

With her head resting against my shoulder, she rakes her nails across my chest. "Tell me about the woman who broke your heart. What's her name?"

"Elyse."

"Is she still in your life in some way?"

"Not even a little bit."

"So what happened? Who was she?"

"We dated for a year and a half, and then I proposed."

"Did you love her?"

"I did."

"So where did it go wrong?"

"You remember when you asked me whether I saw myself having kids someday?"

"I remember."

"Elyse asked the same question. On our second date."

"What'd you tell her?"

"The same thing I told you. It didn't seem fair to hide my feelings. If she wanted kids, and not having them was a deal-breaker, I wanted her to make that decision before we got serious."

"Since you dated for almost two years, I'm guessing she said it wasn't a deal-breaker."

"Exactly."

"And then she changed her mind?"

"No."

Vanessa lifts her head and slips me a curious glance. "What am I missing?"

"Elyse had a kid already. Hid him from me for a year and a half, and only after being engaged to me for six months did she clue me in."

Vanessa's mouth falls open.

"Yeah," I say. "I had the same reaction."

"Where was her son the whole time?"

"Her mother was taking care of him. I mean, can you imagine the lengths someone would have to go to to hide a child?"

"A whole-ass child? Honestly, I can't."

"Me neither. It wasn't that I couldn't love the kid as my own. It was the deceit that burned me up. Essentially, she fabricated this version of herself she thought I would fall in love with, and then she sprung a child on me as if it was no big deal to hide an essential part of her life."

"You broke it off immediately?"

"No. I couldn't turn off my feelings that easily, so I tried. *We* tried, I should say. But I was so pissed off and hurt, those feelings ended up bleeding into every aspect of our relationship. I couldn't let it go, and eventually we admitted defeat."

She's quiet for a moment, and then she caresses my jaw. "I'm sorry that happened to you."

"For so long, I told myself I wouldn't put myself in that position again. Open my heart to anyone. But I'm realizing that isn't fair to the people in my life. Or to myself. Maybe my heart was supposed to be broken so I could recognize the person who's meant to heal it."

I sense the moment she freezes, but then she recovers quickly, snuggling into me with a deep yawn. "Goodness, these postcoital deep thoughts are frying my brain."

Yeah, she's definitely not ready to reveal any truths tonight. Guess I'll play along, then. For now. "Just go ahead and admit it: I tore your ass up, didn't I?"

She laughs. "You did."

"Good night, Vanessa. I'm really happy you're here."

"Good night, Jason. I wouldn't want to be anywhere else in the world."

She's going to be my undoing. I can sense it in my core. Problem is, I feel powerless to stop it.

chapter 26

VANESSA

Sunday morning I blink my eyes open and snuggle into Jason's broad chest. Enjoying the quiet, I take a minute to study his profile as he sleeps. My fingers itch to trace his sharp nose, to brush against his every-o'clock shadow, to caress his strong jaw. Sure, he's what many people would call classically handsome, but there's still a ruggedness about him that appeals to my baser instincts. He's the guy on *Survivor* who gets better looking the longer he remains on the island. I'm floored by the reality that this sweet and sexy man wants to be my boyfriend.

I lean into this feeling of bone-deep contentment for a moment—but it doesn't last long. Within seconds, I remember that my relationship with Jason was engineered to coax him into my sister's arms. No matter how much I want it to, that fact isn't going away. Just as I warned Lisa when I tried to discourage her from using me as a starter ex, there's no coming back from this. Either I tell him now—and risk losing him—or I commit to keeping this secret forever. Considering how Jason's been betrayed in the past, he deserves someone he can trust wholeheartedly. That isn't me. That will *never* be me.

But what if our fresh start begins today? Would my and Lisa's scheme truly matter now that we've abandoned it? If I commit to being honest with him from here on out, where's the harm? I didn't cross any lines or go too far. In fact, Jason doesn't seem at all fazed by anything I said or did; rather than being turned off, he's attracted to the pieces of me that aren't perfect. Jason wouldn't use what he learns about me to his advantage. No, he simply meets people where they are, and I'd be a fool to let someone like him go. Which is why I won't tell him what Lisa and I were planning. It's a moot point anyway. He and I are together now, and I'm going to do everything in my power to make our relationship work. To make myself worthy of his love.

I snuggle closer into Jason's chest, delighted by the purring sounds he makes when he's sleeping. Then an idea comes to me: Wouldn't a new girlfriend do something special to commemorate our upgraded relationship status? Waking him with breakfast in bed is the perfect way to kick off the new me. I can prepare eggs and toast, at least. And coffee. Definitely coffee.

Careful not to disturb him—plainly, sex with me knocked his ass out—I slip out of bed and grab a pair of boxers and a T-shirt from his dresser. After a quick stop at the bathroom, where I use my finger to brush my teeth, I tiptoe to the kitchen and assess what I'm working with. *Lovely.* Jason's fridge and pantry are well stocked, so this won't be hard at all.

I'm whisking eggs in a bowl when I hear the turn of Jason's apartment door lock. Unable to fathom who could be coming into his place with their own key, I freeze. I briefly wonder if I'm about to learn that I'm the other woman, but my gut tells me there's some other explanation. And sure enough, seconds later, Denise strolls through the door, a paper bag and two to-go coffee cups in her hands.

"Shit," she whisper-shouts. "Wasn't expecting you."

"Same," I whisper-shout back.

She holds up the paper bag. "I owed him breakfast."

I hold up the bowl. "I'm making us breakfast."

"Don't let me mess up your plans, then. You two can have the coffee."

"Do you want to join us?"

Her gaze sweeps over my morning-after attire. "Nah, he'd kill me if I stayed."

I laugh. "Okay." I'm hesitant to bring it up, but I'm too nosy not to. "So . . . you and my sister . . . What's happening there?"

"I have no idea. I'm just as surprised as you are, but we're figuring things out."

"Fair enough."

Her eyebrows snap together. "That's all you're going to say?"

"You two are adults. What else is there to say?"

"Refreshing," she says, nodding. After a beat, she adds, "So I'm going to make myself scarce before he wakes up." She sets the bag down. "Take the bagels, but be sure to mention they came from me. I want him to know I repaid my debt."

"Got it."

"Tell me something, though," she says as she approaches the door. "How did he react when you told him? And were you shocked that he knew this whole time? Because Lisa looked like a deer in the headlights when I called her out on that bullshit." She shakes her head, giving me a wide grin. "You guys are ridiculous."

A heavy weight settles in my stomach as Denise waits for me to answer. Unable to face her, I spin around and set the bowl of whisked eggs in the sink.

He knew. All this time, *he knew.*

"Vanessa, what's wrong?"

I drop my chin and let out a harsh sigh. "He didn't mention anything about knowing what we were up to."

"Oh shit, I said too much."

"On the contrary," I say, turning to face her. "You said just enough."

"Sorry," she says, staring at me with sad eyes. "I figured you two would have talked about it last night. I wanted to murder you and Lisa when I overheard you talking in the bathroom at the couples shower. He convinced me to keep quiet." When she sees my eyes widen, she groans. "Aaaand I've said more than I should have. Again."

"No, it's okay. It was going to be an issue at some point anyway."

Because, yeah, who am I kidding? This was always too good to be true, and I should have known he would never be mine. Not for real. And now that I've pulled my head out of my ass, I can see clearly that he was humoring me. The couples shower. The Mets game. The flash mob. The cookout. And so on. Jason kept coming back for more because he wanted to get even with me. And who could blame him? I manipulated his feelings in a shortsighted effort to make up for treating my sister so poorly in the past. *Selfish* doesn't even begin to describe my actions. I don't deserve him, and I never did.

"Talk to him," Denise urges, looking at me with sympathy, and then she quietly slips out the door.

Well, I'm getting the hell out of here. Thankfully, my shoes are in the foyer and my dress is hanging in the bathroom. In less than a minute, I'm dressed and gathering my belongings, including the phone I left to charge on the coffee table. A quick glance at the notifications screen confirms what I already know: Lisa tried to give me a heads-up, but I missed her texts because I put the phone on "do not disturb" as soon as Jason offered me a glass of wine.

And because I'm an unlucky bitch, I hear his low-pitched voice when I turn the doorknob.

"You're leaving without saying goodbye?"

I lean my forehead against the door and gather the mental strength for the conversation I'm unprepared for, then I turn around and face him.

Sleep lines texture the skin of his cheeks, and drowsiness weighs down his eyelids. My chin quivers as I absorb the hurt in his eyes. "I didn't know what to say. Figured it would be best if I left."

His brow furrows as he considers me. "What's going on?"

"Denise stopped by while you were still in bed."

He glances at the food on the kitchen counter, still trying to piece it all together. "You were cooking?"

I nod. "Was going to make us breakfast." I point at the paper cups on the island. "She brought you coffee. It's probably cold by now, but a few seconds in the microwave should fix it." How that's relevant I have no clue, but I'm truly adept at making an ass of myself, so there you go.

"Why are you abandoning everything?"

"She assumed we'd talked last night. About us. About Lisa . . . About our plot to get you two together."

"Right," he says, a muscle in his jaw twitching as he grabs the back of his neck. "Let's talk about it now, then."

Sighing, I drop my shoulders in defeat. Dammit, I *knew* all of this would blow up in my face, but I tricked my brain into thinking I could outwit the inevitable. This conversation is just a formality; Jason and I both know how this will end. "What's the point?"

"The *point* is that I care about you, and I'm trying to understand why you did it."

He's only making it worse and underscoring why we won't work. He's a good person; I'm not.

Jason leans against the wall and crosses his arms over his chest. "Let's try this another way. Were you ever going to tell me?"

"No."

The light in his eyes dims, and it's torture. Because I'm watching the precise moment when any chance of salvaging our relationship dies. "Then you're not who I thought you were."

I've been in this situation before: when my family realized I wasn't nearly as decent as they'd assumed. Their disappointment nearly broke me. Seeing the disillusionment in Jason's expression only reinforces that I'm still that same person. Still letting down the people who care about me. "You're right, I'm not whoever you imagined. I convinced myself I could be better for you, but I wasn't being realistic. You deserve more."

He scowls at me. "You know, in the last few minutes, you've managed to say absolutely nothing. It's one of your many skills, Vanessa: pretending you're revealing something about yourself when you're doing the exact opposite."

I nod. "Harsh but also fair."

I don't mean to be flippant about any of this, I really don't, but I'm hurting, and faking control will stop me from bawling.

"Just go," he says, glaring at me. "I can tell you want to, and I can see that talking isn't getting us anywhere."

I press on the door handle, releasing the lock. Once I get out of his apartment, I'll give myself permission to cry. Just a few seconds more. I can hold it together that long.

"One more thing," he continues, stopping me in my tracks. "I'll be working at your parents' store later this afternoon. It would be great if I didn't see you there."

His words rain on me like golf ball-sized hail, but I don't even flinch. I'm hollow inside. "I understand." Before I step into the hallway, I turn back one last time. "I'm sorry."

"I don't believe you," he says, his eyes hard and unrecognizable.

And that's the problem I'd been trying to avoid all along: Now he'll *never* believe me—even when I'm telling him the truth.

chapter 27

VANESSA

"¡Vete de aquí! ¡Demonio!"

Mami and I are removing items from the shelves in preparation for Jason and his crew's work later this evening. Well, I'm removing items; Mami and the cat are battling for dominion over the store.

"Do you think the cat speaks Spanish?" I ask her.

I'm trying to hide my sour mood so my mother doesn't pry. It appears to be working.

My mother nods as if my question makes perfect sense. "Yes, of course." She narrows her eyes on the ball of chaos hiding behind a stack of Gatorade bottles. "You hear that purr? She's rolling her r's. Now, dogs? They speak English. Bark, bark, bark. ¡Qué feo!"

"I like your theory," I say, forcing a smile.

She sets aside the boxes and places a hand on her hip. "What's wrong, mija?"

Never mind my attempt to mask my true mood. A mother's intuition never fails.

"What makes you think something's wrong?"

"You're asking silly questions. Until today, I didn't even think you realized we had a cat."

"Technically, we don't have a cat. That cat has us."

She stares at me, her expression blank.

"I just had a bad night," I say softly.

Yes, it was actually a bad morning, but my mother's sharp, and I'd like to skip over the details of my and Jason's sextravaganza.

"At the wedding?"

"After."

"Want to talk about it?"

I stick my head between a bunch of Betty Crocker cake mixes to avoid her scrutiny. "Not really."

"Fine."

Do I detect a hint of annoyance in her voice? If so, that's unlike her. My mother's the most chill person I know. "I'm still thinking through what happened. I'm not being cagey or anything."

She shrugs. "You'll tell me when you're ready."

I appreciate that she still has confidence in me, that she thinks we have the kind of relationship where I share my secrets. Sadly, I don't have that with anyone. Sure, people have bits and pieces of me, but the unfiltered version of me who doesn't worry about how I'll be perceived? Or the one who doesn't spin out every negative scenario that could come from opening up to someone? Yeah, nobody's seen that person in a long time.

Jason came close, though, and we all know how that ended.

"Buenos días, mi familia," Lisa singsongs, waltzing into the store as if she's being carried on a parade float.

Well, at least someone's happy today.

"Good morning to you too," I say, giving her a smug smile. "Pleasant evening?"

"An *excellent* evening," she replies with a wink.

How can this be? Why isn't she in turmoil? Her desperate desire to be Jason's one true love got me into this mess, and she's acting as though life's just hunky-dory. Ugh, if I were wearing stilettos, I'd step on her big toe.

No, Vanessa. You must be a better person, remember? Wishing your sister pain is not allowed.

"Can we chat outside for a minute?" I ask her.

"I had a feeling you'd want to." She sidles up to me, then links our arms. "Let's."

Behind the counter, my father looks up from the scratch-off game cards he plays for fun. "Is anyone working around here?"

"You're one to talk," my mother counters. "Have you won three dollars yet?"

He looks at her with triumph. "I won five."

Lisa and I shake our heads, and then we walk out the door.

It's early on a Sunday in El Barrio, which means most of the activity is happening on the city streets: Cars jockey for position as they race down Second Avenue, a sweeper truck maneuvers around a vehicle in the no-parking zone, a woman across the street tends to the plants on her section of the fire escape.

"You didn't answer any of my texts," she says.

"I received them too late."

"You were with him?"

"Yeah." I peer at her, trying to gauge her reaction. "Do you hate me?"

"Hate you?" she asks, her eyebrows squishing together. "Why would I?"

"You had a crush on him. We went through all this trouble to try to line him up for you."

"One, it wasn't that much trouble on my end. I was mostly along for the ride. Two, I've had time to make peace with it. I knew when we were at the spa in Hudson Valley that he would never date me."

"How?"

"Because he couldn't keep his eyes off you. In fact, I knew you were a goner then too."

"How?" I say, unable to keep the skepticism out of my voice.

"Because you *could* keep your eyes off him. Tried your damnedest to. It was like you didn't want to look at him because I'd see right through your act. Am I warm?"

"So fucking hot it's ridiculous."

"Ha, I'm not at all surprised. But don't be too hard on yourself, V. The truth is, I went about this all wrong. I had this idea in my head, and I just wanted to make it happen: Cami would leave, but I'd still be connected to her family. Through him. It would be perfect. Exactly how Cami and I had planned it. Best friends and sisters-in-law. But it was make-believe."

"That's not out of the question, you know."

She cocks her head. "With Denise? Yeah, let's not talk in absurdities. And anyway, once you saw me having oral sex with her—"

"Oh my God, that's *not* what I saw. You didn't have to spell the whole thing out."

"Whatever. We're big girls now. By the way, I finally understand why she calls me Lollipop."

"Get to the point, Lili."

"What I was going to say is that I wouldn't even consider pursuing Jason after being intimate with Denise, not that it was even remotely a possibility, considering that he's infatuated with you."

"Was."

"He can't move past it?"

"He can't move past the fact that I didn't confess to it on my own."

"Did he give you the opportunity to?"

I think about her question for a long moment. Finally, I say, "Yeah, he did. But I ran from each opportunity because I was certain I wouldn't be happy with the outcome. I wanted a chance to be with him. To give him enough reasons to overlook what I'd done first. I was scared."

"Did you explain any of this to him?"

"No."

"So he's operating under the assumption that you're just a lying bitch who was perfectly happy manipulating and fucking him and nothing else."

"Jesus, Lili, that's not how it is."

"But I bet that's the impression you tried to give him. God forbid you should ever make yourself vulnerable and tell the people who care about you what's going on in that head of yours."

"That's not fair."

"No, Vanessa, it *is* fair. You don't talk to us. Not me, not Mami, not Papi. Not unless we badger you into submission. So what do we know about you? Only what we see. Only the little that you tell us. Someday, you're going to have to figure out that you are more than your worst decisions. But in the meantime, if you don't share all of you, your worst is all anyone will ever know. Some people will handle what you tell them with care. But they'll never be able to prove that to you unless you give them a chance to."

"Are you sure you're my baby sister? How are you this mature?"

She rolls her eyes. "We're only three years apart. And I have an advantage over you."

"What?" I say, my brow furrowing.

"I didn't go to Wharton."

"Hey, watch it now."

She snorts, a smile dancing on her lips, and then she pulls me in for a hug. "Jason will be showing up soon. Maybe you can try to open up to him. Give him a glimpse of the real you."

"Not likely. He asked me not to come around when he's here."

She draws back and rests her hands on my shoulders. "Since when have you ever done anything a man told you to do?"

× × ×

La Flor closes at five p.m. on Sundays, a store-hours policy my parents have followed since I was a kid. My mother claims it was instituted to make sure we could have family time; my father says he agreed to the policy because he didn't want to miss Sunday Night Football.

Tonight, Lisa and I are supposed to eat dinner with my parents in their apartment above the store. But dinner won't begin until Jason and his crew clock out for the night. Knowing Jason's finishing up his work, Lisa snags the keys to La Flor's backdoor entrance from my father and tosses them to me.

"Make good use of them," she says, gesturing for me to go.

Standing by the window, I watch for the other two members of Jason's crew to leave, and when they do, I sneak downstairs.

Jason hears me enter the main floor and slowly straightens to his full height. His eyes light up at first, but they dim just as quickly, probably when he remembers what's transpired between us.

"I'm almost done," he says, avoiding my gaze as he packs his tool bag. "I'll be out of here in a minute."

"If I could have a moment of your time, I'd appreciate it," I say, my hands fisted at my sides. "I need a chance to explain."

He looks up at me, his eyes dull and lifeless. "You had that chance this morning."

"Right. And I didn't take it."

"So you've had an epiphany since then?"

Jason isn't like this. Not usually. But I suppose he's taking a page from my playbook and protecting his heart. I can't say that I blame him.

"No epiphany. But I am prepared to speak to you from my heart, which is what I should have done in the first place."

"I'm listening," he says curtly, closing his tool bag with a loud yank of the zipper.

Jason's detached demeanor doesn't offend me. He'd be wise to keep us at arm's length. Still, I want to earn his trust, and I can't do that unless I show him the real me. So I'll tell him *everything*—the good, the bad, and the embarrassing. And although the prospect of opening up to him is terrifying, I'll suffer through it anyway. Because I'd hate for Jason to think I never cared about him. Especially since *nothing* could be further from the truth.

chapter 28

JASON

Vanessa looks like she wants the earth to swallow her whole. I'm inclined to pull her into my arms and tell her all is forgiven, but my brain is acting as a gatekeeper tonight, and it's begging me not to let her back in my life.

So instead I wait—and try not to think about the memories we made this summer.

Taking a deep, weary breath, she flips a milk crate and perches on its edge.

Does she think she's going to change my mind?

Do I want her to?

Fuck, this woman's got me confused.

The sadness clouding her features nearly makes me cave, but I resolve to do nothing but listen to what she has to say.

Finally, she wraps her arms around herself and leans forward. "Growing up, my parents never had much, and that was okay. They loved Lisa and me. They made sure we had clothes. Delicious food. A place to sleep each night. And yeah, we didn't go on family vacations, but we had family game nights. And family movie nights. And my dad even learned how to roller-skate because we wanted to have family roller-skating Sundays too. I didn't need anything else, but my parents wanted more for us. For me. For Lisa. Pretty early on, they realized I was academically gifted, so they put a ton of effort into getting me into private school. I tested well. And I guess I aced the interviews, too, because the next thing I know I was enrolled in grade school at McGreeley."

I set down my tool bag and grab a milk crate of my own so I can sit and face her. "I'm listening."

She straightens, rolls her shoulders, and continues. "I don't know if you've heard of it."

"I have."

"Well, then you know it's where all the rich kids go. The ones whose grandfathers started Fortune 500 companies and had buildings and libraries and schools named after them. Anyway, I hated it. Because I wasn't like those kids. Didn't know the first thing about a proper place setting. Didn't play lacrosse. Had never been on an airplane. I felt so out of place."

I want her to know I'm willing to meet her halfway. I want her to know I care. Because I can't just turn off my feelings that easily. So I ask questions. "Did you tell your parents you were unhappy?"

She shakes her head as a tear slips down her cheek. "Never. I didn't have the heart to. You see, my parents were ridiculously proud of me, and I didn't want them to feel bad, so I sucked it up. And it was fine for a while. Unpleasant but fine. Until I revealed to a classmate that I was poor, not realizing that factoid would make me a social pariah. Once that tidbit got out, I couldn't escape the teasing and taunting. All because my family didn't have as much money as their families did. I wasn't the only one either. Anyone who didn't fit the mold became an outcast. We were never invited to parties. Never invited to sleepovers. The girls would make plans at the lunch table in front of me and joke that they couldn't invite me because I'd steal something from their homes."

"Kids can be so cruel."

"They can. But through that experience, I discovered my superpower: pretending I didn't care. The truth was, I cared so much that I ached with it, but I decided those assholes would never know their words were hurting me. And after a while, the teasing stopped. Because in their minds, it wasn't working. They couldn't get a rise out of me, no matter how hard they tried. I convinced myself that I'd learned some valuable lessons from that experience: Mainly, that people will use what you tell them against you, so it's safest to play your cards close to your chest. When you let people know your true feelings, you leave yourself vulnerable. And when you're vulnerable, someone has power over you."

"You're talking about your boss."

"He's part of this, yeah."

"Not everyone operates that way, though."

"Well, most of the people *I've* dealt with have only reinforced those lessons from way back when." Her lower lips trembles. "Do you want to know my great shame?"

"Only if you want to share it."

She takes a deep breath, then blows it out on a sigh. "When I was in my first year of college, I came home from Philly one weekend with a classmate and my new boyfriend. I figured I'd introduce them to my parents. But when I brought them to my neighborhood, to see where I grew up, they started making snide comments. Made me feel uncomfortable. It was like I was back at McGreeley all over again. And when we got to my parents' store, my boyfriend and friend fell over themselves laughing. Said the place was so much worse than anything they'd seen on social media. By that point, we were in the store, but they didn't know my parents owned it. They were grabbing drinks, and I was trailing behind them, collapsing into myself with each step. They were talking nonstop and slapped the money on the counter as they walked to the door. My mother and Lisa were there. My dad was somewhere in the back. Do you know what I did?"

I think I know where she's going with this, but it's clear she needs to speak it out loud. "Tell me."

"Nothing. I looked my family dead in the eyes and left. Made up some silly excuse to explain why my friends couldn't go to my apartment, and then we headed to my boyfriend's parents' place on the Upper West Side."

"Vanessa."

She sniffles as she wipes away her tears. "See? I'm terrible. I think a piece of me died that day. A piece of my family died that day too. And do you want to know how I know they've never forgiven me?"

"How?"

"Because we've never talked about it. Not a single word has been exchanged between us about that incident. Sure, they dance around it, but what could I possibly say? I didn't know how to explain myself then, and I don't know what I'd tell them now. None of them knew I'd been bullied at McGreeley, because I didn't want to burden them with that information. They'd worked so hard to do the right thing, to give me this once-in-a-lifetime opportunity to change the trajectory of my future. How could I come to them and complain about mean comments in the school courtyard? In the grand scheme of things, it wasn't that big of a deal. Not when they were struggling to put food on the table. To keep the store open. They didn't know I'd failed to acknowledge them because I was reliving a really painful part of my childhood."

"They love you, Vanessa. And you were experiencing trauma. They would have understood."

"But I don't even understand it myself. How does someone *do* that? And live with themselves? And not look in the mirror every day and be disappointed with the reflection staring back at them? And the icing on the cake? I came clean to my boyfriend afterward. Told him what I'd done. I don't know why. Maybe I was looking for him to absolve my guilt. To tell me I wasn't as awful as I thought I was. But he only confirmed that I'd done a terrible thing, and then he said he couldn't ever be with someone like that."

"This is the same asshole who looked down on your family and your neighborhood. I wouldn't give anything he said any weight."

"I understand that now. But back then, it wasn't about what he said. It's what he *did* that messed with my head. I opened up to him. I made myself vulnerable. And he threw it in my face."

"Which is what you expected me to do if you told me about the stunt."

"Yeah," she says, lowering her gaze. "I couldn't imagine a scenario in which telling you wouldn't be used against me. Because if I told you the truth, you'd never forgive me. Not really. Sure, you might convince yourself that you could get beyond it, but it would always be this thing between us. Something you'd hold over my head. The dynamic between us would change. I'd be walking on eggshells, trying to make amends for what I did. And you'd throw it back in my face whenever you weren't happy with me."

I get it now, and still I can't imagine the pain she's been through. My heart hurts for her. For that little girl who felt like she was less than her peers. For the teenager who worried what her college classmates would think of her upbringing. For the woman who was toyed with by someone who claimed to care for her. But none of that changes the one fact that matters: If I hadn't found out about the scheme, she would have kept it from me forever. Our entire relationship would have been built on a lie.

"I wanted so badly for you to tell me. I told myself that if you would just confide in me, I'd be satisfied. I wanted to believe you were different from my father. Different from Elyse. Convinced myself that I could have gotten over all the bullshit if you had just blurted it out without any prompting from me. And I gave you so many chances to tell me the truth, but you never did. So I told myself that was my silly hang-up. And maybe in a sense it is. At the end of the day, though, I just hate being duped. Period. And even giving you a chance to be in my life feels like I'm being a chump. Like I'm inviting you to treat me like one."

She nods, plainly fighting back a new wave of tears, her eyes puffy and red. "How you feel is how you feel. I can't change that. But I do regret not telling you, more than you could ever know. I kept something from you that would have affected how you felt about me, and that was unfair. I guess we don't make the best decisions when the things we want most are at risk. More often than not, we just dig ourselves into deeper holes protecting something that wasn't solidly ours to begin with. The fact that you knew what I was doing the whole time just adds another level of fuckery I can't even begin to unpack."

I wince at the reminder of my part in this fiasco. "Yeah, neither of us is blameless, that's for sure."

"Right. And listen, I'm not telling you all of this because I think we can pick up where we left off. I realize that's not how this is going to go. But I wanted you to know that I wasn't simply trying to save my own ass. I was trying to save what I thought was a chance to be with someone I cared about. It was foolish. And selfish. But I never meant to play fast and loose with your heart. And if it isn't clear by now, please know that I'm truly sorry. For the scheme. For not telling you what I'd been up to. For not allowing myself to be vulnerable with you. For not allowing myself to be vulnerable with anyone, really. That's *my* issue. And I need to work on that more than anything else." She slaps the tops of her thighs and rises to her feet.

"Hang on, not so fast."

Her shoulders drop. "You have questions. Of course you do."

"Yeah, wouldn't you?"

Her mouth twitches. "I'd be all over this like I was running a congressional hearing."

"Then you get why I'm curious. So tell me about the scheme. How'd you come up with it?"

She worries her bottom lip before she answers. "I did it in college. It was my side hustle."

"Seriously?"

"Dead serious. After that whole thing went down with my family and my boyfriend, I was numb. Going through the motions. The money, though. It was too good to pass up. And I wanted to send whatever I made to my family. To try to make up for what I'd done."

"And that shit worked? The scheme, I mean."

"More times than even I thought it would."

"So, what? Lisa asked you to do it for her too?"

"Yeah. I told her it might not work since we were siblings."

"That's a big wrinkle."

"I know. If I hadn't been so concerned about making Lisa happy, I would have refused. But . . ."

"You felt you owed her. Because of the incident at the store. Because you left and never looked back."

She shrugs. "Something like that."

"It's a terrible plan. A person would have to be clueless to fall for it."

"You're not telling me anything I don't already know." Wearing a nervous smile, she adds, "You have to admit, it was fun while it lasted, though."

Fun doesn't even begin to cover what it was. Even now I can feel the pull between us. Can imagine us being this comfortable together for years to come. Can picture myself being the person who's privy to all her secrets. *Fun* is a fling. Vanessa and I could be so much more. But she's doing what she always does: hiding her true feelings because anything else would make her seem powerless in the moment. So I show her how it's done. Because she tried today, and her heart deserves to be cared for. "It was *more than fun*, but it just wasn't meant to be."

"Yeah, I get it," she says, her expression sobering as she surveys my handiwork around the store. "It's looking great, by the way. The floor, especially. My parents are so impressed they're ready to adopt you."

"It's my pleasure to help."

She raises a brow. "Still?"

I nod. "Still."

There's so much more I could say too:

I *still* want you.

I *still* care about you.

I *still* want us to build a future together.

I'm *still* wary of you, although I'm willing to try.

But I don't say any of those things—because Vanessa isn't the only one dealing with a past they're trying to forget.

chapter 29

VANESSA

"How'd it go?" Lisa asks as she lets me into our parents' apartment, her brows knitted in concern.

"I said my piece, and he listened."

She follows me down the hall. "And?"

"And nothing, Lili. We both agreed it wasn't meant to be. Well, Jason agreed more than I did, but I can totally understand where he's coming from, and I'm obviously going to respect his wishes."

"You guys are being so stubborn. There's no reason for you two to be apart. Do you want me to talk to him?"

I whip around and stop her in her tracks. "No, Lili. Don't get involved. This is our issue. We're grown-ass people—"

"Acting like grown-ass children," she mutters under her breath.

"It's not your job to fix this. Please don't interfere."

She throws up her hands. "Okay, okay, fine." Then she takes

my hand. "But I'm only pushing because I love you, and I think Jason could be your person."

"Yeah, well, we'll never know now, will we?" She flinches, so I soften my tone. "But thanks for being here for me. It means the world."

"I know something that'll make you feel better," she says, tucking one of my curls behind my ear.

"What?"

"Mami made flan."

Oh, my favorite dessert. Flan truly can cure everything that ails me. Except my broken heart, of course. But that doesn't matter; I'm not expecting to be cured of that affliction for a long time anyway.

I immediately drop onto the couch. "Mami, you need help in there?"

"No, sweetie," she calls back. "Your father's helping."

I stare at Lisa in shock, and she laughs at my dazed expression.

"He's been helping more and more," she says. "I think he finally realized that she's his equal at the store and he needs to be her equal at home." She whispers the next part: "He even does laundry now. Peep how Mami has a bunch of pink tops. They're supposed to be white. He keeps messing them up, but she won't say a word."

"He's probably trying to get out of it."

"Not going to work. She will wear pink every day of the week if she has to."

I sigh happily. Yeah, I'm torn up about Jason, but I'm reconnecting with my family, and it's refilling my well in a way nothing ever has. "I'm glad I'm home."

"You should tell them that."

"I will."

"All right, everyone," my mother says, carrying two dishes to the table, my father trailing behind her carrying just as many. "¡Vamos a comer!"

"You do know there are only four of us," Lisa teases.

"All of your favorites," my mother says, shimmying her shoulders. Then she sets down the dishes and circles the table as she kisses each of her daughters and her husband on their foreheads. Holding hands, we say grace together, and then we pass around heaping serving plates of chicharrón de pollo, pollo guisado, arroz con habichuelas, and tostones.

My mother jumps up. "¡Ay! Se me olvidó la ensalada de aguacate."

"No one's going to miss the avocado salad, Mami," Lisa says.

My father points a finger at Lisa once my mother's out of earshot. "Psst, she made it, so you're going to eat it."

"Yes, sir," Lisa says, saluting him.

We spend most of the meal chatting about the changes to the store and my parents' plans to slow down before they move on to their next adventure. Lisa shares that she's lobbying for more funding at work and that the principal might allocate budget money for an assistant counselor position. In the back of my mind, I'm listening for an opportunity to tell them what's been going on in my life and finally clear the air about the incident that still makes my stomach turn all these years later. But I conveniently find an excuse not to speak up each time there's an opening.

"Are you excited about the new office?" my mother asks me. "It must be a big deal to be a part of the expansion, right?"

It would be so easy to just say yes and keep the conversation moving, but my experience with Jason has taught me how important it is to be honest with the people you love. "Yes . . . and no."

They wait for me to explain, so I take a deep breath and do just that. "Yes, being a part of the expansion is a good thing. It brought me home. And I get a small raise, mostly to cover the increased cost of living. But I was kind of pushed out by my boss, who I was dating."

My father sets down his fork, his expression hardening. "That pendejo who was here a couple of weeks ago?"

"Yeah," I say quietly.

"Was he married?" my mother asks, her eyes wide.

Oh God, this is excruciating. Maybe I shouldn't have said anything.

Lisa takes my hand under the table. "It's okay, Vanny. This isn't your fault."

I let out a bitter laugh. "Well, it kind of is my fault. I dated my boss. But no, he was single. And you don't have to say it: I *know* it wasn't smart. You both raised me better."

"But he's the boss, so he's supposed to know better too," my mother points out.

"Agreed. It's just . . . It was a mess. He wanted me to keep dating him. I didn't want to get serious. And so he recommended me for the New York office. I think he expected me to beg him to stay, because I'd told him I'd grown apart from my family."

"And it backfired," my mother says.

"Yeah, it did," I say, my eyes glistening. "Because I really want to be here with all of you, and I know things have been strained between us since I left for college, but I'm hoping we can work on that. Maybe we won't get back to where we were, but I'd like to try."

"Why didn't you say anything before?" Papi asks. "You can tell us anything."

Lord, I don't want to do this, but if I'm going to earn their forgiveness, I need to lay myself bare. "Because I never feel like I should be complaining around you. It feels selfish. I never told you I was being bullied at McGreeley for that same reason. How could I? You guys were killing yourselves providing for Lili and me. Worrying about the store. Worrying about putting food on the table. I didn't need to add to your stress."

"What did they bully you about?" my father asks softly, as if he knows I'm ready to clam up at any moment.

"Being poor. They made fun of me mercilessly. Teased me for fun. Said they couldn't invite me over because I'd steal their jewelry. Day in and day out. If there was a character in a book who didn't have much, they'd turn to me in class and ask me what it was like. In the scheme of things, it was silly stuff. To a twelve-year-old, though, it was terrible. I knew you wanted me to succeed. I knew you wanted me to do well so I could help you guys out. So I sucked it up. And by the time I got to college, I thought I was over it. We weren't in high school anymore. But then I came home that one weekend with my classmates." I chance a glance at their faces and press ahead. "They didn't know you owned the store. I was planning to surprise them. And then they started laughing about it. Making fun of the signs written in Spanglish."

"What jerks," Lisa says through gritted teeth.

I wipe my eyes. "I know that now, but back then I wanted to fit in. And it felt like McGreeley was happening all over again.

So I walked out without acknowledging you, and it was by far the worst thing I've ever done in my life, and I've regretted it every second since."

Mami rounds the table, bends at the waist, and presses me against her bosom. "You're our daughter, and we love you. Nothing will ever change that. We don't need you to be perfect. And we don't need you to pretend everything is fine. We're a family, and families help each other through the tough times. They share the good and the bad. And anyway, what matters is who you are now. You're here. You're helping. You're letting us be a part of your life."

"Alicia, give her space to breathe," my father tells Mami. "Your boobs are smothering her."

I manage to laugh through the waterworks as my mother sits down again.

"Nena, you don't have to get us out of SpaHa," he tells me, his eyes twinkling. "We're comfortable here. And you know what? *We* were the ones who felt guilty sending you out into the world without us. We worried about you all the time. But you're doing great, and that's all we wanted. That's all any parent ever wants—better for their children."

"Thank you for being so understanding," I say, wiping my tear-streaked face. "I promise to be more open with all of you from now on."

"Oh yeah?" my mother asks. "Well then, let's start with what's going on with Jason."

Lisa throws her head back and cackles.

"Whose side are you on?" I say, my eyes narrowing on my sister even though I'm holding back a laugh.

"There are no sides here," Lisa says. "Only bochinche."

I drop my chin and stare at my empty plate. "I'll tell you everything, but I need flan first."

My mother jumps up. "I'll get it." And before she rushes off, she adds, "Don't start without me."

I sit up, and we all exchange amused glances. Then I take a deep, cleansing breath.

"You're a good person," my father says, squeezing my hand. "Don't let anyone make you feel less than."

Here's the truth I finally need to face: It's me. *I'm* the one who's always making me feel less than. So maybe now I can learn to give myself grace. My family has certainly shown me how.

chapter 30

JASON

Eric tosses a balled-up napkin across the conference room table. "You know, the point of Tuesday lunch is to give us time to catch up on our lives."

"I know," I say, before popping a potato chip in my mouth. "So what's the problem?"

"Don't do that," he says, narrowing his eyes.

"Do what?"

"Talk while you're chewing. That's grounds for dissolving our business partnership."

"Whatever," I say, eating another chip.

"Okay, fine, but if we're catching up on our lives, what did I just tell you?"

"About what?"

He rolls his eyes. "About anything."

"That I shouldn't talk while I eat?" I ask, frowning.

"No, before that."

"Something about meeting someone."

"And who did I meet, J?"

"A woman?"

"Just a random woman or..."

"A woman you're interested in."

"Good guess, but no. I met Rihanna."

"What the fuck?!? You did? When?"

He reaches over and snatches my bag of potato chips from me. "No, dumbass, I didn't meet Rihanna. I'm just confirming that you haven't been listening to me. I'd be hurt, but I know you're going through it right now."

"Going through what?"

"Heartbreak."

I snort dismissively. "Please. It wasn't that serious."

"Oh really?" he says, drawing back and lifting his chin as he studies me. "So you're not having trouble concentrating?"

"Not at all."

"Is that why you ordered two dozen toilets for the house in Greenwich?"

"What? No, I didn't."

He lifts a folder off the chair next to his and opens it. Smirking, he pulls out a sheet of paper and slides it over to me. "Take a look."

I glance at the paper, knowing it's an order form. Within seconds, I spot the mistake. "Fuck, I did. But it happens. Doesn't mean anything."

"In all the years we've been in business together, nothing like this has ever happened."

"So? I'm entitled to make a mistake every decade. I won't make another one for at least another year."

He pulls out another sheet from the folder.

What the hell?

"This one's an email," Eric says. "From Delroy Oasis, the pool subcontractor. He's wondering why we scheduled him for a meeting with Patricia Barnes to go over her pool plans."

"Because that's what pool subcontractors do—help people with their pool plans."

"Patricia Barnes lives in a condo, J."

"Shit," I say, squeezing my eyes shut. "Okay, I'm a little off this week. But it's not about Vanessa. I'm just tired."

"If that's how you want to play this, fine. I had a feeling you'd clam up, so I brought in reinforcements."

"What the hell does that mean?"

As if on cue, Denise sticks her head into the conference room, then shuffles inside, making jazz hands. "Yah-dah-da-da-da-da- yah-dah-da-duh." Jumping to a stop, she throws her hands on her hips. "Here I come to save your ass!"

I glare at Eric. "This is your idea of helping me?"

"No, this is my idea of helping the business. You're fucking up, and Denise says she knows how to smack some sense into you." He clears his throat. "And yeah, I don't like seeing you like this."

"Where's the lunch you promised me?" Denise asks Eric.

"You had to *bribe* her to come talk to me?"

Eric nods. "Sadly, she doesn't do anything for free."

"I'm right here, asswipes. Eric. Lunch. Where is it?"

Eric flicks his gaze to the ceiling, then gathers the remnants of his meal. "In the fridge. I'll be right back."

"Thanks, papi chulo."

"Yeah, yeah," he says, waving her off.

Denise takes the seat Eric just abandoned and studies me.

"What?" I ask.

"Want to talk about it?"

"No."

"Oh, so you already know what *it* is."

"Vanessa, I'm guessing."

"That's where you're wrong. This is about *so* much more than Vanessa."

"Let me get comfortable for this," I say, sitting back in my seat. "Okay, I'm ready."

"Don't be a dick. It doesn't suit you."

"Sorry," I mutter.

"I'm going to make this relatively easy for you by telling you what went down. All you have to do is correct me if I'm wrong."

"This should be fun."

"After an amazing night of debauchery and sex, Vanessa discovered that you knew all along what she and Lisa were up to. Accurate so far?"

"Wrong."

"Correct me, then."

"After an amazing night of debauchery and sex, Vanessa was ambushed by my younger sister, who, despite knowing I had a date, came over the following morning, brought me some weak-ass coffee, and blabbed for no fucking reason."

"Well, shit," Denise says. "That's quite a correction. But you don't intimidate me. Never have."

"Continue."

"Vanessa, realizing that she'd had sex with someone who was withholding critical information about her that might have affected her willingness to get into bed with him, got pissed and told off that certain someone."

"Hold on, *she* was withholding critical information from *me*."

"That you *knew* about. So she only *thought* she was withholding critical information, whereas you were *actually* withholding information."

"Is this the shit they teach you in law school? How to talk so fast your witnesses can't keep up?"

"I'm flattered you think my conversational skills surpass yours, but no."

"I'm not the bad guy here."

"You're not exactly the good guy either."

I squeeze the back of my neck and sigh. "Then we're both fucked up, and we shouldn't be together anyway."

"Nope, that's a cop-out."

"So what's your point?"

"My *point* is that not everything is simply black or white. There are fifty damn shades of gray, for God's sake."

"That was beneath you."

She tilts her head and twists her mouth back and forth as she considers my words. "It was. Pretend I never said that."

"Done."

"Okay, so my point is that there are all kinds of lies: blatant ones, little white ones, malicious ones, empathetic ones, lies of omission. And your insistence on never forgiving a lie lacks nuance. The *what* of the lie. The *why* of the lie. The *consequences* of the lie."

I hate that she's making sense. "Explain."

"A woman pretends to like the same music I do to get my interest. Eh, it's annoying, but whatever. I'll eventually figure out if we're compatible anyway."

"That's not what we're talking about, though."

"Yes, it is. Be patient."

I drop my head back. "Go on."

"A guy claims he's packing nine hard inches between his legs. Most likely a lie. But why? Insecurities? Society's arbitrary ideas about masculinity? Whatever. The person he's lying to is going to figure it out if they have sex. And maybe it matters, or maybe it doesn't. See? Nuance."

"Where the hell are you going with this?"

"Stick with me." She grimaces a moment, then presses on. "Okay, so this might be a little touchy, but it needs to be said. That woman you thought you were going to marry."

"Elyse."

"Yeah, her. That lie of omission was fucked up. And considering *what* she was lying about, her kid, and the *consequence* of that lie—holy shit, you're now engaged to a woman with a kid when you don't even know if you want to be a father—I'd say you were fully within your rights to be like, 'Bitch, we're through.'"

"I didn't say it like that, but sure."

"Now, our own father's lie, cheating on our mother despite his vows not to, and the consequences of that lie—too many to recount—mean that rat bastard didn't deserve her."

"You're absolutely right about that."

"Now, that kid who knew his father was cheating and didn't tell his mom, well, there's the gray area, wouldn't you say? Because, damn, what's a kid supposed to do under those circumstances?"

My stomach drops. Wasn't expecting her to go there. "That kid wasn't a child. He was a teenager."

"Yeah, but he was also protecting his mother and his family, and he was put in a position where he felt he *had* to keep a secret because the *consequence* of telling the truth was too great."

"Oh-kay."

"Did Vanessa tell you why she didn't confess to the scheme?"

"Yeah, she said her feelings for me had grown so much, and she thought telling me would risk losing me altogether. And even if I managed to get past it, it would be this thing between us. That, considering my feelings about deceit, I'd use it against her."

"Interesting."

"What does that mean, *interesting*?"

"Think about it, Jason. The *what*. The *why*. The *consequence*. I bet if you took the time to truly consider what she did, instead of sticking to your hard-and-fast rules, you'd realize this is one of those lies you might be able to live with. If you care about her enough, that is."

Denise is exhausting, but I can't pretend she's not making me reconsider my position.

"One more thing," she adds, holding up a finger.

"You're not done yet?"

"Not quite."

I look around. "Where's Eric with your lunch?"

"Doesn't matter. I'm on a roll."

"I can't believe I actually agree with you."

"So I'm going to say this last thing, and then I'm going to hunt Eric down and make him buy me dinner too. I think you stick to this rigid standard because you're trying to work through your own guilt. Vanessa didn't tell you what she and Lisa were up to, so you tell yourself she's just as bad as our sperm donor. Or Elyse. But deep down, I think you worry that she's just as bad as that kid who kept his dad's cheating a secret. You can't fathom forgiving her because you can't fathom forgiving yourself. She's not entitled to a pass because you're not entitled to one either."

"You and Eric should open up a psych practice, I swear."

"Or maybe it's time for you to see a professional so you can work through all of this on your own time." She stands and reaches for my hand. "I know I'm a pain in the ass, and you probably think I'm too young to impart any wisdom, but I love you, and I want you to be happy. I just don't want you to give up so easily on someone who might be able to help you get there."

"I don't always agree with your methods, but I admit you've given me a lot to think about."

"Excellent," she says, brushing off her shoulders in a disgusting display of arrogance. "My work here is done."

Before she leaves, I stop her by calling out her name.

She turns around in surprise. "Yeah?"

"You're brilliant. I'm really proud to be your brother."

"And don't tell anyone, but you're my *favorite* brother."

"I'm your only brother, dipshit."

She gives me a cheeky grin. "Exactly." Then she flashes a peace sign and saunters out the door.

chapter 31

VANESSA

"You're a lifesaver, Vanessa. Couldn't have done this without you."

Silas beams at me from his seat in the small conference room at Built to Excel's headquarters.

"It was my pleasure. Truly. You've done all the hard work. I just fancied up the details, added photos, and told them why they should fork over the cash."

"Well, you've done a fine job. I'm tempted to reach into my own pocket and give BTE some money."

"We're kind of looking for more than whatever's in your wallet, Silas."

"Ain't that the truth," he says with a chuckle. "But seriously, there's real heart in this proposal." He holds up the draft of the grant application I completed last night. If approved, BTE will be the recipient of a fifty-thousand-dollar technology grant from the Boilermaker Foundation. "I can tell the person who wrote this has a passion for helping the poor. Understands the barriers. But also understands the triumphs. And this isn't condescending at all. Because Lord knows, I've seen a lot of that in my work."

"I can imagine."

"Are you sure you don't want to make this your next career?"

"Ha. My current employer might have something to say about that. My rent would probably also like a word."

"Yeah, no one's making big bucks here." He sets down the papers and leans forward. "So I know you can handle a grant proposal, but can you handle those kids out there?"

Later today I'll be teaching a class on money management and trying very hard not to bore these kids to death. "I think I'll be okay. I'm just going to go over my presentation one more time."

He smiles warmly. "Did Jason give you any tips?"

"Um, no. We aren't really . . ."

He tips his head to the side. "Oh? I assumed you two were . . ."

"I'm not really sure what we were, but whatever we were, we're not that now."

"I'm sorry."

"Don't be. It's fine. We're just not a right fit."

That's not entirely true, but Silas doesn't need to hear my sob story. The thing is, Jason and I *are* a great fit, but we're stuck in limbo, being held hostage by my poor judgment and his stubbornness. It's a terrible place to be.

"Hmm."

I fiddle with the papers in front of me to avoid looking Silas in the eye. "Yeah, hmm. Uh, I'm going to grab some dinner and eat it while I prepare."

"Right," he says, clapping once then rising from his chair.

"I'm going to get out of your hair. I'll send in the kids when you're ready. Good luck."

"Thanks. I'm going to need it."

"Just be yourself. That's more than enough."

For the first time in a long while, I'm beginning to think that's true.

JASON

"Hey, Silas, what's up?"

"Hey, Jason, you busy?"

"No, I'm walking to my car. Lots of noise out on these streets, though."

"It's okay, and sorry to bother you."

"No bother. I'm done for the evening and heading home."

"Oh, you're still in Manhattan?"

"Yeah, just left the office."

"I hate to ask, but is there any chance you could stop by? I'm looking at a large hole in the rec room's ceiling, and I'm worried it's a sign of something that's only going to get worse. With the kids hanging out here, I just don't want to risk another chunk of plaster coming down on them."

"No need to say more, Si. I can drive over there now. See you in a bit."

"Thanks so much. I'll see you when you get here. Appreciate it."

Thirty minutes later, I park my truck across the street from BTE's home base in Hamilton Heights. This part of Harlem always surprises me. Each street has a different character, so you never know what you're going to stumble across until you're right on it. A walk down Convent Avenue alone is enough to make me want to buy a brownstone here; too bad I'd never be able to afford it. Not anymore. Not with the way real estate prices in this area have skyrocketed as of late.

When I enter the lobby, I see teenagers hanging out in the lounge area. Friday night is reserved for outside speakers and workshops, so I understand why Silas would want me to take a look at the ceiling as soon as possible.

I stop at the front desk and greet the receptionist. "How's it going, Martha?"

Martha, a middle-aged woman who definitely smoked most of her life, answers with a gravelly sigh. "These kids are getting on my last nerve."

"How can that be? They were getting on the only nerve you had left the last time I was here. There are no more nerves to get on."

"Oh, hush," she says, a playful twinkle in her eyes. "You're lucky you're cute."

"Stop flirting with our visitors," Silas tells Martha as he strides toward us.

"Stop worrying about what I do," she replies, her eyes narrowing on him.

"I'm her boss," Silas tells me, the corners of his eyes crinkling. "You'd never know it."

"I'm *his* boss," Martha explains. "He keeps forgetting that."

"You two should stop messing around and get married already."

Silas and Martha glance at each other in surprise, and a flush creeps up Martha's cheeks.

"Right, well, let me show you the problem," Silas says, scurrying away.

A minute later, I'm staring up at a missing tile in the rec room's drop ceiling. "You're saying an entire tile just fell onto the floor and didn't break? Broke off cleanly like that and dropped to the ground?"

"I mean, I wasn't here when it happened, but that's what it looks like."

"No, it looks like someone removed the tile and placed it on the floor. Could the kids be pulling a prank on you?"

He scoffs. "The kids don't have time for games like that. They're not twelve anymore."

"Then could *you* be pulling a prank on *me*? Because this makes no sense, Silas."

"I don't understand it," he says, rubbing the back of his neck. "When I came in, I found it like this, and the first thing I thought to do was call you."

"Fine, fine. I'll get the ladder from the supply closet and take a look."

Silas shuffles to a corner of the room. "It's right here. Figured I could save you some time."

I spend a few minutes up on the ladder, surveying the ceiling with a flashlight. Nothing's amiss, so I fit the tile back into place, climb down the ladder, then wipe my brow with a handkerchief. "You have nothing to worry about. At least not now. If anything changes, let me know."

He places a hand on his chest and sighs in relief. "That's good news. I was thinking there was something structurally wrong. The last thing we need is an unexpected repair bill."

"No, you're good. Besides, you have me if something comes

up. I literally know every person who could fix whatever's broken."

"Good, good." He checks his watch. "Hang on a sec. I need to call in the kids for their workshop. It'll be starting soon."

"What's the topic tonight?"

"Budgeting for Financial Independence."

"Could have used that when I was in high school. Would have saved myself a lot of grief if I hadn't opened a credit card account in college."

"Yeah, that's what I want them to know. The tips and tricks and how to avoid costly mistakes. Want to say hello to the speaker?"

I draw back, raising a brow. "Why would I?"

"Because you know her. The speaker's Vanessa Cordero."

I stare at him for several seconds as all the thoughts of her I tried to push away flood my brain like a tsunami. "Silas."

"Yeah?"

"Is it a coincidence that you brought me here under suspicious circumstances when she just so happened to be the speaker for the evening?"

"I'm hurt," Silas says, not looking hurt at all. "I thought you knew me better than that."

"I *do* know you better than that, which is why I'm asking."

"Just say hello. I asked her about you earlier, and she looked so sad. And because I know *you*, I figured you might need a push."

"How'd this come about? Her being here, I mean."

"She's been helping me out."

"Since when?"

"She called me the Monday after you brought her to Sueños."

"She never mentioned anything about it."

Silas shrugs. "Guess she just wanted to help for the sake of helping."

"What does she do when she's helping?"

"She wrote a grant application, and she's advising me on some tax stuff."

"And today?"

"I think this is a onetime deal. And before you ask, she offered, so I took her up on her offer. She has the right expertise."

"Huh. Interesting."

"Isn't it?" he asks, walking away. "If you need me, I'll be in my office."

"I just bet," I say, staring after him.

His goodbye wave is the only acknowledgment I get, and then he leaves me with a fuckton of feelings I don't know how to handle. Damn, I miss her. There's no question about that. So what's the holdup? In all of this, I've *never* questioned whether Vanessa's a good person. Her presence here today just reinforces what I already know. She's giving back. Without wanting any recognition for it. She's not some evil mastermind hell-bent on screwing me over. Far from it.

The answer hits me like a two-by-four: I'm hesitant to let her back in my life because I'd be giving her a pass on her and Lisa's scheme, *not* because I think she'd lie again. In which case, I'm resisting on principle, when I could be with someone who has the potential to make me happier than I've ever been. Vanessa isn't my birth father. Vanessa isn't Elyse. No, Vanessa could be my person. As if on cue, I can hear Denise pushing me to think about the *what*, the *why*, and the *consequences*, and there's no doubt in my mind: Vanessa matters more to me than sticking to my hard-and-fast rule that a lie can't be forgiven. She and I deserve a second chance. A fresh start. And I'm ready to give it to her. If she wants it, that is. God, I hope she does.

VANESSA

I'm closing my container of takeout Chinese food when someone clears their throat. I whip my head up and see Jason standing at the room's threshold.

A pang immediately hits my belly. As usual, he looks gorgeous. That's no surprise. And yeah, I'd love for him to put me in an orgasm-induced coma, but I miss talking to him, teasing him, laughing *with* him. God, if only we'd had a fair shot to make us work.

I survey his features more closely. He's tired; the slight bags under his eyes are an easy tell. I wonder if he, too, has been having trouble sleeping. Does he think about me? At night? All day? If so, he's not alone. I've made myself scarce at La Flor when I know he's around. Thankfully, he and his crew will be done tomorrow morning. After that, I won't have to worry about running into him at the store. Apparently, I do have to worry about running into him here.

"Hey," I say, forcing a half smile to hide my nervousness.

"Hey," he says, taking a few steps into the room. "I hear you're running a workshop tonight."

"Yeah, I'm looking forward to it."

He tilts his head. "Are you sure about that?"

I blow out my cheeks. "You're right. I'm nervous as hell."

"It's all right. These kids know when someone cares. I bet they'll pick up on your good energy."

"I hope so."

"You doing okay?"

"I'm fine. You?"

"Fine too." After a beat, he adds, "I kind of wish I was more than fine, though. You?"

"Same."

"I was going to ask you what would help get you there, but that's a cop-out. I just . . . I miss you."

Hearing those three words, I take in a sharp breath. It's too soon to know what this means, but that can't be a bad thing, right? "I miss you too."

"Feels like we didn't really get the shot we deserved."

"I was thinking the same thing when I saw you standing there."

"Maybe we could try again?" he asks. "Go on a date? A real one this time."

"That'd be nice," I say, the tops of my ears warming. "But so you know, all those dates were real to me. I just didn't realize it yet."

"That *is* good to know."

Before I can say anything else, the BTE participants begin shuffling into the conference room, weaving around Jason and looking between us curiously.

I shoot up onto my feet. "Um, I need to run this workshop. Maybe we could . . ."

"Right. Another time. I'll call you."

"Sounds good."

"Good luck tonight."

"Thanks."

He walks out, and my knees nearly buckle. That was all so civil and sterile and nothing like our best days together. It kills me to know I'm the reason we're back at the beginning. But it also makes me proud to know that I'm the reason we're even on speaking terms again. I didn't run this time. Instead, I laid myself bare. Maybe our best days could still be ahead of us.

"He's a cutie," one of the girls, Mercedes, says.

"I know."

"Is he your boyfriend?"

"No, but I hope he will be someday."

Perhaps that's not in the cards for Jason and me. But I'd settle for being his friend. Okay, who am I kidding? I want it all: friendship, companionship, and sexship. (Yes, that's a word.) We'll see if he calls.

For now, I have a workshop to get through. These young adults deserve my undivided attention, so I'm going to stop thinking about Jason for the next hour.

Yeah, Vanessa, good luck with that.

chapter 32

VANESSA

I'm sad to say Jason didn't call last night. Which is going to make seeing him today even more awkward than usual.

If I could, I'd avoid him altogether, but my parents are unveiling the improved La Flor to the masses during the 106th Street annual block party. As the architect of the relatively minor but impactful changes, Jason undoubtedly will be there. He deserves the credit, of course, so my plan is to stay out of the way as much as possible and be super polite to him whenever our paths cross.

Unfortunately, Mami and Papi are conspiring against me. Not intentionally, but still. In a clever two-for-one, they're also staging the store for professional photographs their real estate agent can use to entice potential buyers. Given that they asked me to "look nice," I'll likely be in Jason's orbit for a photograph or two. No, I don't generally dress like a sea hag, so I should be insulted by their request, but a Latine child learns early on to fight only the major battles and take the metaphorical Vivaporú for everything else.

When I arrive at the store, the area between Second and Third Avenues is completely closed to traffic and people are milling around the various stands. Salsa music pumps from the speakers, and kids run through the crowd with not a care in the world. Vendors are shouting at their customers as they sell everything from zeppoli to barbecued ribs to alcapurrias. Near the main stage, a group of young dancers, all dressed in white flowy skirts, prepare to dance bomba, a traditional Puerto Rican dance with roots in the island's African ancestry.

The sun is shining, the aroma of sweet peppers and Italian sausage is blanketing the street, and bongos and trumpets are providing a steady beat that people are swinging their hips to. Taking in this sensory experience, I pull in a deep breath of contentment and blow it out slowly. This place has rhythm and soul, a cultural landscape all its own, a hard-fought vibrancy that isn't diminished by its rough edges. It's hard to believe there was ever a time when I was embarrassed to be from here. No more.

Lisa opens La Flor's door and pulls me inside. "Why are you standing outside like you're about to break into song in a Lin-Manuel Miranda musical?"

"Whatever, Lili," I say with a laugh. "I was just admiring the neighborhood."

She steps close, her face inches from mine. "Well, *I* just wanted to give you a heads-up that he's here," she whispers. "And he's been here for a while. He and the guys from his work crew are going to play dominoes with Papi outside. They just went to the back to get the tables."

"Got it," I say, acting calm even though my heart feels like it's pumping in my throat.

"You okay?"

My instinct is to tell her I'm fine, but I'm trying not to be that person anymore. The woman who gives off this overly confident façade to mask her insecurities. I glance at her through pained eyes. "I'm a wreck, Lili. I don't know what to do."

"You don't have to *do* anything. It's a street festival. You're with family. Enjoy yourself. And if he happens to start a conversation, do that thing with your mouth you do so well."

"Talk?"

"Yes, that," she says, her mouth twitching. "That's exactly what I meant."

I let out an embarrassing snort. I'm fine. We're fine. This is all fine.

"You look hot, by the way," she says, eyeing me from head to toe before her gaze lands on my shoulders. "Your arms are insanely toned too. All that masturbating is doing wonders for your physique."

"You're an ass," I say, pushing her away.

"But you love me," she singsongs.

"I do," I say, sobering. "I really, really do."

"No, we're not doing this right now." She grabs my hand and pulls me out the door.

"Where are we going?" I ask.

"To find the piragua man."

Minutes later, we return with cherry piraguas in their useless white paper cones.

"I'm going to get this all over me," I say, groaning.

"So?" Lisa says. "That's the point."

I dodge some of the dripping syrup from the shaved ice treat as it hits the ground and bump into a hard body. Without even looking, I can tell it's Jason. Because I can *smell* him. That perfect blend of cognac and cedarwood transports me to those moments I spent between his sheets. I wish I'd had enough time with him to let his scent soak into my skin. I look up and swallow. "Sorry."

He smiles. "No problem. Bumping into you is always a good thing."

"Hey, Jason," Lisa chirps, wildly waving a hand in front of him. "Good to see you too."

"Hey, Lisa," he says, his gaze not straying from mine the whole time. "You look amazing."

"Thank you," I say, nervously adjusting the fabric of my maxi dress. I gesture toward La Flor. "It's a new place. I can't thank you enough for helping them out."

"It was my pleasure."

"Still?"

"Still," he says, nodding firmly.

It feels like we're talking about more than his willingness to help renovate the store, but I'm too scared to examine what we're not saying. Too afraid to hope for what I desperately want.

Mami pokes her head out from inside the store. "Lisa, time for your shift."

"And what are *you* going to be doing?" Lisa asks Mami.

"Playing dominoes with your father, of course," she replies as she pulls on the apron strings around her waist. Lisa rolls her eyes and slips inside.

I turn back to Jason, who's still watching me with an intensity that warms my skin and makes me lightheaded. It's going to be a scorcher today; that must be why I'm at risk of overheating.

"Your parents convinced me to play dominoes. Are they any good?"

"Very. And they take it seriously."

"So I should let them win?"

"There's no *letting* involved. They're going to crush you."

He laughs. "Thanks for the vote of confidence."

"You're welcome."

"Hey, Jason," my father calls out as he sets up the dominoes. "Let's go, mijo."

"I need to do this," he says, pointing behind him. "But I'd like to talk to you later. Would that be cool with you?"

"Definitely," I say, grinning so hard.

"All right," he says. Then he leans over and presses a soft kiss to my cheek.

Oh. That's a good sign, right? Yes, yes, I think it is.

I watch him join the game, and I'm at a loss for what to do. Go inside? Walk the festival a bit? Out of the corner of my eye, I catch Jason lean over and speak to my father. After a brief exchange, Jason calls my name.

"What's up?" I ask.

"Come join me."

"Join you where?"

"Right here," he says, patting his lap.

"In front of my parents?" I ask, unable to keep the shock from my voice. "Our current relationship status doesn't qualify for such public displays of affection."

He gives me a lopsided grin and pulls a milk crate from behind his chair. "Here, then."

I reluctantly join them.

"You can help me," he says, speaking to me quietly. "Sounds like I'll need it."

I watch the game for a moment and then "Just Can't Get Enough" by the Black Eyed Peas begins playing through the speakers. "This used to be my song in high school. Wore it out."

"I know. Lisa told me."

"She did?" I ask, tilting my head.

"She did."

Before I can press him on why she shared this tidbit about me, a guy in a tank top and basketball shorts hands me a rose.

"What is happening?" I ask, laughing.

Then another guy similarly dressed in casual clothes hands me two more roses. Seconds later, they're breakdancing on the sidewalk in front of the store, a large piece of cardboard serving as their makeshift stage.

"You didn't," I tell Jason.

"I did," he says, holding back a smile.

Soon, I'm receiving roses from a dozen strangers, all of whom are dressed like B-boys in an old breakdancing movie, and then they're dancing together while the neighborhood stares at the woman—*me*—with two dozen roses in her hands.

"Vanessa," my mother says, her eyes flickering with affection. "Sit in the man's lap, ¡por Dios!"

From the store's door, Lisa gives me a thumbs-up.

I scramble up from my spot on the crate and clumsily climb onto Jason's lap. He wraps his arms around my waist to steady me, and I snuggle into him.

"I can't believe you did this."

"Just wanted you to know I can be just as ridiculous as you when the situation calls for it."

"Believe me, I know."

"Do you remember the words to the song?" he asks.

"By heart."

"There's a part about forming a team."

"Yeah," I say breathlessly. "Something about being your queen."

"What do you say?"

"Are you asking me to be your girlfriend?"

"Definitely."

As I think about the parallels between this moment and the song's lyrics, I caress his jaw and bring my face within a hairsbreadth of his. "I can't imagine being anything less, so the answer is yes."

But we don't kiss. Because I'm definitely not doing *that* in front of my parents. And you know what? It doesn't matter. This new beginning is uniquely ours, and we have all the time in the world to celebrate it. We'll get to the good stuff later.

× × ×

That afternoon, we're in each other's arms as soon as Jason kicks the door to my apartment closed. In a frantic dash to remove our clothing, we peel garments out of the way without regard to which one of us is actually wearing them. Our mouths are fused together, tongues sliding and swirling in a heated dance that's showing no signs of slowing. Not even when we're completely naked, our clothes carelessly discarded on the floor.

Groaning, Jason lifts me, and I scramble for purchase, wrapping my legs around his waist and squirming against his hard length pressed between us. His big hands squeeze my ass as he strides down the hall, and then he gently deposits me in the middle of my bed.

I part my legs slightly, teasing him.

His eyes blaze with lust, his pupils flaring as he gives my entire body a once-over and then returns to my face. "Show me."

I don't bother to ask what he means. I know. So I spread my thighs and hold myself open.

"Fuck," he chokes out. "You're soaked."

"No preparation necessary."

He takes a deep breath and strokes himself twice. "For either of us."

"Then why are you standing there?"

"I'm coming."

"I should hope so."

His lips curve into a smile as he climbs onto the bed, and then he lowers himself over me, pressing me into the mattress so we're skin to skin.

"Jason."

"Vanessa."

"Jason."

"This feels right. Tell me you feel the same."

"I do. God, you know I do."

"No more secrets?"

"None."

"You're everything I've ever wanted and never thought I'd have. Te adoro."

"I adore you too."

He nuzzles my jaw, then nips at the corner of my lip. "Take me in your hands and rub yourself. Get it nice and wet."

I moan as I reach for him, and then I'm sliding his tip over my pussy.

"Yeah, that's it," he whispers, squeezing his eyes shut. "What do you want? Slow? Fast? I aim to please."

"Fast. Hard and fast."

He pushes inside me in one swift thrust.

"Yes," I cry out.

"Vanessa," he groans as he shudders. "I'm so fucking gone for you."

"I like the sound of that. And same, same, same."

He balances on his elbows and brushes away the curls that are plastered against my face. "Oh yeah?"

"Without a doubt. Now please move."

He chuckles, his stomach muscles stretching against the softness of my belly, and then he drives into me, filling me to the hilt. With a soft "Jesus," he rises off the bed. "Wrap your legs around my waist."

I slide under the cage of his arms and shoulders and draw him close, enveloping him between my thighs.

He licks his lips once, twice, and then plunges, pounding me relentlessly. Over and over. Again and again. "Like this?"

"Exactly like this," I say with a whimper.

We rock into each other for minutes, my soft cries and his hard grunts the only sounds in the room. Every scrape of his skin against mine sends shivers through me, until an overwhelming surge of heat washes over my body. The telltale tingle hits my spine before I can tell him I'm close. But it doesn't matter, because soon, we're shouting loud enough to undoubtedly annoy the neighbors, shaking uncontrollably as we reach the peak together.

He plants delicate kisses on my chin, my forehead, my cheeks. I work to control my breathing, my chest tight, although the rest of me is limber. We snuggle into each other, his body partly draped over mine as I lie on my back.

"This is the real deal, V. You're it for me."

"Thank goodness," I say, threading my fingers through his hair. "Because you're it for me too."

"When did you know?"

I'm hesitant to admit this, but I'm going to anyway. Because that's the thing about the truth: It may be scary sometimes, but it's always freeing. "The day we worked on the reno in Queens."

He widens his eyes, his pupils flaring. "When we kissed?"

"No," I say, shaking my head. "Before that. When you talked about Sueños and said it refilled your well. I fell a little in love with you right then. I just didn't know what I was feeling yet."

Affection glows in his eyes as he sinks his fingers into my curls and pulls me in for a ravenous kiss.

When our lips drift apart, I tell myself I shouldn't ask a question I don't want the answer to. I might be it for him, but that doesn't mean he's falling for me yet. And I can live with that. As long as we get there eventually.

"Do you hear that?" he says, cupping his ear.

"What?"

"The sound of your brain working overtime."

"Ugh," I say, playfully shoving him off me. "You're the worst."

He scrambles on top of me and threads our hands together over my head. It's a lovely view, seeing Jason's broad chest inches from my lips, his expression soft as he gazes into my eyes. "It took me a while to realize what was happening, but I knew I'd fallen a little in love with you when you sat on that milk crate in your parents' store and just talked to me. I couldn't imagine having that conversation with anyone else, and I yearned to be the person you'd share all your secrets with."

"You weren't ready, though," I say.

"Yeah, I wasn't ready."

"And that's okay," I say, nuzzling his jaw. "We're exactly where we need to be: in each other's arms and looking forward to the future."

"Glad you agree."

"Savor this moment. It won't happen often."

He grins, his eyes flickering with amusement, then his expression turns serious. "Tell me something real."

This one's easy: "I can't imagine living without you."

He beams at me. Fucking beams at me. And I'm a goner just like that.

"Same, Vanessa. Same," he says softly.

So there you have it: the whole sordid mess complete with a happy ending. Ours isn't a typical love story, and I consider that a good thing. The best ones never are.

epilogue

JASON

Two Years Later

"That's a mighty fine ass you've got there, sir."

I'm standing on a ladder, scraping away at the window trim on my latest project, a three-bedroom fixer-upper in Carroll Gardens, one of my favorite neighborhoods in Brooklyn. Below, Vanessa's playfully leering at me, her bouncy curls held back from her face with a turquoise headband. She's a day lounging beneath the Caribbean sun personified.

"Say that again," I tell her.

"What?"

"Sir."

"Ooh, you're kinky too. There's still so much to learn about you, Mr. Torres."

"I was thinking the same about you."

In the two years we've been together, I've learned a lot about this woman—yes, spiders truly do make her skin crawl—but what I've learned isn't enough. It's never going to be enough either. Every little discovery about Vanessa—her quirks, her fears, her flaws, her down-to-the-core goodness—is a treasure. Well, *almost* every one of them. I'll confess I'm sad she really does wear sweats and pink goo on her face to bed. But it's all right, because I get to peel those sweats off her body every night, and seeing what's hidden underneath is like receiving a favorite gift at Christmas three hundred sixty-five times a year.

She holds up a bag. "Ready to take a break? I brought your favorite sushi."

"Yeah, I'd love that."

I climb down, set my scraper on the stoop, and pull Vanessa in for a kiss.

She hums into my mouth, tasting sweet as always.

"Jolly Rancher?"

She nods. "Apple, of course." Then she looks up at the building's façade. "It's coming along nicely."

"Still got a ways to go. Eric's trying to convince the owner to sell it to him."

"Will they?"

"Don't think so. This is a huge investment. Especially in this neighborhood. Anyone would be out of their minds to give it up."

"Especially when you're done with it."

"That's the hope."

I spread out a piece of builder's paper so we can sit on the steps while Vanessa preps our lunch. After we're situated, she sits next to me, close enough that the side of her thigh touches mine.

She hands me Purell, and I sanitize my hands.

"I can't stay long," she says. "Silas is on my butt about finishing the proposal for Carnegie."

That's one of the big changes in our lives. Vanessa left her job at Meridian Financial and now works as an independent grant specialist for nonprofits in New York. Silas hired her first, but she's steadily building an impressive clientele and says her new career fulfills her in a way her old job never did. And because she didn't want David Warner to harass anyone else, she included plenty of receipts with her resignation letter. She says my and her family's supportive reaction to the situation emboldened her to take that step. We don't know precisely what happened to David, but we *do* know he's no longer managing the Chicago office.

"How's Silas doing lately? I need to check in with him about internships for next summer."

"He's good. Still overwhelmed but happy about it. The funding's finally coming in."

"Thanks to you," I say, bumping her shoulder.

"And all of his hard work." She grabs a piece of sushi with her chopsticks. Before she pops it into her mouth, she says, "So what time are you and Nelson heading over to the Garden?"

"Tip-off is at eight o'clock. We're planning to meet at six forty-five." That's another change: my relationship with Nelson. I'm finally treating him the way I should have been treating him all those years ago: like a true father figure. Except we're doing this differently and making new sports traditions. Not sure the Knicks are going to come through for us, but we're giving it a shot. "My mother says I need to have him back by eleven."

Vanessa knows my mother well now, so her playful grimace doesn't bother me one bit. "Speaking of, she called me this morning. Said the holidays will be here before we know it and offered to teach me how to make pernil."

"What'd you tell her?"

"That you could make pernil just fine, and I didn't need any lessons. I think she's still hoping I made up that bit about not knowing how to cook. I told her I was very much not to be trusted in the kitchen."

"It's true. You're a disaster."

She jostles me with her shoulder. "Rude."

"The truth hurts, doesn't it?"

"You're right. Sometimes it does."

Yeah, but love and forgiveness can help heal the pain. Not always, but sometimes. At least that's what my therapist says. I chuckle. "You know, your parents trashed your cooking too. Warned me you might burn us out of house and home."

"My parents?" she asks, drawing back, her brow furrowed.

Shit. I squeeze my eyes shut, mentally scolding myself for that slipup. I guess we're doing this now. "Yeah, your parents. I talked to them this morning. Wasn't going to do this today, but I wanted to ask them for their blessing." I clear my throat. "To marry you."

Her jaw drops. "You want to marry me?"

"More than anything else in the world."

"Jason."

"Vanessa."

"Jason."

"And I was thinking we could live here," I say, pointing behind me. "In this three-bedroom brownstone that's just waiting for Denise and Lisa's future children to run around inside when they visit."

Because yeah, they figured their shit out and realized they're made for each other. As for Cami and Bryan, those two are still in Chile and have no plans for children anytime soon, if at all. They say they're happy to teach children all day and send them home to their parents every evening.

"How could we live here?" she asks, her voice pitched high.

"I'm the investor. Bought this place three months ago. As a surprise for you. If you don't like it, I can sell it to Eric, but I was hoping—"

Vanessa sets her to-go container on the step and launches herself into my arms, her sushi no longer a priority. "Oh my God."

"So what do you say? Ready to be the stylish auntie to my overbearing uncle and live happily ever after with me?"

"Yes, a billion times, yes," she says, her eyes tearing up. "I love you, I adore you, I don't ever want to live a moment without you."

I pull her close and seal our future with a kiss.

When we draw apart, she stares at me in wonder, her gorgeous brown eyes mirroring the love I feel for her.

"As long as there are no spiders and we get to christen every room, I'm game."

"The basement's going to have to be off-limits, though. I'm building an in-law suite for your parents there."

Her eyes go glossy, a tear slipping down her face before I can catch it. "Okay, no spiders and we christen every room except the in-law suite."

"Now *this* is the kind of plan I can get behind. Deal."

She pulls me in for another tight embrace. "We're going to be so ridiculously happy, people are going to hate us."

"Nauseating, probably."

"Utterly in love and so fucking annoying."

Yeah, I can picture it now ... and forever.

VANESSA

It started out as a ruse. As a favor to my then-estranged younger sister.

Luckily for me, Jason ended up being the love of my life.

Red flags: 2. Vanessa: 1.

Doesn't matter. I still came out on top.

acknowledgments

The Starter Ex is my eleventh published work, and I still feel as though my writing career is in its infancy. This isn't a bad thing; a dose of skepticism about one's publishing journey is healthy. But I wish I felt more grounded as an author. I wish I didn't doubt myself as much as I do. I wish I took more chances. As you're probably aware, being in the business of writing (and selling) fiction can be... challenging. So why do it? I'll tell you.

Because it's an opportunity to build fictional worlds that mean so much to me and to others.

Because every book is a chance to stretch my skills, to make people laugh and cry, to touch someone in ways I never envisioned when I first jumped on this publishing roller coaster.

Because my writing helps people *see* and *be seen*. Well, that's what I set out to do, at least.

It should go without saying, then, that the people who support me in this endeavor—the ones who try to ground me, the ones who shore up my confidence, the ones who tell me to take more risks—deserve my deepest gratitude. But it *doesn't* go without saying—because writers are accustomed to saying things in their acknowledgments. In *every* book. So bear with me as I tell a few people how much I adore them (again).

To my husband and daughters: You're my world. Truly. Thanks for your encouraging words and for listening to me babble about my characters. Your patience is appreciated.

To my mother: Thank you for, well, everything. I attribute all of my highs and none of my lows to you.

To my literary agent, Sarah Younger, and my Audible editor, Allison Carroll: Writing this book was a delight. Ten out of ten. Very few bumps. Would recommend this ride as long as you two are manning the controls. Thanks for everything.

To Tracey Livesay, my dear friend and writing partner in crime: We did it. Again. So now it's official: I'm not going on this journey without you. Many, many thanks for your helpful feedback and unwavering support. You. Me. Same.

To my sprinting buddies, including Olivia Dade, Adriana Herrera, Alexis Daria, and Zoraida Córdova: Thank you for helping me brainstorm ideas, reading early pages, or making sure I was staying on task. I admire you all immensely, and I'm lucky to have you in my corner.

To my beta readers (Ana Coqui, Liz Lincoln, and Soni Wolf): Thank you for your kind words, gentle suggestions, and keen eyes. It took a village to write this book, and you're all cherished villagers.

To my Romancelandia compatriots, especially the #BatSignal crew (Michele Arris, Nina Crespo, Priscilla Oliveras, Tif Marcelo, and Tracey Livesay), and my #LatinxRom amigas (Adriana Herrera, Alexis Daria, Angelina M. Lopez, Diana Muñoz Stewart, Liana De la Rosa, Natalie Caña, Priscilla Oliveras, Sabrina

Sol, and Zoraida Córdova): Thanks for always being the sunshine in this grumpy industry.

To Victoria Colotta of VMC Art & Design: Your expertise is invaluable. Thanks for making me look like a professional. Confession: I still visit Canva on occasion. #SorryNotSorry

To Shelbe Renè: Thanks for helping me keep it together. Your creativity and enthusiasm are so appreciated.

To Julia Jacob Mori: This cover is amazing, and your talent is boundless. I'm honored to be the beneficiary of your talent.

To the wonderful people at Putnam who played a role in the production and promotion of this book, especially Kate Dresser, Tarini Sipahimalani, Katie McKee, Jazmin Miller, Regina Andreoni, and Brittany Bergman: Thank you for everything you've done to bring this story to readers. I am grateful to be part of the family.

To my readers: You *better* love it. Kidding. Sort of. No, seriously, thanks for taking a chance on my work. I'm honored.

discussion guide

1. Vanessa Cordero used to run a profitable side gig as a starter ex, employing techniques to make the target miserable. What was your favorite scene demonstrating Vanessa's tactics in action? What tactics would you employ if you were to take that position, and why?

2. Vanessa and her sister, Lisa, share a close bond. So much so that Vanessa takes Lisa up on her request to fake-date her crush, Jason. What prompts Vanessa to give in to Lisa's wishes? Would you do the same for your sibling?

3. As Vanessa performs the role of a lifetime, it becomes clear that Jason might be her most complicated target yet. Why can't Vanessa deter Jason? What does Jason see in her? To what extent are the two actually compatible?

4. Author Mia Sosa includes Spanish dialogue throughout the story. Discuss the ways in which this enhanced your reading experience.

5. *The Starter Ex* explores what it means to be "marriage material" or "dateable," and the ways in which this can be a communal judgment rather than a personal one. To what extent does *your* perception of being "marriage ready" align with that of Jason's mother, Elba? What does this tell you about Elba's intentions?

6. Jason's mother is determined to find Jason a lifelong partner, but just anyone won't do. Why is it so difficult for Jason to communicate his desires to Elba?

7. In some ways, Vanessa's gig offers individuals a greater level of agency when it comes to seizing their romantic futures, because sometimes, your person just needs a little push. To what extent is Vanessa's starter-ex business an empowering mechanism to encourage relationships versus a manipulative tool that might only complicate the life of the couple long term?

8. *The Starter Ex* takes place in the lead-up to a wedding. Discuss how this serves as an effective vehicle to heighten the drama between Jason, Vanessa, Lisa, and Elba.

9. *The Starter Ex* explores the bond of sisterhood, familial expectations, and what it means to forgive yourself for your past mistakes. Which of these themes resonated with you most, and why?

10. This book pays homage to the classic romantic comedy *How to Lose a Guy in 10 Days*. Discuss the similarities and differences. In what ways does Sosa upend this form of the fake-dating trope?

FIND YOUR HEART'S DESIRE...

VISIT OUR WEBSITE: www.headlineeternal.com
FIND US ON FACEBOOK: facebook.com/eternalromance
CONNECT WITH US ON X: @eternal_books
FOLLOW US ON INSTAGRAM: @headlineeternal
EMAIL US: eternalromance@headline.co.uk

RAISING READERS
Books Build Bright Futures

Dear Reader,

We'd love your attention for one more page to tell you about the crisis in children's reading, and what we can all do.

Studies have shown that reading for fun is the **single biggest predictor of a child's future life chances** – more than family circumstance, parents' educational background or income. It improves academic results, mental health, wealth, communication skills, ambition and happiness.[1]

The number of children reading for fun is in rapid decline. Young people have a lot of competition for their time. In 2024, 1 in 10 children and young people in the UK aged 5 to 18 did not own a single book at home.[2]

Hachette works extensively with schools, libraries and literacy charities, but here are some ways we can all raise more readers:

- Reading to children for just 10 minutes a day makes a difference
- Don't give up if children aren't regular readers – there will be books for them!
- Visit bookshops and libraries to get recommendations
- Encourage them to listen to audiobooks
- Support school libraries
- Give books as gifts

There's a lot more information about how to encourage children to read on our website: **www.RaisingReaders.co.uk**

Thank you for reading.

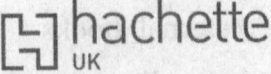

[1] OECD, '21st-Century Readers: Developing Literacy Skills in a Digital World', 2021, https://www.oecd.org/en/publications/21st-century-readers_a83d84cb-en.html

[2] National Literacy Trust, 'Book Ownership in 2024', November 2024, https://literacytrust.org.uk/research-services/research-reports/book-ownership-in-2024